ILLICIT

Acquiescence

A FORBIDDEN ROMANCE

G. ELENA

Edited and Proofread by Jenni Brady

Cover Design by Covers by Jules

coversbyjules.crd.co

For a complete list of content warnings, please check out:

www.graceelenaauthor.com

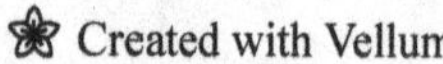 Created with Vellum

Playlist

LOVE ME HARD by Elley Duhé
Good For You by Selena Gomez, A$AP Rocky
So It Goes… by Taylor Swift
Shameless by Camila Cabello
Drew Barrymore by Bryce Vine
Small Doses by Bebe Rexha
Riptide by Saint Chaos
Nonsense by Sabrina Carpenter
The Color Violet by Tory Lanez
Dopamine by Siiickbrain, Maggie Lindemann
Nobody by Selena Gomez
ceilings by Lizzy McAlpine
Kiddie pool by GAYLE
UNDERSTAND by keshi

Prologue

ELIANA

MOVING BACK HOME SUCKS.

Moving back in with your parents at 23? Even worse. There's nothing that can convince me that having to come back to my hometown and living with my parents won't become a dumpster fire of a mess. A colossal nightmare.

I spent the last five years in Florida getting my bachelor's in pre-med and starting medical school. It wasn't easy, but it was a challenge I knew I wanted to face. But then something changed.

Before entering my second year of medical school, I felt *nothing*.

No passion. No enticement. No *desire* to continue this path.

This wasn't me. I never quit. I never let a challenge be too much where I give up halfway. And that's what I felt like when I turned in my withdrawal documents.

It felt like I became a shell of a person I no longer wanted to be. I had to crack that shell and figure out what the fuck I wanted to do with my life. And what did I want to do? I had no idea. But I do know that what I *was* doing was under the control of my parents' decision.

Having my mother come from a family of very successful

professionals, from lawyers to surgeons, I had to fit the mold to please her. And backing down from a challenge to prove to her that I am capable of doing such wasn't my forte. It ultimately led me down the path of wasting the last five years on a dream that was no longer mine.

It wasn't really mine to begin with, anyway. It was all for her and she still didn't seem happy.

So, as much as moving back home sucks, it's the only option I've got left. It better be worth it.

One

ELIANA

MY FEET HIT the pavement as I take proper breaths, the windy air punching my lungs as I finish my morning run.

Only one more block and I'm home. My eyes glance everywhere as I pick up my pace and increase my breathing.

New Haven, Connecticut is beautiful in August. The leaves are displaying more colors, signaling autumn. My favorite time of the year. Even the leaves that begin their descent to the ground bring a beautiful sight around town.

The colors of the transition from summer to autumn are starting to envelope the area as if I'm in a movie. The strong smell of coffee lingers in the air as well as the freshness of the trees after a night rain. It's almost comforting in a way.

Pumpkin patches will be open next month, apple cider will stock the shelves at the closest grocery store, and I can actually use the fireplace in the living room.

As I continue to run past morning walkers, I can't help but smile. Maybe living here again won't be too bad. It's changed so much since I left for college and there are recent developments that I've yet to explore.

I'm finally slowing down as I near the front steps to my

parents' home. It's an old three-story house that sits in a quiet neighborhood with each house stacked next to each other, like townhomes. The house is made of aging red brick and black accents. My parents have lived here ever since I moved to college, but I've only visited for the holidays.

They used to live in the neighborhood a couple of blocks away, but once I moved out, they got their jobs at the nearby university, bit the bullet and moved down the road. They used to commute to a different college for their work before they applied to work at Yale University.

Now, their house is ten minutes away from campus. They can walk to work if they really need to, but my parents never wake up late. They're usually up before the neighborhood is.

My steps falter a little as I slow down and walk up the steps, my legs beginning to feel like jello from my run.

I reach for the small zipped pocket in the back of my leggings for the house key. The door creaks loudly as I make my way inside.

The smell of coffee wafts my way as I shut the door and pull my headphones off my head and let it dangle around my neck.

"Eliana? That you?" My mother's voice drifts down the hall as I kick off my running shoes at the front area in our own makeshift mudroom. I decide to pull the headphones off me and place them on a free hook near the other jackets.

"Yeah, just me," I shout back.

There's a clattering of plates from where my mother is deep in the house. I follow the noise down the dimly lit hallway that rarely gets any sunlight. Pictures of my parents and I litter the walls and some antiques sit on top of dressers and small tables that line the hallway.

I enter the kitchen, brightness finally coming into view from the chandelier above. I see my mother fixing up eggs in a pan and she turns to see me standing there, still catching my breath.

"Sit. I made toast, eggs, and coffee. If you want some bacon you'll have to make it yourself." Her tone is clipped as her dark hair swishes around her shoulders and she turns back to the pan and scrambles the eggs. Her porcelain skin glistens under the chandelier lights, and her expensive golden bracelets jingle against each other.

"Thanks. Where's dad?" I ask as I trudge toward the kitchen island and take a seat on one of the cushioned bar stools.

The walls in this room are stark white with gold accents. The cabinets are a nice light cream color and the stainless steel appliances in every corner make this kitchen seem like out of a catalog. Pristine and clean, just like my mother.

"He's in his study checking emails, looking over syllabi before he heads in for a meeting with the rest of the department. Did you hear the good news? He's the new department chair."

I nod and reach for the glass sitting on the island and drag it closer to me before picking up the pitcher. There's a small cup of chopped lemons ready to squeeze. I pour myself a glass before popping a lemon quarter into the cold water.

I take a long gulp. I forgot to bring a water bottle on my run, unfortunately.

"That's great for him, really. I forgot the semester begins soon, right?"

My mother nods and then turns the knob off for the stove before heading towards me with the pan. I move quickly to grab the plate she set aside for me and lift it for her to plop a portion of the eggs into it. There's a pile of toast near her and she lifts one gingerly in between manicured fingers before placing it next to my eggs. The expression on her face turns sour for a millisecond but I still catch it.

There's a part of me wanting to ask her what I did *now* that upset her with our simple interaction, but I know better.

I give her a weak smile before she makes her own plate and one for my father.

"Yeah, three and a half weeks and then it will be a madhouse here. You know the drill. Papers everywhere. Us stuck either in our offices on campus or here."

I nod. I use a fork to start scooping scrambled eggs onto the piece of toast.

"Does dad usually meet this early with his department? I'd think they'd meet before classes started. Couldn't it be an email?"

She laughs almost condescendingly, her green eyes sparkling. "No, honey. Carlos would rather meet in person than do an email. You know him."

I nod because I know I really do. As much as he loves calling and texting me, he cherishes the face to face encounters more. But Florida was too far for me to do that. There were times where I regretted moving to a college so far away where I couldn't visit him whenever I wanted to.

"Why don't you take his plate to him?" she asks, pushing it across the island. I take a few bites of the eggs on toast before nodding and grabbing the plate. I hop off the stool and make my way back down the hall and then take a sharp right. There's a shorter hallway that leads to a bathroom, a bedroom, and an office.

My mother's office is on the second floor where their master suite is and a guest room. The third floor is just for me, like its own apartment. It has access to the roof, a huge closet space as big as a room, a suite for the bedroom and its own private bathroom. The only thing it's missing is a kitchenette.

Once I find myself in front of the office, I lift my hand and tap my knuckles against it five times.

"Come in," a voice calls. I twist the door handle and push until I'm inside. I allow my eyes to adjust to the different lighting as I take in my dad, scratching his head and leaning over a stack of papers.

"Breakfast is served," I call out as I walk towards him and push the plate on his desk.

He looks up and nudges his glasses up the bridge of his nose before smiling. His brown eyes find mine and he grabs the plate.

"Thanks, *Princesa*. How was your run?"

I retreat a few steps before taking a seat in one of the leather chairs in front of this massive desk. I fiddle my fingers over my lap. "It went well. Really familiarizing myself with the fresh additions to the neighborhood."

He nods before eating some eggs and taking a bite out of the toast. "Wow, your mother really knows how to make the simplest foods taste extravagant."

I roll my eyes at his nirvanic words. He's always full of them. I'm convinced it's his academic brain that never stops taking over. He told me I looked 'exquisite' and 'posh' when I twirled in the living room in my prom dress years ago.

It was a frilly blue dress that looked like a peacock, with the train in the back touching the ground and extending outwards. I shudder briefly at the memory of the horrible dress choice.

"I heard you have a meeting today? You ready for school?" I wiggle my brows.

He lets out a laugh before shaking his head. "I've done this plenty of times. The first day of school doesn't get to me anymore, *Princesa*."

He shovels another forkful of eggs before swallowing and clearing his throat. He wipes his hands over his mustache before pushing his glasses up against his nose again.

"You want to tell me something." I drum my fingers over my knees.

He nods. I can always tell when he's about to suggest a way I can better my life or lecture me. I'm hoping for the former–I'm not in the mood for a lecture.

"Your mother and I talked last night…" his voice trails off before his eyes lift to mine. I wait for him to continue, but he doesn't.

"And what did you guys talk about…?" I press. I've got an

inkling that I'm here for a reason and not just to give him break-fast. But knowing my dad, I have to pull it out of him.

He sighs before folding his arms over his chest and leans back in his chair. "She wants you to find a job."

I scoff before standing up in haste. He watches my movements. "Did she really say that? Do you have a say in any of this?"

He presses his lips into a thin line before shrugging. "I think she's right. You've been here since May and have yet to find something to do. I love having you here, believe me, but your mother thinks it's unproductive of you to just waste your days doing nothing."

"I do *something*," I bite back. His eyes soften and I loosen my body, knowing I shouldn't take my anger out at him. He's just the messenger. "I've tried to apply for jobs. They're all still fully staffed or have the students coming back to campus with secured spots waiting for them. I've tried... *believe me*."

He nods and is silent for a moment. "You can apply for medical jobs as well. Not just retail or whatever else you're applying for."

I shake my head. I'd rather work for the worst retailer than think about that. "That's not an area I want to work in anymore. I told you the whole medical career path wasn't for me and I'm done with it!"

"Which we still don't understand. It promised a wonderful future. A good life. Stable."

"Yeah, but I wasn't happy."

"You're not telling us everything," he starts, placing a hand over his chest. "But you need to tell us enough so we can support you and understand you."

I shake my head and laugh. "She'll never understand."

"She's only thinking about your future."

"To be a neurosurgeon? To be like grandpa? Aunt Beatrice? I don't think so. She shouldn't put that pressure on me when she's a goddamn professor–not even a neurosurgeon herself. I'm tired of having those expectations put on me. I want to do something that brings me joy."

"Well… what does then?"

His question catches me off guard. What does? How the hell would I know? I spent five years of my life thinking medicine was something I wanted to do. I wasted those years on a career that didn't suit me anymore.

"I-I don't know," I admit.

He hums before lifting the fork again and finishing the eggs and toast. He looks at me once he's finished and I continue to stand there, watching.

"What?" He pinches his brows.

"She told you something else."

Just like how he can tell when I'm leaving out important parts of why I moved back home, he's leaving out parts of the conversation he had with his wife.

He clicks his tongue against his teeth before sighing again. "She wants you to decide."

"Decide what?"

"She wants you to find a job in two weeks and if you do, we'll fund you to move out on your own."

"Or?" I ask, because I know this is an ultimatum and there's *always* an 'or' when it comes to my mother.

"Or…" he starts. "She wants you to go back to school. Find a new career path to dive into, so to speak. "

My jaw goes slack and I widen my eyes. I sit back down in the chair and feel the air get punched out of my lungs. My fingers grip the armrest of the chair and squeeze–I attempt to calm my breathing.

"Honey?" he asks with a crack in his voice.

"You're giving me an ultimatum?"

He shakes his head and laughs. "God, *Princesa*, no! This isn't an ultimatum, it's a chance to change your life around."

I roll my eyes. A chance to change my life? They're treating me like a case in a TedTalk. I'm not their charity case to dissect and control.

My eyes slowly glance above my father's head towards the back of his office where a few Egyptian artifacts stay on display in a glass case.

There's a replica stone statue of the god of divine retribution, Ammit, sitting right in the center of the case. The scales of balance dressed in gold sit right next to the statue.

The scales of Ma'at, the goddess of truth and justice, staring right down at me. Since he's a professor in Egyptology, I am well versed in the artifacts he's got around his office. Maybe a little *too* familiar.

It for sure gave me nightmares as a kid, but now I just flip the scales off, and the statues too, whenever I pass the office. I once thought it was cool that my dad was this smart guy who loved to study Egypt and its history, but it got old fast. Especially when my mother found it as an opportunity to scare me whenever I misbehaved.

"I'm not sure a new career path will change things. How different will it be from when I left pre-med?" I scoff.

I don't want to add that there is something inside me pulling at the possible idea of starting fresh. This is what I wanted, right? To quit feeling sorry for myself and not feel tied down to my mother's incessant controlling ways. Maybe this might do me some good?

He shrugs and gives me a pained smile. "I'm just telling you what she told me. You have two weeks."

And with that, he lifts the plate and pushes it towards me. I take it with force before turning on my heel and closing his office door.

I stomp down the hallway towards the kitchen. My mother is gone and my plate is gone as well. I wasn't done eating. I press my lips together and keep a scream down.

If I have two weeks to find a job, then fine. I'll find a job and stick it to her.

I drop dad's plate into the sink before heading towards the front of the house where the stairs are. I run up them as quickly as I can to the third floor, making my steps light so my mother doesn't hear.

Once I'm on my floor, I push through the suite doors and shut them closed. I lean against them, my forehead pressed to the hardwood. I take a deep breath and allow my body to shudder and let the tears fill my eyes.

I've tried since I moved back here to find a job and I wasn't lying to my dad. A lot of places weren't hiring or were simply reserving space for returning college students. I picked the wrong town to move back to.

I take a deep breath before turning around and gathering my things to take a shower. I'll go out again and scout for more jobs. I feel my phone buzz in the mesh pocket on the side of my pants. I pull it out and see my mother texted.

DIABLA

The history museum is opening a new exhibit for Egypt next month and is having an event tonight for early access. They've invited your father and the department of Egyptology alongside other universities. Join us, 7 pm.

I reread the text and rolled my eyes. It's never a suggestion with her. Never has. Never will be. I guess I'll have to go to that as well after I go job hunting.

Another text rolls through and I take a peek. It's from my mother. Again.

DIABLA

Show up for him.

Chucking my phone on the bed, I head into the bathroom to

rinse off this morning's run and nuisance. If only it were that easy.

Now, I'll have to show up tonight and play pretend as the 'perfect' daughter who's still on track to be a neurosurgeon so my parents reputation remains intact.

Needing the instant distraction, I turn the shower on and immediately step inside, allowing the icy cold water to hit my skin.

Two

ELIANA

My phone shows 7:15 p.m. as I near the steps of the history museum. There aren't that many people walking inside, so it's either not that big of an event *or* I'm late.

The gold dress around my legs ruffles in the slight breeze as I walk up the steps and head towards the doors. The noise of people talking and announcements filter the air as I head inside.

Woah. It's almost packed. It looks like a fuck ton of historians and carbon copies of my dad with glasses and business suits. I hold myself back from turning around and leaving. I take a deep breath and remind myself who I'm here for.

As I wait in a small line to check in, I survey the scene to see who I might recognize. There isn't anyone I know, and I can't find my parents in the lobby. Once it's my turn, I tell the security my name and they let me through.

Before I can make my way towards a table in the far right where there are refreshments waiting, I feel a tug on my elbow. I jolt and turn around, letting out an exasperated breath.

"Ana! You made it! I swore you would've stayed home," my best friend since middle school, Lena, screams as she pulls me in for a hug.

I widen my eyes and hug her back. "I didn't know you'd be here! What are you doing here?"

Releasing me from her grasp, her eyes are wild as she studies me. Her curly black hair bounces as she squeals and holds my shoulders. She's wearing a similar dress to mine, floor length with shoulder straps and a tight bodice. Her arms are full of golden bangles that complement her sun kissed skin tone.

"Of course I'd be here, silly! I thought your dad told you?" She waits as I scrunch my nose and shake my head. "I'm his student! Well, his Graduate Assistant."

I knew my dad had assistants every year, but it never occurred to me Lena might be one. I knew she went to Yale and was getting her masters in the same department as my dad. It makes sense though that this would be something she applied for. Lena is the hardest worker I know and always trying to do her best in her academics. It doesn't hurt that the GA program pays for her tuition and gives her a stipend.

Lena and I tried our best to stay connected throughout the five years I was gone—she visited a few times during the first four and we spent almost every holiday catching up. But the last year was so stressful figuring out if medical school was really for me that I couldn't keep up communication with anyone.

"Oh, great," I choke out. I try to force a smile, but she sees right through me.

"I know it's been a while since we last caught up, but this is great! It's so nice to see you. It feels like it's been forever."

I nod. The guilt rips through me that I should've done more. Should've called or even texted her when I needed to talk to or someone to vent to. It wasn't fair to either of us.

She doesn't seem to notice my despair as she smiles and pats my shoulder before looping her arm around my elbow. "I'll take you to your parents. They're in the exhibit already. Your dad loves it so far."

I let her drag me throughout the lobby of the museum until

we step inside the Egyptian exhibit. It's darker in here and I can see copious tall statues of gods and goddesses lining the room. It looks like it goes deeper in the museum, with hallways and crevices that probably have more artifacts and information.

She makes a beeline to a well-dressed couple. My parents.

"Mr. and Mrs. Haros! I found her!" Lena shouts as they turn around and they both smile at Lena. I grimace as I see my mother's eyes catch mine and she glances at my outfit.

"That wasn't what I picked out for you."

"She looks great, honey. You look beautiful, *Princesa*," my father says quickly. He has his arm around my mother's waist and she's decked out in an expensive red dress that swoops to the floor and her dark hair is pinned up.

Dad is wearing a tuxedo with a handkerchief the same color as my mother's dress. They look cute, but I don't tell them.

"It was the same color as yours. I wanted to stand out. I think I look great." I twirl the fabric of my dress to make my point.

Lena nods. "She looks amazing, Mrs. Haros." I give Lena a thankful smile and she winks.

"Well, I guess that's fine," my mother finally says before turning back around and studying the artifacts in front of her. Dad gives me a weak smile before mouthing he loves me and turning back towards her.

"Alright, I think I have to check in with a few other professors, but I'll be back!" Lena says as she releases my elbow. I register her words too late before I can pull her back. She's already leaving towards another area in the room. I look around and realize I still don't know anyone.

Before I know it, I'm heading back out of the exhibit and making a beeline for the refreshments table again. I see a small cocktail tray with various drinks and pick one up that looks like a gin and tonic and take a sip.

Not bad. I take another to keep my hands busy as I head back towards the exhibit. I hold the cups close to my chest as I study the pieces carefully around the room. My parents are nowhere to be seen and neither is Lena.

I'm near the replica of the pyramids when I feel a big shadow next to me. I turn and have to crane my neck up to see who it is.

A man *much* older than me peers at the pyramids, but I can feel the fabric of his sweater slightly touching my bare arm. I hitch my breath as I continue to stare, admiring the crook of his nose. His beard is speckled with salt and pepper strands, as well as his hair. His tan skin looks perfect under this dim lighting. His Adam's apple bobs as he swallows and the simple act makes heat pool in my belly.

He looks handsome and I squirm in my place as he finally turns his head and peers down at me. There's a twinkle in his brown eyes and he presses his lips firmly together.

"Pyramids of Giza," he murmurs. It takes a second for me to realize he's talking to me. It feels like my throat is closing in on itself as he continues to look my way.

He sidesteps a little closer so the cashmere fabric presses directly on my arm. I shudder from the soft contact and his eyes crinkle as he smiles slowly. Even his teeth are perfect.

"What?" I stutter. My hands with the drinks move a little more up my chest, and it feels like I'm stuck. Unable to move under this handsome stranger's gaze.

"The pyramids," he says again, gesturing his head towards the display in front of us. "They're the pyramids of Giza."

"Oh, right," I meekly replied. My brain is mush and I can't think of anything else to say. He continues to study me before he returns his gaze towards the pyramids. I know my Egyptian history, but right now I can't even say one fact even if there was a gun to my head.

I take a deep breath and lift one cocktail and take a long sip. Letting out a deep breath, I stare at the pyramids while my heart flutters dramatically against my ribs. The alcohol courses through my blood and I feel warm already.

"Have you seen the rest of the exhibit?" he asks, not looking my way.

I turn to him and I wonder what the fuck is going on. He hasn't budged and he looks like he's waiting for a response.

"Ar-Are you still talking to me?"

He nods and then turns his head back to me. "Is that a yes or a no?"

I attempt to remember his question... oh, right. The exhibit. "No, not yet. Just arrived."

He nods before gesturing his head towards the rest of the exhibit, and I follow aimlessly behind. I see a waiter walking around with a tray, presumably picking up people's empty drinks, so I hurriedly place mine on there.

He slows his steps, so he's to my left and I feel the heat already rising to my cheeks.

"It's a nice exhibit," I finally say as we walk deeper into it. The hallway becomes darker the further we walk, the only light visible illuminating the artifacts and statues.

Where we're headed, there aren't many people walking around.

"It could be better. Some artifacts don't seem to be like the real thing," he retorts. I turn to look at him under the dim lighting, and his brown eyes glint.

"And you know this, how? You've seen the real thing?"

"Actually, I have," he responds. There's a few people leaving the area that we're entering, so the stranger and I step aside to let them through. I feel his hand press against my back as we make room.

My heart picks up as I feel the heat radiate from his palm to my back. His hand feels *huge* on me and I can't help but bite down on my lip. The thoughts of his hand touching *other* parts of my body run rampant in my mind.

Once the people get by, we resume our walk, but he doesn't move his hand. I'm positive he can hear my heart beating against my whole body with his contact. Silence fills the air as we continue to stroll through the exhibit.

"You a fan of this stuff, then?" I finally ask.

He nods and I have to turn towards him to hear him better, watching his soft lips move underneath the dimmed lighting. "You could say that. I've also been to Egypt a few times."

"Wow," I breathe out. "I went when I was little, but I haven't been back. It'll most likely feel like the first time again if I ever revisited."

He murmurs something under his breath, but I don't catch it. We're nearing an area that juts out to the right, where there's a small room with benches and a movie screen. It's not on, which means it's probably not ready to show yet. Maybe once the exhibit officially opens.

I feel his hand on my back steer us towards the dark room. My heart pitter patters more as I think of all the reasons we're going in here *alone*. But I don't stop him, which frightens me even more. Just willing to go along with what a stranger wants to do. A very *handsome* stranger.

He wants to murder me.

He wants to rob me... wait, I don't even have my purse. My ID and cards are hidden in the case of my phone. My phone is in the pocket of this dress and with the way the fabric sways, it almost looks like there's none. There's a slit on the side that runs from my mid thigh to the ground and I feel the icy breeze as we enter the dark room.

He definitely wants to murder me then, that's it.

Definitely.

But right now my thoughts are becoming fuzzy as the scent around me looms of new carpet and expensive leather. And a hint of lemon.

"What are you-" I start to speak, but he shushes me. I look around the room and see that there's a hint of *light* on the ceiling. *Oh, I guess they got the room ready.*

Stars. There are hundreds of stars on the ceiling.

"The sky of Cairo, real time."

I'm awestruck at the sight. "Really? That's genius." I don't even question how he knows this. For all I know, he could be lying. Those 'stars' on the ceiling could be splattered paint.

"Mhm," he responds as we walk a little further. I twirl a little bit as I continue to look up, feeling his arm continue to be wrapped around me. So, with the angle I'm twirling, his hands rest at the side of my waist, right below my rib cage. His touch almost burns through my dress.

I sense him getting closer and pushing my body further into the dark room.

And I... let him. The scents in the room, the feel of his hand on me, and the way he towers over me makes my mind fuzzy.

I'm walking backwards until I hit a wall and let out a squeak. His lips curl into a devilish smile and it looks so *god damn sexy* on him. My heart beats even faster against my chest. It feels like I'm on a rollercoaster and about to do the initial dip down a hundred feet.

"Who are you?" I whisper.

He leans closer, his breath hitting my forehead. I suck in a breath as he says nothing for a few seconds.

"You can stop me if you'd like," he murmurs as he leans even further until his lips brush against my nose.

I don't push him away, but I don't say anything. My brain is literally melted into putty. If he asked me my name, I wouldn't know it.

"Nod if you want me to continue," he orders. I widen my eyes, processing his thoughts.

Suddenly, my mind goes to where we are. A public setting. Yes, we're closed off from the rest of the people at the event... but my parents are somewhere in the vicinity.

In silent acquiescence, I nod.

And before I even have time to *breathe,* I feel his firm hand on my waist travel down, sweeping down the crevice between my thigh and hip bone. The spongy part that tickles. I let out a whimper at the contact before he leans his lips lower. In an instant, he crashes his lips onto mine.

He moves fast and I can't think of what to do with my hands, my body, or whatever else I have full autonomy over. I let him take charge.

As we kiss, his beard presses against my chin, sides of my mouth and it makes me moan. He momentarily bites my bottom lip and I squeal, a smile pulling at his lips as he continues to *devour* me. Pushing his tongue into my mouth and our teeth almost clacking.

His free hand pulls up to cradle my neck, pulling me further into him. His hand on my hip continues to lower until it passes the slit of the dress. I hitch my breath and he pulls back a little to rest his forehead against mine.

Slowly, his fingers reach the center of my lace underwear and he hitches his own breath.

He hitches his breath. I've never had a man do that before.

I hold back a moan as his fingers press against the fabric and then hook underneath it to move it aside. I spread my leg just a few inches for him to get underneath the fabric easily.

"*Ay, Dios mío,*" he whispers as his fingers meet my already wet pussy. I groan at the contact and I curse myself for how *wet* I got for this stranger. And now he's speaking Spanish? I could literally melt into a puddle right here.

How embarrassing.

But before I can pull his hand away and apologize for being a fuckup, he pulls me in for a kiss again while he runs his two large fingers through my folds and hits my clit. I moan louder at the touch and he chuckles in a deep voice.

"So you like it?" I nod briefly. "*Dilo,*" he commands.

"I like it," I whisper as he continues to kiss me with fervor. Once we're in a rhythm of kissing, his fingers continue to move back and forth against my pussy before he angles his fingers just enough to slip one inside of me.

My hands instinctively run up to hold his shoulders, grasping at the cashmere. He presses himself deeper into the wall, crushing me.

"*Oh*," I squeak out as he pumps a finger in and out of me, causing my walls to tighten at the foreign but *so good* feeling.

"You're so fucking tight," he mumbles as he presses his body even more into me, his erection pressing into my hipbone.

He continues to pump his finger in and out before slipping another one in. I squeeze his shoulders tighter as my vision sparks and I can only see faint images of him and the starred ceiling.

"You like that? My thick fingers getting you off?" his husky voice fills my ears and I feel like I've died and woken up in some kind of heaven.

Pure ecstasy and pure bliss.

I nod my head and moan again before he leans his head and sucks on my neck, leaving bites and small kisses. He continues to grind his hips in a faster fashion, dry humping me.

His thick fingers don't stop. I can feel my arousal already travel down his fingers and onto my thighs. The sounds are *deafening* with how fast he's fingering me and how quickly I'm getting to my release. He shifts his wrist to add his thumb underneath the fabric to rub my clit in circles.

"Oh, I'm about to–" I whine as I lean my head against his shoulder and squeeze my eyes shut. The pressure is wonderful and I can feel the orgasm begin to bloom and signal its burst.

"Fuck, cum all over my fingers. Fucking do it," he whispers in my ear and with those commands, I come.

Violently.

I see stars, my heart feels like it's shattered through my chest, and I can barely hear anything. Not even his grunts as he finishes grinding against me. They just reverberate against my body, sending shivers down my spine.

His fingers slip out of me and I whimper at the loss. I lean my head back to steady myself. He watches me closely as he pulls his fingers close to our faces, popping the wet fingers in his mouth. He twirls his tongue around them, keeping eye contact with me the whole time.

I can feel my cheeks get even hotter as the haze passes. My mind sobers and I realize where we're at. A public museum. With my *parents* so close.

I've never had public sex before and I didn't know how people did it. But apparently I do now.

"*Ven*. Let's finish the tour," he says loudly, causing me to stand taller and nod my head.

Right, the tour. What we were doing before he pulled me into this room.

He says nothing else before he shifts his hands over his pants. If his fingers were that good, I can't imagine his–

His hands reach for my wrist and he pulls me along. I'm drunk off the post-orgasm feeling and I follow him blindly.

Who the fuck is this man?

Three

JULIÁN

It's been three and a half weeks since the event at the museum and since I did something so out of touch with what I'm used to. It was riveting and made me feel *alive*.

Which has been hard to feel with everything that has been going on recently with Laura. She just can't stop forcing herself into my life despite our divorce being final for over four years. She still thinks she can show up at my door or my office and strike up conversation, like nothing has changed.

I almost threw an outright tantrum that night when she showed up at my door, thinking she'd be my plus one to the event. But I slammed the door in her face, finding myself in need of a distraction and I *found* it.

I don't even know her name, but she was exactly what I needed that night.

My footsteps are loud against the hardwood floor of the building as I make my way to my colleague's office. I knock against the wooden door and there's a soft *come in*. I twist the doorknob and enter, locking eyes with the department chair.

"Julián, what can I do for you? Classes don't start until tomorrow," Carlos calls with a smile as he watches me enter. He raises his hand and waves for me to sit down in one of his leather chairs.

His office is homey, and what mine will never look like. I have maybe two decorations and a few artifacts from my trips in Egypt and that's it. Here, there are photos of him and his wife and an old one of them and their daughter; Carlos looks to be about a decade younger in it. I've never bothered to learn the names of my colleagues' children's names.

It was rare for the department to gather outside of the university unless it was for events like the history museum or for faculty dinners. I saw a lot of the family members of the professors I've either emailed or worked with, but it occurred to me that Carlos only brought his wife to those past events. I assume he had everyone join him that night at the history museum though.

My mind flashes back to the younger woman I snuck off with and wonder if she's a new professor at another university or related to anyone that went there.

"Julián?" Carlos' words draw me back to his office and I take a seat in the plush chair before locking eyes with him.

"I'd like to add another course if possible to my schedule and offer a position for a graduate assistant."

Carlos raises a brow before leaning over his desk and laying his elbows on top. "You already teach four undergraduate classes and two graduate classes. I can open a graduate assistant position with that load already."

I lean over and rest my elbows on my knees. I look up at Carlos before sighing. "I can add another course, if you don't mind."

"What's going on?" he asks. I want to take it as prying into my life, but the way his brows furrow and his eyes turn to concern makes me regret walking into his office.

Most of our class schedules have to be approved by the department chair and that's who it is–Carlos Haros.

"Nothing, I'd like more on my plate." I see him open his mouth, so I rush out a lie. "I've got more time than I thought with my schedule. I can do the extra course."

"Is this about–"

"No, no," I interrupt him. He watches me slowly before bringing a hand to brush over his mustache.

I sigh and shake my head. "Carlos, you know I don't like to talk about my personal life. I just have more time, really."

It's obvious that he can see right through my lies, but he doesn't push any further. He nods.

"Alright, but if I see you struggling in any way, I'll reduce you back to your normal load next semester. You can have that graduate assistant. I'll make an application open up this week and have the other professors tell their students."

I nod and stand up. He watches me with curious eyes, but I turn on my heel before he can sense anything else I might be hiding.

"Have a great first day tomorrow," he calls out and I turn to give him a smile before I nod and head out of his office. I almost bump into Lena Ellison, Carlos' graduate assistant, as I make my way down the hall.

"Oh! Professor Estrada, I am *so* sorry!" she mutters as she steps back in shock.

I step away as well and give her enough room. "You're alright, Lena. Excited for the new school year?"

She laughs and adjusts the files in her hands before locking eyes with me. "I guess! Professor Haros already has me copying a ton of packets. He wanted me to work a week ago, but I had to remind him that my contract didn't start until today."

I nod, remembering how grueling Carlos can be to his assistants. If he could live at the university, he would. He even teaches summer classes and during the first two weeks of January where students can take an accelerated course for extra credits before the spring semester starts.

He overbooked himself and would definitely benefit with *two* graduate assistants with how tired Lena looks already.

"That's Carlos for you," I tell her before she laughs and gives me a small wave.

I make my way again down the hall until I'm back in my office. I enter it and almost have a heart attack as I see someone sitting in my desk chair.

"Sweetie, I saw your door open," a nasally voice comes from the person sitting at the chair. I roll my eyes and rub my palm against my cheek and beard.

"Laura, what the fuck," I groan.

She smiles widely, her blonde hair swaying as she moves her head and stands up from my chair.

"You need to add some life to this place. Maybe some pictures of us would help?"

I step inside and close the door behind me. I turn back towards her and furrow my brows. "Why would I do that?"

She shrugs and smiles again. "Because we had great photos taken. You shouldn't ignore how pretty they came out. Especially the ones from our wedding."

"We're not married anymore. It's been years," I remind her.

She waves a hand before getting closer to me and patting my shoulder. I take a step back and clench my jaw.

"Don't be silly, hun. I know we're divorced. That doesn't mean we can't be friends. I have pictures of us in *my* office."

Because you're fucking crazy, I want to tell her, but I keep it to myself as I watch her wide eyes cling to me.

"Laura, you need to cool it. You do this every year. Beg me to spruce up my office before you ignore me the rest of the school year unless you need something from me. And that's just my office. That doesn't count the amount of times you show up at my door."

"You changed your locks, and I had to get some of my things," she counters.

"You took the last of your things over a year ago. I'm not playing these games with you anymore. You need to *move on*."

Her eyes go from excited to hurt. The way she's done it so many times.

The first few years of our marriage, I believed her expressions. Tried to do anything in my power to make it work to get her back to a happy medium. Until I realized this is what she does when she can't get her way.

I'm not her puppet anymore and we've been playing this game for far too long. I cut my strings when we signed the divorce papers and I'm not letting her reattach me to her wooden bar.

"Okay, Julián. I'll go. Sorry I bothered you," she breathes out, her eyes getting glossy with crocodile tears.

I huff out a sigh before heading towards my chair and sit down. She walks slowly to the door, twisting the knob and pulling it a foot open. She turns back, as if waiting for me to ask her to stay.

I say nothing and her face turns to anger before she breathes out in frustration and opens the door wider, slipping out. She slams the door behind her and it shakes the walls.

Typical Laura, storming out to have the last action if she can't have the last say. Or if she can have both, she'll take it.

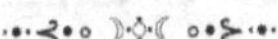

IT'S NEARLY SEVEN IN THE EVENING WHEN I MAKE IT BACK TO my place from the university. It's tiny, but enough for me with everything that has been going on the last four years. It's a two bedroom, one bath apartment and a ten-minute walk from the university. What once used to be Laura and I's conjoined office space, I made it my own and stripped away the walls of any reminder of her.

Now, there's no trace of her left in this place, but she can't seem to let me go on her end.

It took a grueling *year* to get that divorce processed and finalized. A lot of it had to do with Laura not cooperating and refusing to sign it.

She even went to the lengths of going out of the country and begging me to wait until she came back and promising she'd sign them the moment she returned.

That happened three times before I got authorities involved and she complied, signing them the moment she realized she couldn't run away anymore.

But now, I'm still dealing with her shit as much as I try to push her away. It feels like it's just an extension of our marriage beyond this divorce. She still tries to manipulate me with her tactics and I *almost* fall for it every time until I snap back to reality and remember who she really is.

I make my way into my office and drop my briefcase onto the desk. I then head to my bedroom and untie my shoes before taking them off and stripping out of my work clothes.

I grab a pair of gray sweats and a navy long sleeve before heading to the bathroom and showering. Within ten minutes I'm out and dressed in more comfier clothes before making my way towards the kitchen to see what I could eat for dinner.

The moment I open the fridge, I groan. I forgot I was supposed to pick up groceries tonight but got completely sidetracked making sure all the syllabi were uploaded to the university's student portal before classes start tomorrow.

My head hangs as I continue to stare at the empty fridge. Even if I wanted to make a scarce meal to just *eat something*, nothing in here is appetizing. A slice of cheese, a tub of sour cream, and then some random condiments on the side of the fridge.

"Fuck," I groan as I shut the fridge door closed and back up, leaning against the kitchen counter. I cross my arms and close my eyes briefly before pushing myself off the counter and grabbing my phone from the living room coffee table.

I quickly pull up the closest take out places I could run to before anything closes. Even though it's a university town, it's a weeknight and most places with food close their kitchen around nine or ten. There's a Mexican restaurant that I haven't been to before, and it's still open and taking orders. The one I usually go to is a 20 minute Uber away, and I didn't feel like going that far just for some takeout. I could get food delivered, but getting some fresh air seemed like something I'd need anyways.

I click on the restaurant and check the map and see it's only a couple of blocks away from me. I begin choosing some items before completing my order and paying on the app. Heading to the closet in the hallway, I put on some running shoes before grabbing my keys near the door and slipping out.

The wind is picking up—I love this time of the year. Not only because it brings about a new school year and excited students to start their programs with my undergraduate classes, but it also brings about a sense of renewal.

A time for new beginnings and being able to grow as a new person. I can be whoever I want to be and the transition of the weather from summer to autumn really helps with that.

Laura and I got married in the summertime. That might be another reason I love this upcoming season so much. It reminds me of how good my life can actually be if I just do the things I want and not stay with someone who would never want me the way I wanted them.

I try to clear my thoughts from my ex-wife as I walk the few blocks towards the restaurant. The sun has already set and lights outside of shops and restaurants have turned on to create a glow around the streets.

This university town is really pretty when you take the time to walk around and admire it. A ton of tourists come here to experience the autumn and winter seasons, but it's something else when you actually live here.

Once I make it to the restaurant, I pull open the doors and a bell chimes. I let the hostess know I'm picking up a takeout order. She runs in the back and I pull out my phone to pass the time.

> **LAURA**
>
> You're not home? Tried to stop by with some Thai food

I clench my jaw and type out a quick response to tell her I'm out and won't be home for a few hours. This makes her send a string of sad emojis before I leave her on read and click my phone off.

"Here you go, sir!" the hostess calls out as she hands over the bag of takeout. I thank her before heading out into the street. My phone pings and I pull it out again in annoyance.

> **LAURA**
>
> Maybe we can have dinner tomorrow night to commemorate the new school year?

I clench my phone in my fist and honestly don't care if I fucking break it.

I walk faster, staring at the screen, not caring where I'm heading. Just anywhere to get away from her text. From her prying self and always wanting to make up and then make out. She just wants to come over to rile me up and use me.

It's happened far too many times than I'd like to admit. She was a good fuck, but that's all she is to me now. Plus, I'm *really* trying to stop that cycle; it's hurting us both more than we think.

As I continue to walk briskly towards my apartment, I look up just in time to see someone running towards me, trying to sidestep before tripping and landing on her knees and palms.

"*Ah!* Fuck," she yells as she shakes her brunette head and slowly gets up.

"Here, that was my bad. I wasn't watching," I say, switching the takeout bag to my other hand and putting my phone in my sweats pocket before leaning down and reaching my hand out.

"Thanks. That fucking hurt." She grabs my hand harshly, but all I feel is her soft skin.

She steadies herself and finally looks up, a blush creeping on her face as she locks eyes with me. I instantly let go of her hand and take a half step back before I bump into someone behind me and step back to where I was, in front of her.

The girl I fingered in the history museum.

Fuck me.

Four

ELIANA

I'M LITERALLY on my hands and knees.

I'm still trying to register that I almost ran into someone while out on my evening jog. My music was loud, and I was at the tail end of my second mile, working hard to beat the time from my first.

I looked up one second, attempted to sidestep, and *tripped* over myself in front of this stranger. I fell right onto my knees and my palms went straight ahead of me just in time before smacking my face into the pavement. My palms stung instantly from the impact, but otherwise I was fine.

Once I'm officially up and standing, I lift my head to see who the stranger is. That's when I feel the blush creep up to my neck and then my face as I register who it is.

The dude from the history museum that I snuck off and *did* things with. Things that felt so fucking good that I couldn't stop thinking about.

The way his deep voice edged me on, commanded me to do things and just—

My eyes glance down his body where he's wearing a soft, navy long sleeve with gray sweats. I let my eyes travel down the sweats where there's an evident imprint of him that I wished I had the pleasure of meeting that night. I clear my throat, looking back up at the man.

"Sorry, I should've looked where I was going," I whisper before brushing my hands over my torso and tightening the ponytail I'm sure is frizzing out by now.

"It's okay," he answers, watching me slowly.

My eyes glance to the takeout bag in his hand and I smile.

"Getting dinner?" I ask, watching his eyes travel from my face to his hand clenching around the plastic bag.

He nods.

"Forgot to get groceries."

His answer is curt, and it pulls me back to when we were at the museum. When we continued the tour and got to talking, his answers were direct and not as elaborate as mine. It was mostly me talking the rest of the night and then we departed. I didn't notice him leave the museum or catch him in the lobby when I met back up with my parents and Lena. It left me wondering who he was and I became a little distraught after what we'd just done.

He was like a ghost, yet I couldn't get him out of my head. He imprinted on my mind and I even had a few… *dreams* about him. I couldn't help myself.

And at this moment, I realize that I still don't know this man's name. We never exchanged that pertinent information and I truly thought I'd never see him again.

"Well, have a nice dinner," I tell him, grabbing my phone from my pocket and opening the music app to figure out which song I'd like to continue running with.

I was mainly on this run to forget a fight I had with the devil herself. Dad still wasn't home from the university, and she was getting antsy that he was missing dinner.

Even though she and dad had their own schedules during the

school year, she wanted him to join for the night before the semester started.

She, of course, lashed out at me and started bringing up past issues that I thought we resolved. One of them being that I still didn't find a job and agreed to go back to school.

I'd be starting the graduate creative writing program, but an extended version to get the foundation courses I couldn't get with my general education credits from my bachelor's degree.

It would be long and grueling for three years. In her words, creative writing isn't a feasible career and that I would be stuck at home living with them because I wouldn't have a good, sustainable job. I tried to explain to her that there are tons of jobs that would hire me with this degree. Journalist, novelist, or even teaching jobs would be available for me to apply for.

I stormed out of the kitchen, leaving my full plate of dinner and changed into running clothes. She didn't even attempt to come upstairs to talk to me. She stayed in the kitchen, eating by herself by the time I walked downstairs and pulled my keys off the hook.

She remained silent as I opened the front door and looked back, hoping she'd call me back into the kitchen to apologize. But she never did and I made sure to slam the door loudly behind me.

I ran wherever I could, doing my first mile around the neighborhood before venturing out with my second mile into town.

That's when I fell after colliding into a very handsome stranger.

As my fingers continue to scroll through a playlist, I hear scuffing against the pavement and look up to see the man walk closer, his eyes blazing with something I remember distinctly from that night.

"Where you headed?"

My mouth opens and closes, unsure how to respond before I

see his eyes flick from my eyes to my lips and then back to my eyes.

God damn, why does he do that? My legs instantly feel like putty and it's not from the running.

"Going to finish my second mile," I reply, turning my eyes back to my phone before I feel his body push closer towards me, his torso hitting the top of my phone. I look up and instantly I'm surrounded by him.

The takeout bag in his hand brushes against my thigh and I suck in my breath. I'm thrust instantly into his atmosphere once again. It feels like we're back in the museum in the room with stars on the ceiling.

He runs his tongue along his bottom lip before inhaling heavily, his chest puffing out before he exhales at the top of my head.

"Have you eaten yet?"

"I-I didn't. Kind of stormed out of the house when dinner was served. Not the first time." I clear my throat, unsure why I just blurted all of that out. He doesn't need to know the details.

He processes my words before he takes a step back and lifts his takeout bag a little and swings it. "I've got enough for two."

I shake my head and laugh. "I wouldn't like to take someone else's meal."

The atmosphere shifts as the words leave my mouth and I see his jaw clench before he slaps on a smile.

"Don't be silly. I got enough for leftovers. Since I forgot to get groceries." He reminds me.

I mentally slap my forehead with the realization that he indeed told me that part.

But *I* almost ran into him, not the other way around, so I'm a little taken back that he's offering me food after the collision.

"I could use some fuel," I tell him, finally clicking my phone off and shoving it back into the side of my leggings and pulling my wireless earbuds out and stuffing them in the same pocket.

He gives me a hint of a smile before turning on his heel and craning his neck, waiting for me to join him.

The night breeze picks up and he walks us for a few blocks in silence before we near a park that has a few benches and tables. We pick one far enough away from street lamps with just enough glow to see the takeout containers as he pulls them out.

The food smells amazing and my stomach growls in response and I realize how hungry I am after storming out from my mother's antics.

He looks up with a smile as he hears my stomach and pushes the container in front of me and opens it, revealing three steak tacos and my mouth instantly waters.

"These look incredible."

"You've never been to that spot?"

I shake my head.

"I grew up here, but I've been away for years. I just came back this summer and everything's changed."

He nods as he opens the other container in front of him and I notice that it's a smaller portion of tacos.

"Hey, do you want to trade? It's your food. I can get the smaller size."

He looks up at me and shakes his head, reaching into his container and grabbing a taco before I can switch our containers.

"You're hungry, eat."

I nod and start grabbing a taco before picking up a lime and squeezing it onto the steak. I look up to see him watching me with a gleam in his eyes after I followed his orders.

"Are you going to watch me eat this whole thing?" I ask sheepishly, holding onto the tortilla in between my fingers as I wait for his answer.

His eyes squint for a second. "Do you want me to?"

I feel the heat rise to my cheeks before I even realize why. With the way he's watching me slowly, taking in his words, I blush and shake my head.

"N-no, I'd rather us both eat. I don't enjoy having the attention on me," I confess.

That's one thing I hate the most, is unwarranted attention on just me. He's silent for a second before nodding and lifting his own taco and taking a big bite. I watch as some of the steak juice and salsa dribbles past his lips. He licks it clean before lifting his eyes towards me.

There are butterflies swarming my stomach as I watch his eyes grow dark, just like they did at the museum, and I can already feel my core tighten at the thought of him fingering me that night.

My eyes glance at his fingers… his very *thick* fingers as they grasp the rest of the taco. Before I know it, he's lifting his hand and licking his index and middle finger to rid them of the salsa that spilled on them as well. My tongue goes dry and I gulp, realizing there's no drink to wash this down with.

"*Come*," he says with more authority and I get back to my senses before lifting the taco to my lips and taking a bite.

The steak is perfectly cooked and the lime adds the finishing touch. The salsa is not too spicy and I can't help but groan at all the flavors. I didn't realize how hungry I was until this bite.

He flashes a small smile before we finish our tacos in silence. I want to ask him a ton of questions, but I don't know if that's something you do with someone you barely know that had their fingers inside of you.

Plus, the first time we met, we barely talked.

"Thanks for letting me have your future leftovers," I say as we get up half an hour later. He grabs the container from me and we walk towards the edge of the park and he throws the containers in a nearby trash can.

"Thanks for having dinner with me. Didn't want to go home quite yet."

"Yeah? How come?" My brow raises, and he gives me a shrug as we walk back the way we came.

"Ex issues."

I stop in my tracks, and he turns his head before stopping as well. He's about five feet away from me and I stand my ground. His response wasn't something I was expecting. We barely talked about our personal lives the first night and here he is already talking about an ex. I'm not sure what I should be feeling right now, but it definitely caught me off guard.

"What?" He asks.

"Nothing, it's not the answer I was expecting."

He laughs before waving at me to join him again. I take a couple of steps before we're walking in line again.

"I have exes. You probably do too. I'm not going to lie to you and say something else happened tonight for me to not want to go home."

"Oh," I simply answer. I rack my brain for a better response, but nothing comes to me.

"Trust me, I would've asked you to eat with me at my place. But that's just somewhere I don't want to be right now."

He… what?

"Really?" I ask, turning to look at him and he nods.

"You didn't think I forgot what happened three and a half weeks ago?""

I bite my lip and he catches it, smiling before I see his eyes travel from my eyes to my lips again.

"Maybe next time," he says under his breath, walking a little closer so our arms are touching. I can feel his muscles through his long sleeve.

Fuck. Images of that night at the museum flash my mind and I gulp, attempting to block those images and memories away.

The way his voice was so fucking deep and his fingers brought me to another realm. I clear my throat and I notice that we're nearing a quieter part of the neighborhood near the Mexican restaurant.

The streets aren't as lit over here and I side step to be closer to the walls of apartments that we're passing by.

"What's your name? I never caught it."

We're slowing our steps and I can tell he doesn't want to leave as much as I don't want to. Thoughts of *who* I'll have to go home to make me wish I could follow this man home. But I still don't know him, and that would be the stupidest thing to do. Or I'd be able to finally get a glimpse of those dreams and fantasies I've been having the last two weeks.

My arousal will always triumph over my stupidity, as much as I hate admitting.

"Julián." He stops in his tracks and I do too. He steps closer towards me and I back up, finding myself pressed up against a brick wall.

"Last name?" I ask.

"I'd prefer if we stuck to first names for now," he whispers. I feel a weird tug at my chest with his abrupt answer, but the butterflies in my stomach push past that feeling.

He's towering over me and my breathing picks up.

Oh my gods. He needs to step away before we do something again.

"Now," he states, lifting his hand to brush a strand of hair that's escaped the ponytail and tucks it behind my ear. The contact of his finger on my cheek brings a shiver down my spine, and I close my eyes.

"Hmm?"

"What's the name of the girl I made cum with my fingers under the stars?" His voice drops an octave, and I open my eyes in shock.

"I-uh, it's Eliana."

There's a twinkle in his dark eyes as he nods and leans in closer, his beard tickling my cheek.

"You want to know what I would've done if I brought you home?" His lips touch my ear and I visibly shiver. Every muscle in my body is wound tight and will surely snap under the pressure of his words.

I nod my head desperately, wanting to know what exactly he'd do.

"I would've let us eat before I devoured *you*."

"Oh my gods," I breathe in a whisper as I feel the rush of arousal flood my core and my breathing quicken. I look up and see his eyes gleam. He licks his lips before leaning closer, brushing his lips on my cheek before right over my lips.

"I would've spread you out on my kitchen counter and *feasted* on you. A full five course meal, if you will. And that's before I fuck you *deeply* and *roughly*."

I gasp and lift my hands to rest on his chest before he closes the gap between our bodies. I can feel his clothed erection hit my hip and I groan, closing my eyes.

"*Dime*," he demands, and I whip my eyes open before licking my lips.

"Yes," I spit out quickly.

"Yeah?" he asks, a twinkle in his eyes and a smile forming on his lips.

His hand travels down my side before grasping my ass and gripping *hard*. I squeak out again and nod. He chuckles in a low voice before pressing further into my body, causing me to squish myself further into the wall. My hands clasp in a fist around the fabric of his long sleeve and he groans.

"Please," I breathe out. All I can think of is this man and nothing else. It's like we're in our own little bubble and not even in a public setting. On a street where anyone can walk by.

What was it with this man and public settings?!

"Oh," he murmurs before moving his lips to my ear and nibbling on the lobe softly. This causes me to thrust my hips forward into his clothed erection, pulling another groan from the both of us.

"You sound so fucking pretty when you beg, *amor*," he whispers in my ear.

I close my eyes and clench my thighs together from *everything* that this man is making me feel. I can already tell that I'll soon soak my underwear if he keeps talking to me like this and if he keeps rubbing his erection on me.

The need to go home before I go full on feral intensifies. It won't be long before I let this man take me right here, right now. The museum was one thing, in a low lit room with a slim chance of someone walking in… but this is different.

I find my voice and some confidence in the way he's talking to me to respond to him.

"M-maybe you'll hear more of it next time."

My fingers let go of his long sleeve, and he pulls away, nodding. "It's late. I have to work early tomorrow."

I nod, but don't respond. I don't want to tell him, *Yeah, I have to wake up for school tomorrow*. It'll feel too juvenile regardless of my age.

Before I can say anything, he steps back and allows me to have more breathing space. I inhale and exhale sharply before rubbing my hands over my cheeks and tightening the ponytail.

He shifts his sweatpants and I watch as he pulls out his phone and grimaces at whatever is on his screen. He then shakes his head, typing something before swiping his finger and a bright screen casts a glow against his face in this lighting. He turns his phone towards me and I see that it's his contact list. He's opened an entry to add a new contact.

I slowly take his phone in my hands before entering my information. Instead of putting my last name, I enter the initial.

Eliana H.

"Here," I murmur as I hand him back his phone. He looks at the contact, smiling, before clicking his phone off and shoving it back into his pocket.

"I'm this way." He points his thumb towards our left.

"And I'm this way," I respond, pointing in the opposite direction.

Before I can make a fool out of myself and do anything stupid, I give him a small wave before making my way past him. He waves back and then treks towards his way home.

I bite my lip and pick up my pace to get further from where we just were.

My phone pings and I pull it out, glancing at the screen to see a text from my mother asking where I am. I let out a tired breath before increasing my speed to a slight jog to get home before another argument ensues tonight.

Five

JULIÁN

THE FIRST DAY of school in the fall semester as a professor will always be hectic. The chaos that ensues the moment I step foot on campus will always fill me with energy, but also leave me drained and exhausted by the time I get home.

I'm up before the sun and I always make sure my clothes are pressed. The university seems to prefer to have their first day of classes on a Wednesday which I don't really mind. Coffee pot is on the moment it hits 6:15 a.m. and I'm in the shower. Once I'm changed and ready for the day, I grab my briefcase.

I do most of my work at the office and try not to take anything home and have gotten into a fairly good routine where I can manage my time between classes to finish grading and having office hours with students.

Now, with Carlos opening up a position for me to have a grad assistant, it'll help me keep this schedule.

It also allows me to have someone in the office or department floor if Laura attempts to come around. I'd just make the assistant whisk her away at a moment's notice.

A flawless plan.

Once I make it to campus, it's busy already with kids hustling to the dining hall for breakfast before their morning classes.

In order to get to the Egyptology Department, I have to trek across campus from the faculty parking lot to the Liberal Arts building. It's only two years old, and it's improved more than the previous building I was working in. It houses all the majors that go from History, Literature, Creative Writing, English, Sociology and more.

Luckily, the building is so huge that the Egyptology department and the creative writing department are on opposite wings and different floors, so Laura and I never have to cross paths.

Although I worked at this university longer than Carlos has, he has seniority with his teaching experience and was offered the department chair position.

I was offered it first, but I didn't want it. I love teaching and delegating students, not other professors. It seemed more like a management or supervisor position that would make me reduce my teaching hours that I just couldn't sacrifice.

Syllabus week can be daunting for new students, so I try to make it a fun time getting to know each other. Once we level up to other undergrad years, I still try to keep it light during syllabus week, but we keep the introductions to a minimum.

No one needs to play two truths and a lie every fall semester. Especially if you're a junior or a senior.

I have one night class this week for graduate students, so I'll have a busier schedule once we're in full motion every Tuesday and Thursday. Carlos decided to only add another undergraduate course to my schedule, so my nights won't be as busy as I hoped.

IT'S ALMOST NOON BY THE TIME I FINISH GETTING LUNCH WITH Carlos after teaching two undergrad courses this morning.

I wave to him as I get close to my office door and notice that it's not shut, but ajar. I look around the hallway, but no one's near. My hands fall on the door, pushing before I suck in my breath and survey what's in front of me.

Laura is standing near my bookshelf to the left, her arms crossed and in deep thought.

"What are you doing here? I thought we discussed this."

She twists her head with a mischievous grin on her face. "Oh, honey! How was lunch? How is your first day going? I brought you some snacks for the rest of your day."

She points towards my desk where there's a small black box wrapped in a red bow. I take a good look at her, and she's wearing a tight, black formal dress with long sleeves, and her legs and curves are highlighted.

She tsks and I pull my eyes back to her face.

"Like what you see?"

I shake my head. "*Ni si fuera ciego.*"

Her jaw goes slack for a moment, but she recovers quickly. "Still on for dinner tonight? My place."

I finally get inside my office, but keep the door open. I walk towards my desk, dismissing her eyes that are following me. I place my briefcase onto the chair and thank the heavens that I brought it with me.

Who knows what kind of fucked up shit she could've done while I was gone? Although she isn't *crazy,* per se, she's shown me the lengths she goes to if she doesn't get what she wants.

It's daunting and I never want to be in that position again.

I like my sanity intact.

She paces the front of my office. It's not small, but it's not exactly huge. There's an empty desk to the left of where I'm sitting, which would be the graduate assistants if they ever needed to work with me in the office.

Besides that, I have two chairs in front of my actual desk for meetings and then some bookcases that have my textbooks for the courses I teach, as well as other textbooks and biographies.

Her hand lifts to drag a finger along a shelf on the far left of where I'm sitting. She lifts it and examines her finger as if she's looking at any dust particles it must've picked up.

I dusted everything this morning, so there aren't any.

"Could use some cleaning," she mutters. I roll my eyes and cross my arms as I continue to watch her.

"Why are you here?"

"I can't check in?" she asks with a bite to her tone. She turns and walks towards me, but I back up. She halts in her steps, her eyes watching me cautiously.

"No. And I can't have dinner with you tonight."

"What?" she laughs. "It's not like you have plans."

It's easier to lie to Laura now that we're divorced, so my response comes out easily. "Maybe I do."

Her eyes turn to slits as she continues to examine me as if I'm under a microscope. Once she's satisfied, she turns on her heels before pacing again.

I sigh and hang my head back.

"It's going to be a big year for us. My students seem great and I can't wait to meet more of them later this week."

I whip my head back up and stare at her. Her blonde hair sways as she turns to look at me from another bookcase.

"That's usually how it goes with new school years. New students to meet. But I'm not sure how that becomes an *us* thing?"

She laughs and shakes her head. "Oh, sweetie. We'll have plenty of faculty dinners we'll be invited to and can be each other's plus ones."

Yeah, right.

"I don't think we should do those anymore, Laura. You know it won't end well for us. It's a toxic cycle that we need to stop. I've said this time and time again—you need to respect that we're over."

Her eyebrows raise and her eyes widen. Before I know it, there are tears surfacing her eyes. *Great.*

I don't like it when she cries, especially in my office or on my side of the building. It makes it look like *I'm* the bad guy the way she storms out, making a scene.

"Don't, Laura." I warn.

She sniffles. "It's okay. Just thought it would be nice to be together in that kind of sense for this school year. I miss you."

"We're not doing this right now, or ever again." I push with more venom to my words.

That's until she locks eyes with me and lifts her chin. "You don't mean that, honey. I'll let you have tonight off. I'll see you tomorrow."

And with that she leaves the office, but not before making it known that she's wiping her eyes for anyone that might see her in the hallway.

I let my eyes roam the room before I finally focus on the bookshelf. The one Laura was standing near when I first arrived.

"What the fuck?" I whisper, walking closer and noticing that she added a small picture frame of us. It's *younger* us by a few years. When we were married.

I grab the frame and clench it between my hands, the slightest sound of the material cracking from the pressure.

"Jesus Christ, she'll never let it go."

I can feel the increase of anger in my body and it instantly fills my head with rage.

She comes in here and thinks she can hang around my department? Who does this woman think she is?

And then leaves a picture of us as if we're still together? We've been divorced for *four* years and she thinks a picture in my office can erase all of that?

Not on my fucking watch.

I chuck the frame into the trash can near my front door.

I'm so angry, I'm having difficulty breathing and my chest is heaving. It feels like all I can see is red when I stare down at the frame. That's all I see, and that's all I'm feeling.

Rage and… the feeling of entrapment.

No matter where I go, Laura is there. At work, at home… nowhere is safe. I try so hard to clear my thoughts from her, but she's plagued my mind. She's like a relentless parasite sinking into my skin, burrowing her way into every avenue of my life.

She has since the moment I met her. And now, I can't get rid of her as much as I'm begging the universe to.

My fists clench at my sides. I have to talk to Carlos to make him aware that Laura can't step foot on this side of the building.

I know he probably won't have any authority over the matter and he'll question why I'm finally telling him what's going on with Laura. Like, what's *really* going on. All he knows right now is that we divorced and there are some attachment issues on her end. It's become too much for me. It's suffocating.

I charge past the trash can and almost make it out of my office door and into the hallway when I collide with someone.

Someone with brunette hair that falls past her shoulders. Her perfume is sweet and her voice is one I recognize instantly.

"I'm *so* sorry! I wasn't watching where I was—"

She stops the moment she turns to look at me and I swear her breathing stops just like mine. Her green eyes widen and dart from my face to the hallway.

"Julián? What are you doing here?"

"Me?" I exhale, almost laughing in shock. "What are *you* doing here? At my university? In my building?"

I instantly think the worst–that she followed me here, but there's no chance. She doesn't know where I live and I haven't texted her yet since last night. I *meant* to, but things have been so chaotic with getting ready for the first day back.

"Your university?" she laughs, her eyes finally settling back from shocked to a relaxed expression.

"This is my office. Are... Are you a student here?!" I start to panic and think back to the fact that I never got her age.

Fuck, what if she's an undergrad student? Although that age isn't *illegal*, it isn't the age group I thought she'd be in when we first did things. She doesn't look eighteen.

"Kind of... but I see the look in your eyes and I want to let you know..." she begins to whisper, but her voice trails off. I walk backwards into my office so no wandering eyes or people passing by will stare. I pull her along with a quick grab of her wrist.

"Let me know what?" I wait for her to finally be in my office before I let her wrist go and shut the door, locking it.

I run my hands over my beard and rub my eyes. Fuck.

"I'm not an undergrad student, so don't worry. And I'm not even in this department. I got... lost."

Her green eyes look at me expectantly and I try to keep my cool, but she's on campus with me right now and it feels like a fever dream.

"I'm not going crazy, am I?" I laugh, backing up in disbelief.

"No, but I think I am. You're kind of looking at me like I'm a stalker. I swear I was just walking the halls and got lost. It's my first day on this campus."

I nod, but my body is still on edge from Laura's unexpected visit and my hands seem to keep shaking with rage.

I need to cool it before I do something I'll regret.

"I just—didn't expect you here. I meant to text you last night, but now you can see that I've been busy," I chuckle, waving around my office.

She seems to relax more at that. She looks around the office and I'm thankful for a moment for chucking the photo of Laura and I before Eliana saw it.

"So, you're a professor?" she inquires.

I nod, stepping closer to her. She's wearing an outfit that hugs her curves that makes it hard *not* to stare. Sage green velvet pants with a tight fit white shirt, some gold jewelry and cute converse.

It's the most basic outfit that I've seen already many times in my classes this morning and walking around campus, but she makes it look even better on her body.

I can't help but close our distance and find that being this close to her… my anger seems to dissipate.

My mind is in a trapped bubble of *her*. I'm no longer bothered by earlier events with my ex-wife. Sure, my body is still going through the stages of anger, but my mind isn't as troubled anymore.

And it scares the living shit out of me that this woman can make me feel this way. But she always has—since the moment I met her. She made me forget about Laura's bullshit that night. And then again when Laura kept texting me while I went to get tacos. Eliana happened to be the perfect distraction every single time and it's become a habit I'd like for her to continue.

She's my lifeline right now, and I don't want to let go.

I want to be consumed by her.

"Julián," she breathes, watching me get closer to her. Her hands instantly move up when I close our distance to touch my chest. I lean down and get close to her ear, nibbling on it.

I can hear her breathing pick up and my cock instantly hardens at the thought of her breathing heavily under me. Naked and moaning my name.

"Eliana," I whisper in her ear before nibbling her earlobe again. She shudders and grasps my dark gray sweater in her fists.

Her hands are smaller than mine and it's almost cute with how weak her grip truly is on my sweater.

I'd ruin her, if she'd let me.

And everything in me *really* hopes she does.

"What are you doing?" she whispers again, adjusting herself to push me a little, but not enough to move my body.

"It's been a rough morning, *distráeme*."

I didn't mean for it to come out as desperate as it does, but my mind is racing again with fervor for her and weaning off the rage from Laura.

I need to forget Laura and focus on *Eliana*.

She pulls back enough to stare at me. Her eyes cloud with confusion before nodding.

"We can go somewhere—"

"No. *Aquí*," I demand.

Before she can respond, I pull her flush to me. I step back and collide with the empty desk. Its edges are sharp against my legs, but I twist us around so she can be pressed against it.

She squeals softly before I lift her thighs enough to have her sit on the desk. I spread her legs and stand in between them. She's breathing faster, her chest rising and falling rapidly, and I smirk.

My hands run along her thighs before moving closer to her crotch. She tries to clench her thighs, but she can't.

"People will hear us," she whispers. Her green eyes slowly look up at me underneath her lashes and...

I'm done for.

"I don't fucking care who hears. You can scream as loud as you want. Be as vocal as you'd like, Eliana."

Her eyes widen, but there's a faint smile on her lips and the growing blush that sits on her cheeks. It starts to spread like wildfire over her temples and even down her neck. It's adorable on her.

I lean down, running my hands further up her body and latching my fingers to the buttons of her pants.

"Wait," she speaks up. My hands lift from her pants and I look at her for a moment. She nibbles her lip before taking a deep breath.

"I need to know that you're okay with this," I say. "With your *words*."

She registers my response and she nods her head. "Okay. I'm fine. I've just never done this, ever."

I can still hear the hesitancy in her voice. I want to make sure she knows exactly what we'll do.

"As much as I'd like to fuck you right here and right now, I'm going to be pleasuring just *you*. I want to take my time. And when you're ready, then you'll let me have my way. But not today, Eliana. We could christen this office in different ways that make you scream my name," I respond before my hands move back to the buttons and begin pulling them out one by one. My fingers find the zipper quickly, pulling it down.

"O-okay," she stutters finally.

She squirms underneath me and clenches her thighs again, holding me closer to her with the movement. This only causes my erection to grow, and I have to stop myself from flipping her over right here, tearing off her pants and diving into her pussy.

I take a deep breath to regain a sense of control before I move my hands to the waistband of her pants. I drag them and watch her eyes spark with something.

Curiosity? Arousal? Maybe both.

Once I pull down her pants to her ankles, I pull off her converse and then her pants and let them litter the floor.

"The door?" she speaks up as my hands move to her panties. I chuckle and shake my head.

"It's locked. *Créeme*. No one's getting in."

She finally nods before I continue my work, grasping the waistband of her black panties and she groans with the skin to skin contact.

"Lean back," I order while pushing her body down. Her lips quiver before a gasp escapes.

She's balancing on her elbows and watches me as I finally pull down her panties to her ankles and then let them fall.

Her pussy is *dripping* already, calling my name.

"Remember to tell me if you'd like to stop." I remind her.

She nods. "Yes, sir."

I look at her and move my hands to her thighs, clenching hard with my fingers–they'll certainly leave marks tomorrow. She breathes in deeply with the force of my hands and my cock twitches at the sight.

Before she can say anything else, I lean close and wrap my hands around her waist, pulling her closer to the edge of the desk.

I get on my knees and wrap her legs over my shoulder. She shudders again and I laugh, rubbing my beard against her inner thigh. I can see her pussy clench at nothing and her thighs continue to close around my throat.

If this is how I go, then so be it.

Eliana whimpers as I get closer to her pussy and breathe out heavily, causing her legs to clench again.

My beard tickles her slit before I waste no time in licking a long stripe along her pussy.

"*Oh!*" she groans, squirming her body. I lift my hands to steady her, one over her covered stomach and another on her leg.

I don't bother responding, but I lick again and find a rhythm in lapping up her pussy. She continues to grow wetter at the motion and her moans and whimpers just get louder.

Her legs continue to clench and her body moves, her core rubbing along my face until she's riding me as I continue to eat her out.

"*God*, your beard—" she exhales heavily.

I chuckle against her, and she shudders at the vibrations. I move my hand from her thigh to rest my thumb over her clit before I apply pressure and swirl it in circles to match my lapping with my tongue.

"Oh, fuck, I'm close," she moans.

My cock strains harder against my pants and I try to focus on just her. But it's *hard*.

"My tongue isn't even in you yet," I tease. This causes her to shift and she moans.

With that, I move my mouth until I press my tongue inside her and she squeals a little louder, like music to my ears.

"Just. Like. That," she says in shaky breaths.

My thumb rubs in circles even faster and my tongue continues to move in and out of her, tasting her and relishing in her juices.

She's close and I can tell by the way her pussy clenches around my tongue.

"*Fuck*," She moans before she comes all over my tongue. I take no time to lap it all up.

"Julián, please, too much," she murmurs, attempting to grab my hair to pull me off.

I finally do one more lick alongside her pussy before I lift myself up. Her legs drop with the motion and I get in between her again so she can't clench her legs.

I wipe my mouth and she's breathing heavily on the desk. There's sweat outlining her face and there's an after-orgasm-glow that makes her look like an angel with a halo hovering above.

She catches my eye and laughs. "That was something. I hope no one heard."

I lean over the desk, planting my hands on either side of her torso. My face gets close to hers and her chest moves up and down in an even more rapid motion.

"You thought we were done? Not a chance, *Corazón*."

Her eyes widen and her gaze flickers from me to the door. It's locked, and she isn't being as loud as she thinks she is. Her moans are quite soft in this office.

But I can make them louder.

"What?" she asks, watching me with panic.

My hand moves from her thigh to her pussy and I move a

finger up and down her slick folds. She shudders and closes her eyes.

When she opens them up again, she's relaxed again, and she moans at the touch as I drag my finger over her clit. She pulls her bottom lip between her teeth as she takes in the sensation.

"Please," she whispers.

"Say that again?" My brows raise. My finger moves from her clit and teases at her entrance.

She squirms under my touch, and her face turns to begging.

"*Please*, please, Julián. Don't stop." Her hands move to my shoulders and try to bring me closer, but she's not strong enough.

"Only if you're a good girl, then I'll continue to finger fuck you. And then maybe I'll flip you over and fuck you with my cock. Make you my dirty *slut*," I tease, knowing that won't happen, but it's nice to see her instant reaction.

Her eyes widen, pupils blown with desire. I want to devour her right here, right now. But I need to take it slow.

"Please, Julián. Please, *sir*," she moans.

And with that, I come undone—unwilling to hold back.

Six

ELIANA

JULIÁN IS RELENTLESS, and I can see it in his eyes.

The moment he heard me beg… there was a sudden *switch* in his persona. I instantly saw it in his demeanor.

It's something I've never seen before in a man. I've had a slew of partners in the past, but they were never like this. They were always one sided or simple, *basic* movements. They performed like they were in a porn movie, trying to hit spots but missing.

No dirty talk. Or at least the way Julián does it.

The way Julián can ignite a fire within me, in all areas of my body. It makes me want to be whatever he wants.

My breathing continues to grow heavy under his watch and under his body. His finger teases my entrance and I know that he'll give me what I want.

But do I know what I even want right now? I was thrust into this room so suddenly, and all I wanted to do was make him feel better.

I close my eyes and try to focus back on what we're doing, instead of trying to figure out the many reasons he's here and why he needed a distraction.

"Open your eyes," he demands, and my eyes flutter open.

"Y-yes," I hesitantly respond.

"Good girl, you listen so well," he murmurs before inserting his finger inside me.

I jolt from the sudden intrusion and he lifts his hand to press against my stomach, traveling it up my body until it reaches my neck.

His fingers wrap around my throat gently, his calloused hand causing shivers to run down my spine.

Without notice, he moves his finger inside me, pulling me into euphoria. I can't help but moan and close my eyes tightly.

Instantly, he removes his finger. I open an eye and see that he's staring.

"What?" I groan, throwing my head back before his fingers around my throat tighten and pull me back to look at him.

"I didn't say you could close your eyes, did I?"

I attempt to open my mouth to respond, but it's so dry I can't let out a syllable. It's like it's suddenly full of cotton.

"If you don't want this..." He teases, releasing his fingers around my throat and taking a step back.

"No, *no*," I groan, lifting to snatch his wrist that was on my throat. I close my legs enough to encase him between me and he smirks.

"No, *what*?"

I continue to stare at him incredulously. He steps back toward me, but even closer and I can feel his cock through his pants poking my inner thigh.

Fuck, use your words, Eliana.

"I-I," I stutter out. I take a deep breath and swallow. "No, I don't want you to stop. *Yes*, I want this."

"Do you?" He smirks again, removing his hand that was enclosed in my palm onto my thigh. The contact of his calloused skin on mine... makes my mind go into a frenzy.

I can't help what I do next. It's the needy part of me that craves his touch and whatever else he'll allow me to have.

I release his wrist and clasp my fingers around the fabric of his sweater and pull him swiftly. This catches him off guard, allowing me to pull him with ease. He gasps before I close our distance and kiss him.

"Does that work for you?" I ask once our lips separate. We're nose to nose and his brown eyes have tiny, golden specks in them.

They're beautiful, I don't think I've ever seen such pretty brown eyes like his. I can't help but feel even more butterflies flutter in my stomach as he maintains eye contact.

Julián doesn't respond. He latches his lips on mine again, but *deeper*. He pushes his tongue past my lips and through my teeth. Our tongues touch and we both make inaudible sounds.

A spark ignites in my brain from his sounds.

We continue to kiss with intensity before I feel his hand move in between our cores again and run along my slit, gently caressing my clit before he uses his body to push me to lean more. I let him guide us.

If he wants me outstretched on this desk, then I'm fine with that.

I gasp as his fingers enter me again, this time moving it around to find the spongy part in me that makes me moan. Once he finds it, he chuckles, causing vibrations to fill my body.

"*Fuck*," I groan, moving my hips to ride his finger.

With this motion, he teases another finger before entering it. His thumb finds my clit and I swear I see stars and lift my eyes to see him watching me for a reaction. He parts our lips just enough for us to breathe and for him to smirk. My chin is bruised from his beard, but I don't care.

He leans in again, biting my bottom lip, pulling it until it snaps back in place.

"You think you can fit three?" he questions, with a gleam in his eyes. "You're not quite ready for my cock just yet. But I'll need you to be, for when it's time."

I take a deep breath before nodding. He takes his time, pumping his two fingers in and out of me before entering a third one. I clench his sweater in my fists and close my eyes.

He stops his motions and I flutter my eyes open again, seeing him shake his head.

"What did I say, *Corazón*?"

My breathing grows heavier and my fists clench harder around the fabric, attempting to bring him closer than he already is.

"T-to not c-close my eyes," I finally stutter.

"*Mmm*, and yet you keep disobeying me."

I shake my head and grind my hips against his fingers, attempting to get back to what we're doing.

He tsks under his breath before lifting his free hand and clutching my chin, squeezing my cheeks and lips. It's rough and I have to breathe through my nose.

"If you're going to disobey me, then you'll have to be punished."

His voice is low, and it almost vibrates with how close he is. His eyes flicker to a darkened shade and I can't do anything but simply nod. With his hand still clenched around the bottom half of my face, I can't verbally answer him.

This is a much darker side of him I'm teetering on the edge of meeting. A part of me wants to push him away and tell him I can't do this right now. And the other half is bent on seeing if he's going to go by his word. If he'll really *punish* me the way he says he will.

I guess I'll have to see.

I nod again, causing him to release my face and place his hand on my collarbone, pressing me down to lie completely on my back. His fingers move again, but this time faster.

"Oh!" I squirm under his touch and he shushes me. I clamp

my lips together and watch him as best as I can from this angle, but he's not looking at me anymore. He's watching his hands. Like he's mesmerized by the movements.

His thumb presses against my clit and moves in faster circles. I moan and clench my thighs around him, feeling the rise of another orgasm fill my core and whole body. If I close my eyes, I'll see stars. And I don't want to be punished like he said, so I keep them open.

And I swear there's fucking tears lining my eyes with how badly I want to close them shut before I orgasm.

"Almost there, baby?" he whispers, thrusting his fingers even deeper than they were.

They hit the spongy part and I cry out, my hands grasping the desks edge. Before the coil can snap—

Julián pulls his fingers from inside me and takes all touch from me.

A whine escapes my lips. There's no smirk on his face and I gulp, feeling a sense of *danger*.

This is my punishment, isn't it?

"Julián," I whisper, finally feeling a tear fall from my eye. His face twitches at the sight before he turns back to the stone expression.

"What's wrong?" He cranes his neck.

I squirm and feel a bubbled cry leave my chest as I lay my head back down and look at the ceiling. It's white and freshly painted.

"Please, I didn't mean to disobey."

"So you learned your lesson?" I feel him move closer.

I lift again, so he can see me. I murmur out a quiet *yes*.

He places his hand on my thigh again and moves it in up and down motions. My skin is so sensitive right now from the intense feeling of wanting to orgasm that my whole body shudders and I have to take a deep breath to steady myself. Goosebumps rise from his touch and it's almost intoxicating.

His three fingers are still glued together in the same position that they were in while inside me. They're wet and he keeps them at his side. That's until he closes the distance and lines his fingers again at my entrance. He watches intensely as his fingers enter me. I choke out a cry and flutter my eyes.

"Thank you, sir," I whisper, moving my hips to grind his fingers at a better angle.

He mumbles in confirmation before he begins the movement of his fingers in and out of me. It's faster and his thumb goes back to its position at my clit. I clutch the desk again with my fingers.

My body heat is rising, as does my racing heart. I'm close again to an orgasm and I'm grateful I'll get the release.

"Almost there," I moan to Julián. He huffs out in response as he picks up speed. I clench my thighs around his body again, circling my hips against his fingers.

"Oh—" I slip out.

That's until his fingers pull out of me quickly and his hand on my thigh lifts.

"Fuck!" I whine, banging my head against the desk. I look up at him and the anger in me is taking over the pleasure I'm feeling.

I narrow my eyes and attempt to throw daggers at him with my stare. He lifts his fingers to his mouth and licks them one by one. Then he leans over the desk, placing his hands on opposite sides of my legs, palms flat on the wooden surface.

He sighs and shakes his head, and I take the moment to lift myself to a sitting position. My pussy is still trying to clench around *anything* and I wince at the movement of sitting up. Fuck, I need a release soon or I'll have to do it myself. He's already punished me enough.

"Please," I beg, lifting my hands to touch him.

"You disobeyed me," he whispers, shaking his head. "I told you what'd happen."

"But I let you deny me *twice*. Please, just let me have this."

He's silent for a moment. He doesn't move. His eyes stay stationed on mine and it even looks like he's not breathing.

I cup his face, my fingers brushing through his beard.

"I promise to listen," I whisper.

"And you'll take the punishment if you don't? Because they'll just get worse."

His words are sharp, and I feel his jaw clench underneath my touch.

I nod. I don't want to tell him I'll *try*, but who in their right mind will remember this? The moment I'm with him, I forget everything and I can't remember my own last name.

It'll be the death of me, but I agree anyway.

"Good, now get your clothes on. I have a meeting soon."

I see his eyes flicker to a lighter shade and his face relaxes in my hands. He watches as my eyes widen and my lips quiver.

He's going to leave me like this? On the verge of an orgasm and just expected to walk out of here?

He leans in and grabs my wrists, pulling my hands down from his beard before he kisses me. He then moves his lips to my ear. I take in a sharp breath, waiting for what he could say next.

"If you're a good girl and don't satisfy yourself, I'll text you my address for tonight."

My body quivers underneath his words, and he chuckles, brushing his beard alongside my ear.

"B-but I don't think I can wait," I confess. I am this close to running to the bathroom and just satisfying myself, as embarrassing as that sounds.

He growls in my ear. It's low and sends sparks throughout my body.

"If you can't wait, then I can't give you the proper reward."

He finally leans back and he stares at me, watching for any sign that I'll listen this time.

He's already denied me twice. I don't want to think what he

could have in store for me if I showed up with an after orgasm glow.

I could try to fake it, but my mind is telling me he'd fucking *know* if I gave myself an orgasm and showed up at his place.

"Okay," I concede. He nods and bends down to pick up my panties and pants. He helps me slip them on before he pulls me off the desk and I slip on my shoes.

He takes a step back and I turn on my heel to head out of his office, but he catches my elbow and twists me around. I squeal at the motion, but I'm silenced with his lips on mine again and a groan falling from his lips. I lean into the kiss and it's not helping with where my body is right now.

My hands fly to his chest and press hard, pushing him off me. Our lips tear away from each other and he grins.

"Stop, you're so bad," I laugh while backing up again. I run my hands through my hair and turn to see him flash me a smirk before I turn the lock and pull the door open.

I slip out and check the hallway for anyone before I make my way to a nearby bathroom to fix my makeup that's positively ruined. Once I'm done with that I head toward my dad's office down the hall.

I try to steady my breathing and contemplate turning around and going home, but I told him I would visit him after my morning class.

Rounding the corner, I find my dad's office, knocking on it in five swift motions. He calls out loudly for me to open it. I push the door open and see Lena hovering over his desk, pointing at a file.

My dad is pressing his glasses up the bridge of his nose and nodding at Lena before he lifts his head and smiles.

"*¡Princesa!* You came, I thought you'd gone home."

Lena stands from her leaning position and waves. "Hey, how's your first day?"

I shrug and let out a shaky breath. They thankfully don't

notice. "It's going. Just had one class. But the majority of my classes are on Tuesdays and Thursdays."

He nods and so does Lena. She gathers her things on a nearby table, lifting her book bag over her shoulders. "Professor Haros, I'll see you later, after my class?"

My dad smiles and nods, waving her off. I give her a smile as she leaves before walking closer to his desk. His brow raises as he studies me standing; I can't exactly sit down right now with what just happened in Julián's office.

If I sit down... I don't even want to think about that.

I'm surprised I haven't soaked my panties with how wet Julián got me with two orgasm denials. I try to clear those thoughts while standing in front of my *father*.

"Will you be home for dinner? Victoria—your mother, will have to skip it. She has a lot more issues than she thought with her coursework online."

I pinch my brows. "Is she having that same issue where she uploaded the wrong type of file?"

She did this last year and didn't seem to remember that she had to make it the right type of file to upload to the computer system. I helped her fix it over the phone, but she didn't seem to pay attention or even thank me.

He nods and takes a deep breath, letting it go slowly. "We can just get take out, *mija*."

I nod, thinking back to Julián and if he'll even text me at all with his address tonight. I'm not used to *this* much attention from a guy. I've had my fair share of partners, sure, but this is different. It's addictive and all consuming. There hasn't been a day where I don't think about him or fantasize the things he'd do to me.

Something in me has doubts he will even text at all. He's a professor, for one, so he's already got such a busy schedule.

"That sounds great. I'll see you at home."

"Maybe go see your mother before you go home. Just so she can feel like she got to see you."

I huff out a breath and feel all my arousal from Julián leave my body. Victoria Haros is the perfect cockblocker, I'm not surprised.

"*Fine.*"

"Love you, *Princesa.* I'll see you in a few hours."

I nod and turn on my heel, scurrying out of his office.

··⋅⊰•◦)◦◊◦(◦•⊱⋅··

MY MOTHER WASN'T IN HER OFFICE EARLIER TODAY, SO I DIDN'T have to see her. But, now it's almost eight in the evening and neither my father nor Julián have contacted me.

I assumed my father would've texted, but he hasn't even done that. I've been in bed going through files on my computer and getting everything ready for this week. I enjoyed having my laptop organized with everything needed for the semester.

But it seemed like I had *too* much time. Once I was done, I glanced at the clock and noticed that it was past dinner and dad still wasn't home.

I also noticed that my phone had no message from an unknown number claiming to be Julián. I don't like this harrowing feeling that's slowly taking over, I thought he'd stay true with his word.

Even as the clock nears ten p.m., I still get no text. I hear the slam of the front door, though, and I run down the two levels of stairs to see my dad get in, looking exhausted. He lifts his head to give me a small smile before he walks towards his office on the first floor. I linger in the second floor's hallway before I head back upstairs.

I wanted to go down there and ask him what's going on and

why he never answered my texts or my calls earlier, but I couldn't make myself do it.

Instead, I ran back into my room and hopped in bed, pulling the sheets over my face and shutting my eyes. Disappointment ached through my bones for more than one person. My dad, Julián, and even my mother. Skipping dinner wasn't on my agenda, but I couldn't fathom walking downstairs.

As the night neared closer to midnight the disappointment boiled into anger, causing me to toss and turn. The growling of my stomach didn't even push me to get out of bed–I was somewhat of a stubborn mess.

Sleep didn't come easy, but it did eventually.

THURSDAY GOES BY WITH ONE CLASS THAT WAS MORE OF AN introductory course. I attempted to stay focused, but I was worried about my father... and Julián. My classes today were at ten in the morning and then two back to back at one in the afternoon.

As I head out of my class, waving to a classmate, I feel my phone buzz in my pocket. I pull it out of my tan plaid pants before widening my eyes.

It's from an unknown number and I open it quickly, glancing around to make sure I don't bump into anyone as I head out of the building.

UNKNOWN

Want to grab a coffee at Crescent? My treat.
As an apology.

Then another filters in.

This is Julián, by the way.

I want to text something angry, but I don't. My stomach flutters at the thought of seeing him again and that takes over all the disappointment and anger that coursed through my body the last few hours. I save his number before replying.

ME

A coffee and a scone would do.

I make my way out of the heavy doors before I feel rain hit my face. I quickly pull out the tiny umbrella from my bag, opening it.

Thankfully, I dressed with durable shoes that wouldn't get ruined with a puddle. I make my way across campus to the nearby coffee shop, *Crescent Cafe*. It's just off campus enough where it's not deemed an on-campus coffee shop, but it's close enough where I can walk there.

There's usually a hybrid population of classmates and locals that go there, but it's the best coffee I've been able to try out this summer. My phone pings again and I look down at the opened message.

JULIÁN

Deal.

Perfect. I increase my speed as my shoes slosh against the wet pavement and try to bypass any puddles.

The sky is a dull gray, and it feels like it's been months of fall already despite it only being September.

In five minutes, I'm shaking water from my umbrella and closing it as I enter the cafe. It's not as busy as I assumed. The smell of baked goods surrounds me and brings the simplest of a smile to my face.

I glance around the cafe before I spot Julián sitting at a table in the far corner. I see him look up and catch my gaze before standing up and grabbing something from his briefcase. He's got his computer out and I watch as he closes it just enough before walking towards me.

"Hey," I murmur as he gets closer.

It feels *weird* being here with him in such a public setting. We had the dark room in the museum, the night at the empty park, and then his office.

This was new for me and I can see he's a little nervous as well. He laughs and nods his head towards the front of the cafe where the baristas are.

"Get anything you want. I kind of was in the middle of an email I needed to finish. Here," he states, opening his weathered wallet in his hands and pulling out a titanium card. I hold back a gasp as he presses his card into my open palm. I take the heavy card and he winks at me before he turns on his heels and walks back to his seat.

"Oh," I whisper before I glance back at the menu. There are new fall items out and just looking at the bakery glass cases makes my stomach growl. I head over to the register and order an apple cider latte and a cider donut. I add in a blueberry scone when my stomach growls loud enough for the barista to hear.

Once the barista tells me the total I look down at the card and notice just his initials are on the card, not his full name.

J.E

I give the barista my name before handing her the card and she swipes it, handing it back to me with the receipt. I make my way towards the area of the cafe where there's a long empty counter where completed orders sit.

In no time, my order is ready, and I grab my items. I head towards Julián and he finishes typing, looking up and reaching his hands out to grab the items from my hands.

"Thanks," I sheepishly say before I take a seat across from him. There's enough space if I wanted to whip out my laptop as well, but I watch him close his laptop instead and put it away in his briefcase. I remember to hand him the card back and slide it on the table before he takes it and slips it back into his wallet.

He runs his hands over his beard and sighs, giving me a

pained look. I furrow my brow before grabbing my hot latte and pulling it to my lips, taking a sip. The hot liquid warms my body from the rainy weather outside.

"I'm sorry," he starts.

His apology seems genuine and I place my latte down before leaning my body closer. My ribs hit the table underneath my brown top. It's a V-cut out with buttons along the center. I feel my breasts get pushed up with the motion and Julián's eyes flicker down quickly before going back to my face.

"It's okay, I kind of got busy," I lied. I know he's talking about last night.

"It's not okay. I'm a man of my word, I meant to text you. This entire week has been *a lot*." He rubs his beard again and then the bridge of his nose.

"It's fine, Julián," I reassure him as I take a bite of the donut.

He watches me chew, licking his lips briefly. He leans his arms on the table and crosses them. "I'd say tonight, but I have… obligations."

"Plans?" I ask, smiling.

He's silent for a moment as if he's mulling over the right answer.

"You can tell me you have plans, you know. I won't get upset." I try to assure him, trying to sound casual despite feeling anything but.

He shakes his head. "They're not exactly obligations I'd like to attend to." He leans closer, dropping his voice an octave. "There's other *plans* I'd much rather do."

My cheeks grow hot at his words and I clear my throat, reaching for my drink. I sip it for a few seconds before placing the cup down and he narrows his eyes for a few moments.

"Another night then," I reassure him.

Now that he's texted me, hopefully he'll continue to do so. I don't want to bother him, but if he's free he can message me. I know how stressful the first weeks of the semester get with my parents, so I can't imagine how he's feeling.

"Tomorrow night, I'll get us dinner. Tacos and then maybe a movie."

My chest tightens at his words, and heat pools in my belly.

"Like a date at your place?" I question, feeling a smile rise to my lips.

He flickers his eyes from the table to my face before smirking.

"You can call it that. But I think we have other things to take care of as well."

He watches me and my cheeks feel like they're burning. Actually, my whole body feels like a tea kettle about to explode. He smiles at the response and reaches over to break off a piece from my scone, taking a bite and eating it before licking his thumb and pointer finger.

I feel my mouth go dry and pull the latte to my lips for a distraction. My fingers drum against the ceramic mug in rhythmic beat. He's going to make me go feral at every place we're in. This isn't fair.

"What?" He laughs.

I take another big sip before shaking my head. "Nothing."

He smiles and winks before lifting his arms and leaning against his chair. I feel his shoes kick against mine. I flick my gaze from his face down towards his chest and then his crotch. The table is small enough where I can almost see his thighs.

His thick thighs and–I exhale heavily and center my thoughts on anything else.

"Do you want to walk back to campus?" I suggest finishing my latte and working on finishing the donut on the table.

"I'd love to," he replies with a soft smile. He gathers my trash and hands me the scone and donut on a napkin. He waits for me to get up before he grabs his briefcase in his other hand and pushes in our chairs.

We head to the front of the cafe and he throws the trash away before opening the door for me to go through. Once we're outside I realize that more students are walking around the streets, presumably leaving the dining hall or class. I look at Julián who is running his hand through his curls.

"I forgot that it probably wouldn't look innocent walking side by side," I whisper. His lips curl into an almost devilish grin.

"It's not out of the norm. Some professors catch up with students outside of office hours," he reassures me.

My shoulders relax at that and he nudges me playfully before he starts walking towards the crosswalk. I giggle and follow him, but attempt to keep my hands to myself. To hold his hand would definitely be inappropriate, as much as I want to.

So, we walk side by side and make sure not to throw too many smiles and flirtatious glances at each other the closer we near our building. It feels nice though to be out in public with him like this.

And I think he enjoys it too.

Seven

JULIÁN

DINNER WITH LAURA IS FUTILE. She brought over some Italian dishes and insisted on putting them on a heated skillet as if she cooked them herself. She made a big show by placing the food on my nice plates.

The moment she knocked on my door and strutted her way into my place, she started digging around for those plates and preparing the stovetop. Like she lived here and knew every nook and cranny.

I made a mental note to re-organize the kitchen so this won't happen again. I had to make *another* mental note to myself to stop letting her get away with this kind of stunt.

There was a reason she's doing all of this, but she won't admit it to me. I know she wants another go, but having another intimate relationship with her is not even on my mind anymore.

If she came to me with this proposition sooner, sure, I would've obliged—but now I know it wouldn't have been good for me. She drained me until I had nothing left and I'm still working on picking up the pieces. I wasn't a saint, but I didn't go to the lengths she did, and that's what made us different.

"You like the Alfredo pasta? I added some pepper to the

sauce," she pipes up from her place. She's sitting across from me, twirling her fork around some noodles. She lifts the fork to her lips and drags her eyes towards me as I watch her take a bite.

She chews slowly, her expression teasing. A scowl crosses my face as I take a twirl of the pasta on my plate and eat it. I don't want to respond to her obvious delusions because it's not a fight I want to waste my energy on. If she wants to pretend she cooked this meal, then have at it.

She clears her throat, waiting for me to respond. I think for a moment before smiling.

"It's okay. You know I don't really prefer pasta as a takeout meal. Chinese food or pizza would've been fine."

Laura rolls her eyes and huffs out loudly as she places her fork down on the plate a littler harsher than necessary. "You were always so critical. It's just pasta, sweetie. It's just as good as any of those takeout meals."

"I'm not saying it's bad. I just prefer to be at the restaurant eating it instead of ordering it to go. Or cooking it from scratch," I add a smidge of sarcasm to those last few words.

She watches me slowly, her brows knitting together. She then peers at me with her accusatory expression I've become very well accustomed to.

"Well, it's not like you gave me a choice..." Her voice travels until her eyes meet mine. My jaw grits in annoyance as she continues, "You didn't want to eat anywhere in public with me. So this is what I had to do."

Her words are sharp and she quickly inhales as she picks up the fork again and twirls it aggressively, pulling an enormous chunk of noodles and placing it in her mouth.

It's quiet for a moment as her chewing takes over the silence. My mind is racking for an answer, but I can't think of one. I suddenly feel transported back to the times we were married.

Her always having to have the last word. Her expressions seemed accusatory when there was no reason for it. Her sharp and serrated words cut into me, pulling bits and pieces of myself as she yanked the imaginary knife out.

My heart begins to thud louder in my chest and I feel like I'm going to lose myself once again. The anger that comes over me whenever we find ourselves in this predicament isn't a feeling I prefer to be consumed by.

She knows how to get under my skin though and push my buttons—she knows how to manipulate me into thinking it's *my* fault when I get to this headspace. She has a way of making me think it's my fault I get so angry. It's an entrapment that's suffocating. A cycle that Laura always seems to put me in.

She clears her throat and I finally look at her, noticing the way her eyes get glossy. She sniffles and looks up at the ceiling, as if attempting to not let herself cry.

"Laura, *qué quieres ahora*?" I mumble, letting the fork fall from my grasp. It bangs against the plate loudly and she *tsks* under her breath.

"Julián Estrada, you need to fix your table manners."

She says nothing else as she stares back at me with narrowed eyes. She blinks a few times, her eyes still in a glossy state. I don't know what the fuck she's wanting to say, but I want her to get out.

I don't know why I agreed to letting her come over. I don't know why I *let* her come over. I should've sat in the dark and pretended I wasn't home. I could have easily left my apartment for the night. The thought of getting new locks on the door crosses my mind as she sniffles across the table.

My eyes roll and she gasps. "Julián, you care about me. Stop lying to yourself." She lifts her fork again and twirls more pasta and takes a ginger bite.

I fix my eyes on her mouth as she chews, and my lips turn to a scowl. Heat is bubbling inside me and I know I'll soon be at a boiling point that won't stop. I'll get her truly upset and she'll put me in a position where *I'm* apologizing to her.

I can't keep apologizing for the way she manipulates me into doing things I don't want to do.

"So, fall break will come here fast. Are there any faculty dinners you've been invited to yet?"

I cast my eyes onto hers, and she smiles, finally. I shake my head and sigh. I push my chair back and it scrapes loudly. "No, Carlos hasn't invited me to anything yet. I don't even know if he plans to do something at his place. I offered to do it here, but it's too small."

"Yeah, we wouldn't be able to contain all those people."

Her words hit me hard, and I suck in a deep breath. I dig my heels into the ground and push myself off the chair and stand tall. She watches me slowly, her lips curling into a small smile before turning back to a straight line. But I catch it.

"¡*Ya, basta*! We're not a *we*, Laura. Stop acting like it. And *stop* trying to insert yourself into my life! We're *over*."

I pick up my still-full plate and make my way to the kitchen and dump it into the sink. The plate and silverware clatter loudly and I almost think the plate breaks in two, but it's still in one piece. Laura gasps again behind me and her chair scrapes as well.

"You don't have to be so rude about it. I just wanted a nice dinner with my hus–" She stops herself before clearing her throat. "With my ex-husband and see how things have been the first week of school."

I hear her footsteps trail behind me and I jolt from my place when I feel fingers curl around my bicep. She leans her head on my shoulder and I take a side step.

"Laura, get the fuck out," I say through gritted teeth. My voice cracks in the process from the growing anger.

"Honey, you know you don't want that." Her curled fingers turn flat as she runs her palm up my arm before moving across to my chest. I take a deep breath from trying to pry her fingers off, but she takes it as if I'm breathing deeply *for* her.

"See? You can't hold back. You want this just as much as I do."

I shake my head and don't think, grabbing her wrist harshly. She yelps from the tight grip and I push her off me, taking a step back. I run my hands through my hair.

"You fucking hurt me. Look!" She reaches her wrist out and I don't see any bruises or marks.

"You'll be fine, Laura. You always are. Now, get the fuck out of my place."

I don't let her get near me again as I make my way towards the front door. I pull the door wide open. The hallway is quiet save for a faint sound of a tv playing across the hall, but it's barely audible.

"Out, *now*," I say again. I turn to where she's still standing, holding her wrist with her hand. Her dramatics used to get me, but not anymore.

She huffs and grabs her coat that's over her chair and leaves her plate on the table as she reaches for her purse from the kitchen counter. She hangs her coat over her arm and pulls her purse over her shoulder as she marches towards the door. Her blonde hair sways with her movement and her eyes are like daggers.

"I-I don't know what's gotten into you, Julián. But you're not the man I used to know."

Her words don't pain me anymore and I actually *like* hearing them coming out of her mouth. If I was younger and more naïve, those words would've broken me. I would've begged for her to stay until I could be myself again.

But I like who I am now. I'm not the broken Julián she used to make her punching bag.

"*Ándale, pues*. Before you make me do something I'll regret." I spit out. She's silent before slipping out of the door and down the hall. I slam the door shut and lean my head on it, allowing myself to cool down.

But just like yesterday, my thoughts are swimming and I feel rage take over my body. What helped me yesterday was having Eliana miraculously step into the hallway at the same time I opened my door.

I told her earlier at the cafe that I couldn't see her tonight. But I don't know what I'll do if I don't. I need the release she gives me and I don't fucking care if it becomes a crutch for me. Her body and her *moans* tame me. Like I'm in another world and there's no Laura. No worries about my past. Just *her*.

I lift my head from the door and make my way to the kitchen counter where my phone is face down. I check the screen and see I have a few school emails, but that's it. I swipe the screen and go to the messaging app before typing in her name.

ME

Come over.

I type in my address and hit send. I clean up the kitchen, tossing Laura's plate into the sink as well. The rage is still boiling and I almost throw her plate onto the wall just to see it shatter everywhere.

My phone pings and I see a text from Eliana.

ELIANA

At dinner with parents. Sorry.

My fingers grasp the phone tighter and I type back a reply. I'm fucking desperate and I don't care how it makes me seem to Eliana. I need her.

ME

Por favor.

While I wait for her response, I toss my phone on the counter and lean my palms on the surface. I try to take a few deep breaths, but it doesn't work. It feels like one of those panic attacks I used to get when I was stuck in arguments with Laura.

She wouldn't let shit go and would berate me until I couldn't take it anymore and my body reacted in a way I couldn't control.

It felt like asthma—like my lungs were closing in on themselves and I couldn't breathe. I'd cough and lean over to see if I could get a better angle of breathing, but nothing helped. It wouldn't be until Laura calmed down that I'd be able to breathe better.

The sound of the phone breaks me from my thoughts and I take another deep breath as I see her one word response. I expect a firm *No*, because she doesn't owe me anything. But I see her text and my body relaxes a bit.

ELIANA

On my way.

Eight

JULIÁN

THE MOMENT ELIANA knocks on the door, I rip it open and pull her in by her raincoat. The material is thin and I almost break the fabric from my pulling, but I don't care. She yelps at the sudden movement as she stumbles into my place.

"Julián! I almost thought you gave me a murderer's address!"

I don't respond as I slam the door shut and push her against it. I press my body against hers, trapping her in. Her eyes gawk and I take no time to close our distance, kissing her with fervor.

She gasps in between our mouths and that makes me kiss her harder. My erection is already growing and I can feel some of the panic and anger from Laura's visit dissipate.

My tongue pushes past her lips and she moans as our tongues slide against another. Her arms move from her sides to run along my chest until her hands wrap around my neck and she pulls me even deeper into the kiss.

After a few moments of kissing, she finally moves her hands back to my chest and pushes, separating our lips. We're breathing heavily and her cheeks are flushed.

"What's going on?" she asks softly. Her emerald eyes search

mine, but she comes up with nothing. Her clenched fists on my sweater relax a little.

I sigh and close my eyes, leaning my forehead against hers. "Nothing. Just wanted to see you, *Corazón. No podía esperar.*"

"Well, it's past dinnertime, so I'm assuming there are no tacos?" she teases and I chuckle, shaking my head in defeat. I lift my face to see a smile spread across her face.

"No, no tacos. Just some trashy pasta in the sink."

She raises a brow. "You don't like pasta?"

I shake my head. "It's not the pasta, it's who—" I stop myself. Her eyes stay on mine as I stay silent and wish I said nothing.

"Oh," she finally breathes out. Her hands fall to her sides, and I curse Laura for coming over and fucking up my night. But we agreed to meet for dinner and I was stupid enough to keep the promise.

It's not in me to break a promise, even for people who deserve it to be broken.

"It doesn't matter," I say with more force. I can feel the annoyance and the anger bubble up again and it reminds me again why she's here.

Do I care for her? I think so. But my mind isn't letting me go there right now. I just need the release. That's all that matters right now.

"Eliana," I say, stepping back and taking her hand to pull her with me. Her brows stay pinched together as she follows me with no fight.

I finally take my time to see that she's wearing a soft, blue turtleneck underneath the raincoat. She's wearing leggings that flare out at the bottom. Her clothes cling to her curves well, and I want to devour her until she forgets her own fucking name.

I pull her forcibly closer to me. She yelps with a soft smile on her face as we get closer to the kitchen. The table is cleared off from dinner earlier, so I spin her around enough to push her against it. I lean down and wrap my hands underneath her knees, pulling her up in one swift movement until she's sitting on top.

"Oh!" she squeals as she watches me lick my lips and place my body in between her legs. She takes a deep breath, her brunette hair clipped back and slowly falling out with her movements. Strands are falling over her face and I instinctively reach my hand out to move them back behind her ear.

Her cheeks flush even more with the contact and I grin, loving the way she reacts to my every movement. The anger is slowly dissipating again, and I lean to rest my head in the crook of her neck. I inhale her sweet scent and let my hands roam up her thighs until they're resting on the sensitive part where her hips and thighs meet. She stiffens from the contact and her breathing grows heavier. I lift my head a little to place a few kisses on her neck.

Her legs tighten around me, and I know she's getting just as needy as I am. My cock is straining hard against my slacks. Laura wouldn't have approved if I ate dinner *in my own fucking place* wearing pajamas or anything comfy.

With the thought of earlier, I let my teeth bare and take a bite at Eliana's soft skin right on her collarbone. She jolts and squirms.

"Julián! Oh my gods," she squeals. My hands tighten on her sensitive skin, and she squirms again.

"Let me have my way with you tonight," I whisper as I move my lips from her collarbone to her neck until I'm at her ear. She shudders at the contact.

"Yes, *please*," she murmurs in a low voice.

I smile and bite her earlobe until I grasp her sensitive skin harder and she squirms even more. I move my lips until they're brushing against her cheek and then her lips.

My mouth devours her as we continue our kiss and her legs tighten more around me. I'm grinding my hips against her core and she moans through each movement. I push my tongue into her mouth again and I increase my pace. I will bruise her lips for sure tomorrow from my force.

Just the thought of her bruised from my touch, in this way, makes my mind go feral. I groan and move my hands to remove her clothing. She lets me take off her coat and then lift her turtle-neck over her head before we connect our lips again.

"Oh, my gods," she moans again as I place my fingers back at the waistband of her leggings. The fabric is not as thick as I'd expect. I could rip it if I wanted to.

"Didn't take you as the religious type," I chuckle as she pulls her head back.

Her brows shoot up. "Sorry bad habit."

"With what I plan to do to you tonight, you won't be screaming just their names," I promise her.

Her lips quiver as she takes in my words and she nods, before I place one hand on her chest and push her back. "Lean back on the table."

She obeys and falls back as I lift my sweater over my body. "Take off your bra," I command and she obeys by moving her hands to snap off her bra and throw it to the ground. Her nipples are pebbled and I lick my lips at the sight.

Without a thought, I lift my fingers to brush over her right nipple, softly twisting it. This elicits a moan from her lips before I do the same to the other. "So fucking beautiful," I praise.

Her upper body is even more beautiful than I could ever imagine. I could stay here all night worshiping her.

I pull my own undershirt over my head and throw it to the growing pile of clothes on the ground. Moving closer to the table, I place my fingers on the waistband of her leggings, pulling them down. She peers at me from her place, lifting her hips just enough for me to slide the fabric down. It dangles at her ankles and I lift each foot to get the leggings off before it plops to the ground. I then hook my fingers on her panties and with one tug, I break the seam on the side. She gasps.

"Oh my gods, you destroyed my underwear!"

I laugh as I take the fabric and pull it from her body. I bunch it in my fist as I wrap my hands underneath her knees again and drag her body closer to the edge of the table. She squeals from the movement.

I lean over her just enough to see her face. I lift my hand with her panties. "Open," I demand. She widens her eyes but obeys. Her soft, pink lips open slowly and I push the fabric into her mouth. She moans from the action and I know she's tasting herself.

"Don't you dare spit it out, or you'll get punished. Got it?" I say firmly. She nods her head and I move my hands back to her knees, lifting them until her legs are on each shoulder.

Her breathing is erratic as she watches me closely. I finally look down and see how wet her pussy is for me. I caress her thighs before moving one hand down, sliding a finger down her folds. Her back arches from the touch and she moans loudly.

"Remember, keep that inside those pretty lips," I remind her. She moans again as I brush my thumb against her clit.

"Fuck, I'm going to have fun tonight," I exclaim. Her thighs tremble from my words and it makes my cock strain even more against my pants.

I don't let her calm down as I lean down, licking the inner sides of her thighs before licking a *long* stripe along her folds. She jolts in place and her moans are muffled. I can't help but let out a grunt myself. My tongue goes along her wet folds again and her pussy tastes like the best thing. I can die between her legs and I'd be perfectly happy with it.

I move my thumb against her clit again as I increase the pace of my tongue. Her hips continue to grind against my face and I groan, enjoying every bit.

"God, Eliana, your pussy is so fucking delicious." Her hips grind harder against my face and I insert a finger inside her. Her scream is muffled, but it's loud enough to know how much she's enjoying this.

"I just want to tie you up on this fucking table every night and feast," I continue as I move my finger at an antagonizing slow pace. Doing so makes her walls clench, so I add another and that brings a muffled scream. My tongue slides along her folds as she gets wetter and my fingers pump in and out of her easily.

I press my tongue against her clit and she moves her hands to my scalp, grasping my strands tightly. I moan in pleasure and add a third finger in.

"Fucking come for me, baby."

She moans loudly before her thighs clench tightly around my neck. I increase my fingers at the sound and my tongue swirls along her clit more. Finally, her back arches and her pussy clenches around my fingers before I feel her orgasm. Her wetness pools out of her pussy and drenches my hand as I continue to lap up her juices and finally pull my fingers out.

She cries and her thighs tremble hard. I hold onto them to steady her as I lift my face and lick my lips. Her eyes are brimmed with tears and her chest is heaving with every breath.

"We're not done yet," I remind her. She moans and shakes her head, her breathing erratic.

"You want me to stop?" I raise a brow and she shakes her head again, her lips opening to push the panties out. I reach over and pull the fabric out.

"Please, more," she begs. Her face is red and I brush my hand over her cheek, pushing back strands from her face that are stuck from the sweat that's beading at the top of her forehead.

"Get up and turn around. I want you laying facedown on the table. At my mercy," I tell her.

I take a step back and reach my hand out for her to grab. She slowly takes it, allowing me to pull her up and off the table. I lace my fingers around her neck.

She swallows, and her eyes look up. I squeeze my fingers around her throat and she doesn't move. Like she's okay with me snapping her neck right here. She fucking likes it as much as I do.

God, she's perfect for me.

"I want you clenching around my cock. And I want you screaming my name as I slam into you," I say abruptly, letting her neck go. She gasps and takes a couple breaths before nodding and turning around, leaning over the table. Her ass is up and in full view of me. Her pussy is still glistening for me.

I take my time slipping off the belt from my pants and sliding the fabric down, kicking them off to the side. I push down my boxers and my cock springs free. It's more painful to stroke it as I attempt to get myself lubricated enough with my spit. My tip drips with pre-cum.

She turns her head back to watch me, and I slap her ass. She squeals and I line my tip with her entrance. I pause for a moment as her eyes go wide. I raise a brow and that's when I realize that it's going to be the first time we've had sex. Everything else has been oral.

"I know this isn't the best time to ask this, Eliana," I start, backing up a little. She cranes her neck toward me and waits. "I'm clean, but I want to make sure…"

She smiles. "I'm clean too. I meant to ask, but I tend to get caught up in everything whenever I'm with you."

I breathe a sigh of relief. "Want me to grab a condom?" I ask softly.

She shakes her head and smiles. "I'm safe, too. Get a shot every three months. I prefer no condom Julián. I want to feel *all* of you, please."

I step closer once again to tease my tip with her entrance, this time making contact. Her body jolts and a small moan leaves her lips. I glide my cock along her folds as she squirms. "Well, then. That's perfect," I respond as I continue to tease her entrance.

She mewls loudly and moves her gaze back at the table and I smirk.

"If my fingers were too much for you, baby, then you're in for the real treat." She gasps again at my words and I push my tip inside her. She moans and I close my eyes from the feeling.

I hold myself back from slamming into her, to the hilt. I let my tip move in and out of her, stretching her out even more. I stroke the rest of my length as I curse under my breath and push even more inside her. She squirms and I place my other hand on the small of her back to keep her steady.

"Fuck, *todavía estás tan apretada*. You really are my *slut*. Think you can take my whole cock? *Qué nena tan perfecta*."

And the last word, I slam my hips into her ass and my cock drives into her and she screams loudly at the sudden stretch.

"*Ah*! Oh my gods," she cries out. I grind my hips against hers, moving the hand that was around my length towards her thighs and then her pussy. I find her clit and start rubbing it slowly. Her walls clench around me as she adjusts to the girth and length.

"The gods aren't here to save you, as much as you scream for them tonight. You'll have to deal with me," I reply with a groan as I slide out of her slowly and slam my hips again against her ass.

She jolts and cries out again. Her sounds are intoxicating and I want to hear them on repeat. So I do.

I continue to thrust harshly into her and I'm almost to my release as my cock hits her in every spot. Her thighs tremble and she's no longer able to keep herself upright. I move my hands to her hips to keep her steady as I continue to fuck her deeply.

"Fuck, I'm going to come," she cries out as I drive my hips against her once more. My orgasm is approaching, and I bite my lip and groan.

"Come all over my cock," I tell her, and she cries out as she tightens around me.

"Fuck," I moan as I continue to thrust into her. "Where do you want me?"

"Cum in me, *please*," she moans from her place. She turns to head to lock her eyes with me. My chest heaves with each breath and I can feel the sweat bead at my forehead and dribble down. My chest is hot and sweaty as well.

"Yeah?" I groan as I slam my hips against her again. She nods.

"Please," she says louder. "Fucking cum in me!"

"My pretty whore, so fucking needy," I grit through my teeth and I slam my hips once more before my release snaps and my cum streams out of my cock and into her. I moan loudly and lean over her body, my cock twitching from the feeling as I lay my head against her back.

We're both breathing hard as we take a moment to gain our strength back.

She clenches her walls around my sensitive cock and I groan, biting her soft skin on her back. She squirms under my hold and she lets out a squeal.

"Julián! That tickles!"

I chuckle as I lift my head from her body, and I pull out of her slowly. She whimpers from the movement and I lean over to kiss each side of her hips before I step back and will myself to go grab a wet towel to wash her.

"Stay there," I tell her. I head into the hallway and then the bathroom to grab a hand towel, wetting it. I look in the mirror for a moment and see how sweaty and red my body is. But what I notice for once is a smile stretching along my lips.

Fuck. I haven't smiled like that, even with Laura from sex. I brush the idea of my ex away from my mind as I walk back into the kitchen and wipe the towel along her pussy. She whines from the sudden contact against her sensitive skin and I kiss her hips again.

"There, all done."

She pushes herself off the table and turns around slowly. Her eyes travel along my body until they fall on my cock. Her eyes widen and then her cheeks flush.

"What?" I ask her, watching as her nipples get hard again and I'm not sure if it's from arousal or from our bodies finally calming down and cooling off.

"Nothing, I had fun," she murmurs before cocking her head to the side. She lifts her hands to cover her breasts and I shake my head, taking a step closer.

My hands wrap around her wrists and pull them down. I lean down and her head cranes up to look at me.

"You never have to be shy around me."

She bites her lip. "Just a little self-conscious. You know, naked in a man's kitchen that I barely know."

"You never have to feel that way around me. And when you do, I'll get on my knees and worship you like the damn goddess you are."

She glances down at my chest before I move my hand to her chin and force her to look up at me again. Her eyes are sparkling and I smile before leaning in and kissing her lips. She melts into it and I groan, feeling my cock get hard again.

What was once deemed as a way to get a release from the anger I felt, has soon become an addiction. Not just to her sex, but to her presence. Her aura. The feeling I get when I'm around her.

I'm fucking gone for and I can't let her go.

I won't.

Nine

ELIANA

The morning is quiet as I wake up and let my hands smooth over the sheets. One minute I'm placing my head on the pillow and the next I'm waking up what must be hours later.

I open my eyes and let my vision clear before I remember where I am. Not home. There's shifting on the mattress, like another body, and I whip my head to the right to see Julián turning over in his sleep and facing me.

His hair is a tousled mess and I fight back a smile that threatens to split my face. He's beautiful when he's sleeping. The rise and fall of his chest is mesmerizing as I take it in.

He sighs in his sleep before reaching his arm and moving it across my chest and curling it around my waist. I squeal as he drags me closer towards him until we're nose to nose.

"Julián," I whisper, attempting to hold in a laugh.

He stirs once more and his hold tightens on me, right on my hip where I'm the most ticklish. I jolt and let a laugh slip out, making Julián finally open his eyes.

"Morning," I whisper again. My heart lurches at the way his eyes continue to flutter open and widen the moment he takes me in.

His lips curl into a smile and he sighs again, pulling me in closer than I already am. I squeal once more from the force and giggle as he buries his face in my neck. He kisses my skin softly, his beard scratching me and causing shivers down my back.

My very naked back and body... I completely forgot we went to bed like this. After another round of sex on his couch and the bed of course. We couldn't stop the moment we started on that kitchen table.

He asked me to stay over and with the way he looked at me last night... I couldn't say no.

"Have a good sleep?" He asks as he remains nuzzled in my neck. I nod and wrap my arm around his shoulder until I can caress the nape of his neck, my fingers grasping his growing salt and pepper curls.

"The best. But I have to go soon. I have class and need to meet my advisor later."

"Right," Julián sighs.

I laugh and smile as he leans closer, rubbing his nose with mine. I inhale deeply before closing my eyes.

"What about you?" I ask slowly. He shrugs and closes our distance and kisses me, causing me to let out a soft moan.

"Doesn't matter," he whispers before kissing me deeply and shifting his body to be closer to mine underneath the sheets. Suddenly, his erection hits my hip and I let out a gasp. Flashbacks of last night run through my head, remembering how *big* he was. I was shocked he could even fit.

He pushes his tongue into my mouth with my gasp, and I feel like I'm floating. His hands travel along my bare skin until I feel like putty underneath his touch.

"Please," I beg him softly. He lifts his head before nodding and going back to kissing me before traveling his lips downwards. He leaves a scatter of kisses along my neck, collarbone, chest, and then takes his time with each of my breasts.

My body arches for him almost immediately from his tongue

swirling along my nipples. He sinks his teeth into my breast and I mewl loudly. He doesn't stop; he keeps going down and shifting his body until he's hovering over me with the bed sheet slowly falling off his back.

"You make the most beautiful sounds, baby. And they're all for me? For my cock?"

This causes another animalistic sound to escape my lips as he places his rough palms on my knees and spreads me wide to move himself between them. He continues to travel his tongue lower and lower until he reaches my crotch. My heart is beating against my chest and I can *hear* it in my ears. All I can *feel* is his touch. It's so much, but I need more.

"*Please*, Julián," I beg harder. I arch my back once more and move my hands to grasp his curls, but he moves his hands instantly from my knees and grabs my wrists tightly. He looks up and his brown eyes cloud with darkness.

"Hands to yourself. If you hold on to me, I will not let you come. I'll edge you for fucking hours." There's a tensity to his words.

"But—" I start, but I stop myself from the way a singular brow raises. His jaw clenches and I gulp, feeling heat pool my lower belly and honestly my *whole* fucking body.

He smirks before dropping his head back towards my body and I dare to touch him. My mind flashes back to his office the other day when he denied me twice just to never let me come at all. He made me leave and I was distraught the rest of the night.

His tongue glides right over my pussy and I jolt, my mind coming back to the present. He groans as his hands go back to my hips and then to my thighs, holding me down tightly as he slides his tongue over my clit. I attempt to raise my hips, pressing myself further onto his tongue.

It feels so good to be in this position with him. I haven't had this much sex in 24 hours. My body is still spent from last night on the table and the couch.

"*Oh,*" I squirm under his touch as he lowers his tongue through my folds and teases my entrance. I want to clench my thighs at the sensation, but his hands keep me from doing so.

"So fucking sweet and so fucking wet already for me, baby. It's like you're made for me," he mumbles, just loud enough for me to hear. This praise makes me suck in my breath and I feel dizzy.

This whole dirty talk coupled with the praise has never really occurred to me in intimate relationships in the past. But the way *he* does it and says these things, they make me feel like my mind and body are floating. I'm in dirty talk heaven and I didn't even know that was a thing.

"Right there," I moan as he teases my entrance with his tongue again before I feel a stiffer feeling and realize it's his finger.

He twirls it in my arousal for a moment, causing another ripple of sounds to escape my lips and I drag my hands to fist the bed sheets. I shut my eyes tightly as he pushes a finger into me and continues to suck and lick my clit. The sensations make me on the brink of passing out, but I persevere.

"Think you can handle two? Of course you can, my needy baby. You want my fucking cock stuffing you, don't you?"

I cry out from his words as he fits another finger inside me and continues to pump them in and out of me while his tongue swirls along my clit. I press the back of my head back into the pillow and with how tightly my eyes are shut, I see stars.

"Come on baby, I know you want to come all over my fingers. Do it for me, *please.*" The coil tightens within me, the flood of emotions rises in me from his words and then I feel the coil snap.

My back arches one more time before I squirm and my orgasm takes over. He continues to suck on my clit and fuck me with his fingers before I have to move my hands to his head and grasp his curls tightly to push him off me.

He *growls* and grabs my wrists firmly. I finally look up and my heart stammers against my chest as he lifts his head. His lips and beard are shiny from my juices. He licks his lips before his thumb smooths over my skin in small circles. His hold remains tight around my wrists though as he pushes himself off me and moves up, shifting his knees on the mattress so he's hovering directly over me. His cock is hard and bobbing against my thigh. The tip of it is pink and glistening with pre-cum. I widen my eyes at the length, once more forgetting how big he is.

"I told you not to do that," he breathes out. His eyes are dark and stare into my soul and I feel my breath hitch for a moment.

I don't feel fear in any way that's logical. I fear what he's about to do to my body because of what I just did.

And for some fucking reason my body aches for him. Like his tenacity and dominance urges me on.

"Sorry, sir," I whine, my lips going dry from the nerves tingling my body. He smirks before releasing my wrists, and they fall limply at my side. I don't dare to move them again. He leans down, positioning his palms against my ears. His face is close to me and he breathes out again and it blows against my chest, causing my nipples to go hard from the feeling.

"I already made you come, but I can still keep my promise to edge you until you're fucking begging me for mercy."

I gulp and shake my head. "Please, no."

I'd never make it out alive if he edged me the way he did in his office. Even with an orgasm out of the way, my body is reacting quickly to his body language and his voice so that it doesn't feel satiated.

"No?" He chuckles. It vibrates against my body and I shut my eyes again, hoping I don't get wetter. But I do and it's getting exhausting how reactive my body is to him.

"Don't edge me," I whine.

He *tsks* under his breath before pushing his hips closer to my core and his cock rubs against my inner thigh, inching closer and closer to my entrance. I buck my hips forward, but he doesn't move.

"But you disobeyed," he reminds me. I want to grasp his wrists that are fastened near my ears, but I don't dare.

I lean my head closer, and he does the same, our noses brushing against each other again. I inhale his scent.

"Please, Julián. I'll be good, I promise," I whisper. His eyes twitch at my words.

He's affected by me just as bad as I'm affected by him, I know it. We can't starve each other from what we truly desire. He huffs out a breath before leaning his hips down even further until his cock slides between my folds and I cry out.

"Fuck, please!" I scream. His teeth clench together and he groans loudly. His hand travels to my throat before wrapping around it. His fingers are slow, with a feathery touch, *before they aren't.*

His fingers tighten around my neck and I gulp against his palm, my breathing getting strained. I suck in a breath and he groans, pressing his cock against my folds again. I squirm against him, attempting to bring some friction between us so I can get off again.

I just need another orgasm. I'm willing to beg all morning for it, if I have to.

"You're so pretty like this, struggling to breathe. I'm the one allowing you to breathe, baby." His words are husky and fill my mind. His praise makes my belly swarm with butterflies, and he clenches his fingers tighter around my throat, causing my heart to beat a little faster.

"Please, fuck me."

He bares his teeth and moves his other wrist to lower between our bodies. He aligns his cock with my entrance and pushes slowly into me. He breathes out loudly and I gulp against his hold.

My breathing is straining even more and my vision prickles.

Faint stars and blackness fill the outer edges. But I attempt to take in shallow breaths through the airway he allows me.

Something sickening in me is happening where I wouldn't mind for his hold to tighten even more to the point I pass out. But he doesn't. He keeps himself from teetering off the edge of pushing me to the point of passing out while he pushes himself even further into me.

His cock stretches me out and I lean my head back, my mouth agape as he seats himself fully in me. My pussy clenches around him and he groans, his hold on my throat lessens.

I gasp for air and his fingers don't tighten, no–they smooth over my throat comfortingly.

"Fuck, you're always so tight for me, baby. Like I didn't wreck you last night. I could get used to this tight pussy. Fuck you every day. You'd like that, huh? Get stuffed by my cock daily, like the whore you are."

I mumble out in affirmation as he pulls out and then leaning over, moving his hand from my throat to grasp my nipple and squeezing it. His hips snap forward and his length fills me once more and I cry out loudly.

He does this motion again, leaning his head towards my ear and sucking on my earlobe before trailing some sloppy kisses along my neck. He thrusts into me again and again, his speed horrifyingly slow. Agonizingly brings me to my climax, and then pulls me away from it.

I can't keep up with this pace and expect an orgasm. I need him to move faster. I lift my hips and circle them, attempting to speed up his thrusting, but he groans and moves his hand from my nipple to my hip, squeezing it and holding me still.

"*Slow*," he demands in my ear before returning his lips back to my neck. I nod, feeling my legs shake and my heels dig into the mattress.

He's not punishing me by withholding an orgasm. He's

fucking edging me with his slow thrusts. He knows I won't ever get to my climax like this. He fucking *knows*.

And I honestly believe this is more tortuous than denying me an orgasm. Because I may not orgasm at all from this speed.

"Please, I want to come!" I beg. My lips part as his hips roll and push his cock deeper into me.

"Mhm, not yet, baby. I love seeing you distraught like this over me. Over my cock filling you up."

I cry out again as he slips out and then pushes himself into me at full force. The mattress slams against the wall and I'm sure whoever is his neighbor is sick of us by now.

"Julián."

There are tears that are brimming my eyes and I need him to speed things up. I *need* him to. I've become almost completely feral for a release.

He doesn't respond, but he pushes himself up and moves his hands over my knees and lifts them over his shoulders as he steadies himself. The angle drives his cock further into me and I cry out. His forehead is shiny with sweat and he licks his lips.

He looks beautiful even in this state as he thrusts into me once more.

"You'll be a good girl?" he asks as he moves his hand, smoothing it over my thigh until his thumb connects to my clit. He rubs soft circles over it and I cry out some more, the tears falling from my eyes.

"Yes I will, sir. Yes, please," I blabber mindlessly. My brain is mush and I don't care what he asks of me. I'll agree to anything he wants at this point.

"Good. *Fucking.* Girl," he responds as his thumb swirls faster along my clit and he snaps his hips at full force with each word, pushing me almost to the headboard.

He continues this brutal pace, and I clench the sheets tightly. The coil tightens once more and this time he doesn't tease or stop the thrusts. He continues until I'm screaming out his name.

"Come for me!" he demands and I clench my walls, the coil snapping and wetness pooling out of me. I come all over him before I realize it's not stopping and I'm doing much more than just that.

"Fuck, so fucking beautiful. Got my cock all fucking wet. I love when my baby squirts. So fucking filthy." He snaps his hips again and *again*, causing me to be on the brink of another orgasm. I scream and curse his name as he gets himself to his own climax.

My body shakes completely, and he has to hold my legs up before they collapse on the bed. I have no energy to hold them up myself.

"Want me to come in you again?" he asks, disrupting my thoughts. I find his eyes and they wait for me as he continues to thrust in me. But with the way he's looking, they're soft and waiting for my permission.

I nod my head and he licks his lips and grunts loudly, snapping his hips a few more times, sloppier movements, before collapsing over me and I feel warmth fill my insides.

I wrap my arms around his back and he nuzzles his head against my neck once more.

"Fuck, you're perfect."

I hold back from responding. I don't want to ruin this moment.

Whatever this is.

He kisses my neck before lifting his head and kissing my lips.

"Let me clean you up," he says before slipping out of me slowly and getting up from the bed. His body is tense and his muscles protrude in his arms. His thighs are thick with muscle as he walks from one side of the room into the hallway to grab another towel to clean us up.

I lay my head back and take a few deep breaths.

ELIANA

"MISS HAROS?" The blonde speaks as I enter her office. Her smile is big and bright as she beckons me in and I close the door.

Her office is small but vibrant. The walls are littered with bookcases, which are full of books and decor. There are some picture frames on her desk that are facing away from me. She's got two nice leather chairs in front of her desk and she leans forward, placing her elbows on the desk.

"Thank you for meeting me. I know it's really early in the semester," I tell her. My eyes rake over the rest of her desk where her name plaque is.

Professor Estrada.

"Of course! I'm glad to have you as a graduate student. I hope the first day of classes went well?" The blonde speaks up as she continues to smile. Her eyes sweep over my face and then my body.

I had to race home to find new clothes this morning after Julián's. He ripped my underwear off last night and I couldn't come back to campus with what I wore to his place last night.

I also had to cover up his marks on my neck. They didn't

hurt, but there was some color to it and if you looked hard enough, you could see the outline of his fingers. It kind of turned me on seeing the marks. Seeing the aftermath of what we did. The imprints on my skin, reminding me it actually happened.

"Yeah, it went really well. I think I have your class this afternoon."

She nods and briefly glances down at a few papers. Probably my schedule. "Right, you've got me. It'll be fun. I try to make classes fun, at least," she laughs.

"Do you think I'd be able to stay on track? I know I'm only taking four classes, but that's full time according to graduate school standards."

She nods and waves her hand, dismissing my worries. "Of course. You're already taking all the introductory classes necessary. Next semester, you'll really be diving into the coursework for Creative Writing. My class is actually one of the first to give you a feel for it. Not everyone who comes into the graduate program has a bachelor's in Creative Writing, so foundation courses are essential the first semester."

I breathe a sigh of relief. I was worried that I wouldn't be on track and that I'd be wasting my time. It's been so long since I was back in school with classes that weren't specific to my medical degree. I don't think I took an elective since my sophomore year of undergrad.

Even though electives in grad school pertain to your field of study, it'll be nice to have some options to choose from. I might try that poetry elective I saw online when I was looking up possible schedules.

"And your father works here," she adds. I lift my head from looking at my knees and her smile is wider. There's a gleam in her eyes.

I clear my throat. "Yeah, he's in the Egyptology department."

"It's a great degree. He's a smart man. I believe I met your mom too at a past dinner. My husband actually works in that department as well."

My eyes glance at her hands that clasp over one another. She's got a wedding ring on and I wonder who her lucky husband is.

Who Mr. Estrada is.

"Most likely," I tell her. "I haven't really been around for those, but you probably met her at them. I just moved back." I kindly skip over her mention of her husband, not sure how appropriate that'd be to discuss during my advising meeting.

She nods and laughs. "Right. I think your father mentioned that when I passed him in the halls over there. Welcome back. I'm sure your parents missed you."

My fingers start to pick at each other, wearing down the cuticles. I give her a small smile before shrugging ever so lightly. "Yeah, they're happy I'm back. Happier that I'm back in school where they work."

She smiles before unclasping her hands and finding a pen, scribbling and circling a few things on the papers. She lifts the papers and leans them over towards me. I grab them and see that it's a tentative schedule for the next couple of semesters.

"You can keep this just in case. You can move some classes around if you'd like in the future. But as long as you take the required courses, you'll be fine."

I nod and thank her. I stand up from the leather chair and she fixes her eyes on me. "Thanks, Professor Estrada."

She looks deep in thought for a moment before she laughs. "I look forward to seeing you later today in class. Remember, I'm always here if you need anything. I'm just a knock away."

I give her a big smile and nod before I turn on my heels and head for her door. I look back as I whip the door open, and she gives me a small smile before I shut it.

My hands are holding the papers tightly as I head towards my mother's office, where I kept my bag. We got a quick, early lunch to catch up on how it's been going lately, but it was futile. She kept asking questions that when it came time to return to campus, I felt knots in my stomach and threw up the food we had. I had to run to the bathroom and forgot my things in her office and then got sidetracked by not wanting to be late meeting my advisor.

By the time I reach my mother's office, it's slightly ajar. I knock and open it wide, seeing my dad inside, sitting on one of the cushioned chairs in front of her desk. My mother's eyes find mine and her lips fight back a smile.

"Hey, just left my bag. Had a meeting with my advisor." I walk inside and head for the other chair where my bag is. I pick it up and drape it over my shoulder.

I turn to my father and he smiles. "Hey, *Princesa*. Heard you and mom had lunch?"

She snickers from her place and I nod, not daring to look her way. She knew she ruined my meal and knew exactly where I went. This wasn't the first time she made me throw up because of her stress.

"Who's your advisor again, sweetie?" my father asks as he leans back in the chair and folds his arms over his chest.

I shift my weight on my feet and look at my mother before looking back at him. "Professor Estrada. Laura I think is her first name."

He nods and smiles. "Ah, she's something. Great professor, you'll learn a lot from her."

I look back at my mother who peers down at him before giving me a strained look. "She's something, for sure. I haven't spoken to her a lot since the whole *ordeal*."

I furrow my brows and look between my parents. "What ordeal? Did something happen to her?"

My father shakes his head and takes a deep breath. "I haven't introduced you to the other Professor Estrada yet."

"Her husband?" I ask slowly. Flashback of conversation to

Professor Estrada mentioning her husband working in the same department as dad comes floating to the forefront of my mind. My mother snickers again and this time I'm the one peering down at her from my place.

"Something like that," she responds before lifting her phone from her desk and tapping the screen, opening it.

I look back at my father who shrugs and gives me a strained smile. "Something like that. Doesn't matter. She doesn't let her personal life affect her students."

"She seemed really nice," I tell him. Whatever the hell is going on in her marriage has nothing to do with the students or with me in particular.

Dad hums before nodding. "I have to get back. Got a class soon. You do too right, honey? I can make us dinner tonight."

I nod and look back at my mother who is typing out a text on her phone. She glances up at us. "I'm having drinks with Mary, sorry."

Mary is another professor in her department.

I shrug. "No worries. We'll survive."

He laughs loudly before I step close to him, patting his shoulder before heading out of the office with my belongings.

My phone buzzes in my pocket and I make sure I'm far enough from my mother's office before pulling it out and seeing the text.

> **LENA**
>
> I need a girls night out. Your father is driving me nuts already.

I smile and type out my response and hit send.

> **ME**
>
> Definitely.

In an instant, Lena responds.

LENA

Yes. Fucking yes. We can go far away from
this campus. I don't want to bump into any
students I'll have to see Tuesday.

I laugh as I read her text and respond back with an *okay* before closing my phone and heading down the stairs until I'm in the lobby area of the building and heading out. I need some coffee if I want to survive this class and then study some.

I was already getting some assignments completed that I didn't want to push off until the last possible minute. I wasn't a procrastinator, but I didn't want to get into a habit of pushing things off and then becoming one. It helps that it's Labor Day weekend so we'll have Monday off.

I head to Crescent Cafe once I'm out of the building to get another one of those tasty scones I got while I was with Julián.

Eleven

ELIANA

LENA IS OVER, running her fingers through her curls after applying some mousse. She's sitting at my desk with her makeup products strewn all over the surface. She's leaning in close to the mirror in front of her.

I am still trying to decide on an outfit. I'm standing in front of the closet, arms crossed over my chest, and chewing on the insides of my cheeks. After showering, I did my hair and makeup while I waited for Lena to come over.

I didn't bother acknowledging my parents, who were in the kitchen when I went downstairs to let Lena in.

"Just pick the first one you tried on." Lena's voice floats through the room. My eyes glance at the hangers that hold the outfit I first tried on *almost an hour ago*. Nothing felt right.

Nothing fit the way I wanted it to. I groan and shake my head, turning to look at my best friend. She's got a pretty black, shimmery top on and tight black jeans. Her golden tan skin seems to only glow even more with the clothes and the gold jewelry she's got on.

Lena's eyes reach mine through the mirror and she smiles softly. "You've never had *this* much trouble finding an outfit.

Remember your 21st birthday? You bought the first dress you tried on."

"This isn't the same," I snicker.

"I still say go with the first outfit. It made your boobs pop."

I laugh as I spin back towards the closet and sigh, lifting the hangers with the first outfit I tried on. A golden top that dipped low in cascading fabric down the chest. The straps were gold chains. The pants are a nice tight, black leather.

"It doesn't make me look like a tube of sausage?" I ask, eyeing the clothes a little more.

Lena snickers behind me. "Absolutely not. It makes you glow *and* the pants make your ass rounder."

I think of her input and decide to wear the fucking outfit. I clutch the hangers to my chest and head to the bed, tossing them onto the mattress before stripping out of the sweats and over-sized tee I'm currently in. Lena is still trying to fix her curls.

As I pull the top over my head, the golden straps are like ice cold on my skin. I hiss before grabbing the pants and dragging them over each leg. I forgot how *difficult* it can be putting on leather clothing.

"Hot *mama*," Lena squeals. I turn to her and lift my hands to my waist and raise a brow. She smiles widely and wiggles her brows. "I'm serious!"

"Okay, okay," I giggle. "It's not that bad. But I don't think I'll be able to pee with the pants."

"That's why you drink more alcohol than water. You won't have to worry about that. Don't break the seal."

I quirk a brow. "You're really encouraging me to drink more alcohol than water? Since when? Where did Lena goody-two-shoes go?"

She laughs as she finally finishes her hair and checks her make-up. I head back to the closet to find shoes to go with the outfit. I spot a pair of golden heels and grab those. Once I get those on, I find a small black purse to throw my things inside.

"Ready?" I ask Lena. She turns to me and nods, getting up and slipping on her own heels.

"Remember, if I find a cute guy *or* girl to take home, don't let me."

I chuckle as I grab the handle to my bedroom door. "Why's that? You don't want a hook up tonight?"

Lena sighs as her brown eyes find mine. "I'm just trying to do this new thing where I don't date while I'm in school. I had my fun this summer."

I nod. "That's fair. *Me*, on the other hand, I won't be doing that."

Lena nudges me with her elbow. "Really? Anyone in mind?"

My mind flashes back to Julián and I instantly feel the fluttering in my core. And other areas. "No, but that doesn't mean I *won't*."

"*Hmm*," Lena murmurs before we make our way down the stairs and out of the house. Even though we live close to college bars, Lena didn't want that. So, we're waiting for a Lyft to pick us up and take us a few miles away to where locals and older crowds go.

By the time we make it to the small bar, show our IDs to the bouncer, and make our way inside, I feel my skin rise with nerves. My fingers find each other and I'm picking again at my cuticles.

"Let's get a drink!" Lena yells in my ear, to be heard over the loud music. It's a mix of rock and metal that I rarely listen to.

"Sure!" I respond as I follow Lena's lead to the bar. I scan the area and see how many people are already here. Definitely an older crowd, barely any college aged people. I take a deep breath and know that Lena is already enjoying it with the atmosphere.

There's a few bar stools empty that we hop on as Lena orders our drinks and pays. Once the bartender pushes two drinks towards us, Lena hands me one and lifts her own for me to clink against.

"To the new year and new *things*," she yells over the music. I nod and smile, clinking my plastic cup with hers. We drink and my lips instantly purse at the strong alcohol.

"A vodka sprite? Really?" I ask, peering at Lena. She giggles and leans her head back, her black curls following the movement.

"You'll get the next round then," she laughs. I nod.

We continue to drink as we people watch–what we love to do best–before Lena hears a song she really loves and begs me to go to the makeshift dance floor at the back.

"Come onnnnn!" Lena whines, pulling me by the wrist. I quickly put the plastic cup on the countertop before she drags me to the dance floor and we join the other few people that are dancing to the music.

Lena sways her body to the beat of the music and I copy her, feeling the drink loosening my muscles and my mind. I don't really go on the dance floor, but for her I will. We're dancing for the next three songs before Lena points to the bar to get another drink. I thankfully agree and link my arm around her elbow.

As we drink our second *and* third drink, we spark up conversation with the bartender. His name is Owen and he's got a wife and two kids. He's been managing the bar for a few years now and likes to bartend as well since that's when he first discovered his love for mixing drinks and talking to customers.

"You know, we've got a small patio out back. Most people don't know about it," he finally tells us as we order another drink. I look to Lena who's eyes open in mischief and a smile erupts from her lips.

"Yes! I love those kinds of hidden gems."

Owen laughs as he nods his head towards the back of the bar. Both of our heads snap to where he's looking and that's when we see a metal door that barely looks like a way out. It's blending really well with the wall and that's why we didn't even see it when we went to the dance floor.

"Let's go!" Lena says, whipping her head back to the bartender and grabbing our drinks. He winks at us before I slip out of the stool and follow my best friend who is already making a beeline for the patio door.

I have to run a little to catch up with her and pray she doesn't trip and fall. I'd be too worried about her wellbeing and she'd curse herself for dropping the expensive drinks. With what they're paying her for her GA position, she's told me countless times how much she's been trying to save. "Hold on, Lena!" I scream and giggle as she slips through the door and I have to pick up my pace.

I push the door and feel the cold weather against my skin. I suck in my breath as I let my eyes adjust from the darkness of the bar to the twinkle lights that are hanging over trees and such outside. The patio is cute and there's a few tables as well as some steps that lead to a grassy area with more picnic tables. There's more people than I thought would be out here and I hear loud laughs coming from one corner, but I keep my eyes on where my friend might have gone.

"Lena?" I call out, pressing my lips tightly as my heart rate increases and I can feel the alcohol really do its thing.

"I'm right here," Lena speaks up behind me. I whip around and almost scream.

"Jesus, you scared the crap out of me!"

Lena giggles before giving me my drink. The outside is wet and sticky and I try to ignore the feeling as I take a big gulp. This time it's a tequila Red Bull and it's not bad.

"Oh shit," Lena whispers beside me. I look up at her and furrow my brows.

"What?"

Her eyes glance to the right of me, where the back of the area is. Where the loud laughter was coming from. She glances back at me and rolls her eyes.

"I just saw some professors. I swear this town isn't big enough."

I glance slowly at the crowd of men, but I can't make them all out. There's some where their backs are to us and then some where the fairy lights above them barely make out their faces with the light.

"Who's there?" I ask.

"Let's go find out. I just recognize one. Professor Rhodes was my art professor when I had to do some prerequisites a couple of semesters ago."

"For Egyptology?" I raise a brow.

She nods and huffs out a breath. "Yeah, it was informative, though. But I wish we went into more detail on how it connected to my degree. I didn't need to know the color wheel at this age."

I can't help but let out a laugh and she playfully punches my arm. "Ouch!" I playfully yelp.

"Oh, you're fine," Lena grumbles before nodding her head toward the professor group. "Let's go say hi to Professor Rhodes, at least. He's like five years older than us, so at least he's not ancient."

"Stop," I laugh, following her though.

Lena doesn't stop, she walks down the steps and heads towards the group with her head held high and I follow. The grass isn't too wet from the weather, but I can still feel the heels dig through the dirt and curse myself for following Lena.

Once we get to the group, Lena squeals. "Professor Rhodes? It's Lena!"

The group stops talking, about four of them, and one of the blonds looks to us and smiles brightly. He's handsome and looks as old as Lena mentioned. He's got green eyes that stay on us.

"Lena?" Mr. Rhodes calls out.

"What are you—" Lena starts, but then she stops once the others that had their backs turned finally look at us. That's when *my* own breath hitches at the sight of someone I didn't expect to be here.

But then again, it makes sense. My mouth gapes open and I almost spill his first name before I shut my mouth. But Lena laughs before she speaks up again.

"Professor Estrada? What are you doing here? Isn't this bar a little *young* for you?"

The other guys let out a few *oooh*'s with her playful joke and Julián glances from Lena to me. His brown eyes turn a darker shade once they find mine, and his jaw clenched tightly. And with that movement, it feels like the other night when he ripped my panties and ate me out on his kitchen table.

Fuck.

"You know Professor Estrada?" Professor Rhodes speaks up, patting Julián on the back.

The last name sounds familiar and I try to rack my brain to think of where I might've heard it. The alcohol already coursing through my veins doesn't help with the task.

Lena nods, but doesn't go into detail before realization finally hits me.

That's when my world *stops*. It feels like the air has been sucked out of my lungs and I take a small step back, barely able to hold onto my cup. Actually, I can barely grasp the fucking wet cup and it falls from my grip. It splashes the remaining liquid all over my feet and Lena's and Julián steps back a little to avoid his shoes from getting wet.

"Woah," one of the other guys says.

"Ana! What's wrong?!" Lena gasps, touching my elbow. I take a deep breath.

"Is she okay? Does she need to sit down?" Professor Rhodes asks. I shake my head and Lena just smooths her hand over my arm over and over again.

Finally, Julián clears his throat and I look at him. "Are you sure? Do you need to go home? One of us can take you."

I shake my head.

"That's so nice of you, Professor Estrada, really," Lena speaks up. But as far as I can tell, their voices are starting to get drowned out. The noise gets muffled around me as the gears in my mind start turning.

Professor Estrada. *My* Professor Estrada. My *advisor*.

Was he? Is he? *Married?* To the blonde professor that's my advisor?! It doesn't make sense. He would've told me. My eyes attempt to glance at his left hand and there's no ring.

"She looks like she's going to pass out," one of the guys speaks up. That's when I flutter my eyes and try to take a few deep breaths. It's like a panic attack is oncoming and I need to breathe fresh air even though I'm already outside.

"No, no," I mumble, but even my voice sounds distorted.

"It might've been the drinks, she usually isn't like this," Lena's voice travels to my ears.

That's when I feel strong hands grab both of my arms and pull me away from the small crowd. I flutter my eyes closed and gulp, taking a deep breath. The hands holding me don't feel like Lena's.

"She just needs to sit down and catch her breath," Julián's voice speaks up.

"Okay, do you need me to help?" Lena's voice drifts.

"No, no, go mingle with Professor Rhodes. I'm sure you guys have some catching up to do. I was going to call it a night, anyway. She just needs some space–I'll take care of her. Go, have fun."

"Okay, thank you so much, Professor."

Julián laughs beside me and it causes chills to run down my spine. I can already feel my body reacting to his *hands* touching me and now his *voice*.

"Call me Julián, Lena. Please."

"Okay, Julián," Lena laughs before I flutter my eyes open

again and struggle to take a deep breath. I feel my body shifting and Julián is holding me tightly against his chest.

I want to tell him to stop and that this is embarrassing enough as it is and that people probably think I'm way past wasted. I'm just struggling to breathe and need a moment.

"I can walk on my own," I mumble under my breath, but Julián doesn't catch it. I'm starting to look around more and see other people on the other side of the patio look at us.

Julián finally reaches a small patio table and sits me at one of the chairs. I open my eyes and take a deep breath, feeling the cold metal chair dig into my body and shock my system a little. Like splashing your face with ice cold water to get out of a panic attack. This is doing just the same.

Instead of Julián sitting in the other chair, he crouches down and is eye level with me. His brown eyes search mine and they're full of worry.

"*¿Estás bien?*" he asks, voice full of concern. His hands rest on my knees and I take a deep breath and grab his hands, attempting to push them off me. He gives me a concerned look before moving them to the chair's armrests.

"You're married?" I finally breathe out.

He takes a deep breath and shakes his head. "I can explain."

Twelve

JULIÁN

ELIANA HAS tears in her eyes and I fucking hate seeing her this way. How did she know?

I want to explain it to her, about Laura, but I need to tread lightly. I don't want anything getting back to my ex-wife and I really don't need Eliana getting involved in that shit.

"Did Lena tell you about me? That I was married?" I finally ask. I want to brush her fallen hair behind her ear, but I keep my hands placed on the armrests to be safe.

She sniffles and my heart breaks. My fingers hold the armrests tighter.

"Eliana, please," I beg, inching closer to her, so it feels like it's just us right now. I don't care who walks by and sees me like this, but I want her to feel safe in this little bubble.

If I had to get on my knees, I'd be on them in an instant.

"I'm not a homewrecker," she states.

"Who told you I was married?" I press again, harder. It feels like my heart is hammering against my chest more forcefully than ever. I hate seeing her this way and I just want her bright eyes and blinding smile.

We haven't talked much since yesterday morning, but I figured she was just as busy as I was.

"Your *wife*," she spits out. She finally looks at me with her dull green eyes and my chest cracks.

Laura? What the fu—

"What do you mean, my wife?"

She sighs and shakes her head. "Does it matter? You're married and you really made me believe–" She stops talking and presses her lips firmly together.

I raise my brows. "What did I make you believe?"

"Nothing, forget it. Clearly, this can't happen again." She tries to push her knees forward to stand up, but I grab her knees firmly and press her back down.

"*Espera*," I demand. Her eyes are getting glossy again and I hate that. I hate every second that she's looking at me like I just broke her.

"Julián, this can't happen. It was stupid, and I can't believe I was fooling around with a *married* man."

"I'm not married. I was, but I'm not anymore," I say firmly. I need her to believe me, but she's clearly decided. Her eyes glance at my hands and they briefly stay on my left one.

"Where's your ring?" She sniffles. Her hands move from her body to my hands and that touch alone calms my own nerves. It makes my heart skip a beat and it curses me silently for how much I feel for this woman.

"Don't have one anymore."

She finally drags her eyes up to my face and I trace random shapes on her knees with my thumbs and she takes a deep breath, leaning in closer. We're almost nose to nose and I lean in more, despite how much my knees are hurting from this prolonged crouching. I need to stand and stretch, but she needs me more.

"Julián," she whispers. Her hands move from mine to my beard and she holds me softly, breathing me in. Her eyes flutter and my body melts at her beauty. Her green eyes find mine and I can't help but push past any other thoughts of people around us or what they'll see.

"Eliana, please," I beg once more in a whisper.

"I *can't*," she pleads. Her fingers run through my beard, my cheeks, and then the sides of my face until they're in my hair.

"I just want *you*," I breathe out. "I'm not married and I can explain it another time. But please, don't go."

"But I–" she tries to argue, but I won't have it. I lean in and close the distance between us, kissing her. Her fingers tighten around my hair and I moan in her mouth before she does the same.

She pulls me closer and I almost fall into her lap. I grab her plush thighs tightly to hold myself up and she lets out a soft mewl in my mouth. I catch her lip and nibble on it slowly before pushing my tongue past her lips. She tastes sweet and I need more.

It's slow and intoxicating, and I can drown in her kiss. I've already drowned in other areas, yet this woman has got me aching for every inch of her.

"I *need*," she starts, attempting to break the kiss. I shake my head and kiss her more.

"Let me have this, Eliana, please," I whisper as our lips part.

She nods and whimpers as my hands travel closer to her inner thighs. My fingers clutch at the leather fabric and I groan, fluttering my eyes closed. I'm already getting hard just from the sight of her, but these pants are doing other worldly things to me.

"If I could pick you up and bend you over this table and fuck you, I would," I whisper.

She gasps and lowers her hands from my hair and onto my chest. Her green eyes aren't as glossy anymore and it eases the knot that was forming in my chest. But I can think of a few other things that we could do that could make the both of us happy.

"We can't," she whispers softly.

"They're probably waiting for us to return. I want to make sure you're okay before we do."

She looks at me before looking over my shoulder and squinting her eyes to look at the back part of the grassy area. She returns her gaze and takes a deep breath. "Yeah, I feel better. Less panicky."

"Was it about my ex-wife? I need you to believe me when I say that we got divorced years ago. It's a lot to process, I know— but believe me, Eliana."

She looks like she wants to answer, but then she just shakes her head no.

"*No. Dime, por favor*" I press. My hands are still inching toward her inner thighs and I drag my point finger closer to her clothed pussy. She whines softly, biting her lip.

"I told you I'm not a home wrecker."

"And you're not. Let's not ruin the rest of the night like this. Come on, you can meet the rest of the professors I usually hang out with. Get some more insight into my life." I nod my head towards the back of the patio.

She finally nods. "Okay, sure."

I get up, groaning as my legs stretch and I curse myself for being in a crouched position for longer than usual. I push the pain away as I reach my hand out to Eliana and she grabs it softly, wrapping her fingers around it. I pull her slightly to get her off the chair and she smiles.

We head back to the group where Lena is laughing loudly with Malcom Rhodes. He's younger than me and we just met tonight through a mutual professor. But it seems like they're hitting it off.

Once we're closer to the group, Eliana lets go of my hand, and I look at her for a moment. She gives me a small smile before she walks faster and heads towards her friend.

"Ana! You okay?" Lena yells, grabbing Eliana by the shoulders and hugging her, kissing her head. I smile at the interaction before I head to the other guys.

The main professor I go out with is Kane Olsen. He works in the English department and we've had a few events together with our departments. He's a cool guy and near my age. He's with us tonight, making the conversations go smoothly between us all. He's more extroverted than Hall and I.

Professor Hall isn't here tonight, despite inviting him out. He's the only Egyptology professor I go out with. He's got a wife and two kids though. Professor Haros is a little older than me and tends to stay home with his family. I don't blame him, though. I would too if I had a family and all. Malcolm brought another professor that I've already forgotten the name of and they're quiet. They keep walking away to flirt with women that pass by.

I glance over at the girls who are seemingly in deep conversation. Malcom Rhodes has stepped back from Lena and rejoins next to me and raises his brows as he catches my eye contact.

My lips pull to a smirk as I brush his shoulder with mine. "How's your semester going?"

He laughs before shrugging. "It's going well. All the excitement with the new year will wear off soon for my students once they get into the bigger projects."

I nod. "That's what always gets them. I'm trying to fit in an assignment to make my students go to the new Egyptian exhibit at the history museum."

Malcolm takes a sip of his beer before responding, "That's what I try to do for mine. Make them get outside and go to the museums around here. But let's not talk about work."

I press my lips firmly before nodding. *Bad habit.* Being around Laura for so many years and both of us being professors just meant constant discussions about work, no matter the environment. We could be having dinner for our anniversary and we'd be talking about our troubling students.

"You're right."

He shakes his head, "No worries, man. How's you and your wife? Laura, right?"

Right when Malcolm lets out her name, I feel the tension in the air. Particularly the air between Eliana and me. I can *feel* her gaze burning through me. Her and Lena aren't that far away from Alex, Malcolm, and I.

"I–uh," I cough. "We actually divorced a while ago. I thought you knew."

His eyes bug out. "Shit, no. Sorry, that must've been rough. I wish I knew."

I shrug. "It's okay. Wasn't that big of a deal. It was time."

It's not something I want to really dive into at the moment with him, so I leave it at that. It briefly reminds me of the conversation I had with Carlos Haros regarding wanting to add more courses to my schedule–he asked if it was because of personal problems. My eyes quickly glance towards the girls and I can see Eliana staring daggers at me for a moment before Lena nudges her with her elbow. I focus back to Malcolm whose eyes avert from me and Eliana.

Shit.

"Well, if it was time and not that big of a deal…" He lifts his beer can and I don't have a drink anymore so I just lift my fist and bump it with his can.

"Are you seeing anyone?" I ask nonchalantly.

Malcolm finishes taking a sip before laughing. "No, no. Too busy. But it's nice to come out like this. Meet people and such."

I want to look at Lena in this moment, but I don't need to be so fucking obvious. They click really well and it's nice to see them laughing like that. But I don't want to meddle with someone else's relationship.

"Yeah, that's the best part of being back out there," I confess. I think back to the time I was officially divorced. I was scared as shit to get back out there, but I knew I had to. I had lousy dates, but they still helped me break that shell.

"Is that so?" Eliana's voice drags me out of my thoughts and she's next to me, Lena towing behind her and completing our circle. Alex has been on his phone for the last few minutes but he finally looks up and nods as if he heard our whole conversation.

"Yep, the best," Kane chimes in.

"Why are we talking about dating with our professors?" Lena laughs.

Malcolm shakes his head and laughs loudly. "You tell me, Julián asked and I answered."

"Alright, well I think they're asking us to change the topic, so we can," I mutter, eyeing Eliana whose lips are pursed.

"Do you guys usually come here?" Eliana speaks up.

We all nod. "This is kind of our spot," Kane chuckles. He takes a sip of his own drink. Lena smiles.

"Well, it's going to be ours too. We didn't want to go to a bar near campus and run into any of my TA students. I already have a hard time going out to eat without seeing one of them."

"That's the worst. I once saw someone I *failed* while trying to get a bagel across campus. It wasn't a splendid morning," Malcolm scoffs.

Lena laughs louder than usual and I almost chuckle, but I cough to repress it. Eliana catches my eyes and although there's still some curiosity and anger swirling in her irises, she smirks.

"That's horrible," Lena laughs. "I'm glad I just have a class to TA and then majority of my work is in Professor Haros' office."

Eliana clears her throat and Lena turns to her, nudging her with her elbow. I notice Eliana's fingers finding another and picking at the cuticles. I don't think I've noticed this habit of hers before. She glances at Malcolm briefly.

"Well, you girls are more than welcome to crash our weekly

hangouts here. We do try to take more shots throughout the night, but we'll try to keep it appropriate." Kane smirks.

Eliana is the one to laugh next. "I think we're already past the whole 'inappropriate' stuff the moment we walked up to you guys."

"That's if Julián can keep up with us," Malcolm jokes. I roll my eyes.

Lena suppresses a laugh as Eliana shakes her head with a smile on her face. "Yeah, yeah. Just because I'm the oldest here doesn't mean I can't take shots. I might regret it in the morning, but I've got thick skin."

"I bet," Eliana murmurs, almost too quiet to hear. I give her a wink and her cheeks grow a rosy color. She continues to have her fingers picking at each other and it takes everything in me to stop her nervous tic.

It also takes everything in me not to nibble on her pink, plump lips that are pursed at the moment. I don't fucking care if her friend is right here or if my colleagues will see. She makes me wild and free. She makes me feel like I'm young again, chasing this high that so many love.

I haven't felt this way in a while, not even with Laura. They say if you're really in love you'll have spurts of this high with your partner, but it ended with Laura almost as soon as we got married.

"I will, however, be ending my night soon," I add. Malcolm sighs and shakes his head, patting my back.

"It is getting late," he mumbles.

"Not that late," Kane laughs. "I can get a few more shots, now that we've established it's not inappropriate to take them with our TA's and students."

"Oh, I'm not in any of your guys' classes," Eliana confirms. "I'm in the creative writing department."

Ah, that makes sense.

"Wait—" Malcolm speaks up but I stop him before he can even mention Laura's name.

"That's good, that means I'll buy the first round next week." I promise the group, but keep my eyes locked on Eliana.

Her cheeks get redder by the second and I want to offer to take her home, but *that* would be highly inappropriate in front of the guys.

"You've got yourself a deal, Professor Estrada!" Lena squeals. I shake my head and the guys laugh.

"Please, call me Julián. Professor Estrada makes me sound pretentious," I joke. Lena nods and Eliana is silent.

I take this as my cue to leave. I don't want to ruin their night, but I don't want to stay any longer if I can't be close to her. It's killing me inside and I'd rather take her home and fuck her until she can't remember her own name.

Within minutes of finishing our drinks and Kane offering to buy the next round, we head inside. Lena is talking with Malcolm and Kane is leading the pack. I stay in the back of the group with Eliana, who's messing with her fingers in obvious nerves.

"You okay?" I ask. She nods and huffs out a breath.

"I just want to take this shot and kind of forget about my panic attack earlier."

I nudged her with my elbow. "Hey, it's okay. We didn't really talk about that, so I do apologize if it blindsided you. It was never my intent. Laura… is just very complicated and I didn't want you to be in the same air she breathes."

"Too late for that," Eliana mutters. I nod, knowing she's her advisor now.

"I know, it sucks, but that doesn't mean we can't keep seeing each other," I confess.

She takes a deep breath and I hold my own, waiting for her response. We're walking up the steps towards the door to bring us into the bar. I open it, letting her go in first. She gives me a small smile.

I'm back to her side and she continues to stay quiet until we're near the bar. She finally whips around, causing me to crash into her frame. She holds onto my arms and I steady my hands to her waist. I look up briefly to make sure the others aren't looking and thankfully I have this moment alone with her.

"What?" I ask.

"I want to continue this, I do. But we need to talk more about things. We don't have to go into detail *here*, but I just want you to know that if you want to continue seeing me then we have to talk."

I nod. "I agree."

Her eyes go soft and she lifts herself on her tiptoes, her lips getting closer to mine. She's beautiful and it takes my breath away every single fucking time. Her green eyes sparkle as I focus on her. My grip on her waist tightens and her eyes flutter closed for a moment.

"I'm going to go take a shot and *maybe* I'll call you tonight," she teases, biting her lip and stepping back. Our hands fall from each other and I want to pull her back in, but I don't.

"At least let me know when you're home safely," I press.

She nods and smiles brightly. "Of course, *Professor*."

I can instantly feel my pants tighten at her words and I curse myself for getting hard a few feet away from our friends. I press my lips tightly together before she laughs and steps further back, finding her way back to the group who's finally gathering the shots from the bartender.

Malcolm catches my eyes before looking at Eliana and handing her a shot. My eyes try to not leave hers, but I have to go.

I don't need them questioning things. We're all already getting along fine and I don't need them to know I'm seeing her.

She's not any of our students, but I don't need word getting back to Laura.

Fuck, Laura.

My mind goes to my ex-wife and I remember I haven't checked my phone since seeing Eliana here. I pull it out and see that I've got a missed call from her.

I look back up to the group and they're already on their next shot. I make my way out of the bar. I'll have to call her on my way home.

What does she want now?

Thirteen

ELIANA

THE HANGOVER on Saturday lasts the whole day while I try to study at home. It didn't help to have Lena over and her waking up early to get on campus to grade more assignments. I tried to tell her to not do that on the weekends to prevent burnout, but she assured me she wouldn't be there too long.

She was loud when she got downstairs and saw my parents. I treaded lightly in the kitchen while I got some breakfast and hydration. The headache was pounding harshly against my temples and I almost told Lena to shut it before my head exploded.

I attempted a run, even in that hungover state, and barely made it home in time to puke my guts out. Professor Hall kept buying us shots despite our protests to switch to cocktails. Malcolm seemed too enthralled with Lena to protest with me. Lena didn't seem to mind at all and didn't look like death this morning when we woke up, which I was jealous of.

Hours later, and many more bottles of water drunk and Tylenol pills taken, I'm finally feeling a little more human. It's nearing dinnertime, but my parents already let me know they have some kind of benefit dinner to attend. I don't mind though.

I want to get a jump start on some assignments at the library and then grab dinner.

I'm heading toward the same Mexican place I bumped into Julián last week and get flashbacks to that night at the park. I texted him late last night when Lena and I made it home, but we have talked little since.

Lena asked much about what Julián and I were doing on the patio of the bar when I had my panic attack. I couldn't tell her *yet* that I was sleeping with a professor. And *now* I couldn't tell her I was sleeping with my advisor's ex-husband. I'm not sure how well that conversation would go and I don't know if I'm ready for it.

I'm not even sure if I've processed it all yet. My emotions were all over the place last night. I do feel some relief though knowing that I'm not fooling around with a married man. But it still doesn't pull me out of the guilt of not knowing him as much as I should to continue things.

My feelings are increasing by the days while being with him.

I don't even know what department he teaches. I know he's on the same floor as my father's office, but I can't remember if they were in the same hall. I don't think I'd be able to handle *that* conversation if Julián ended up being my father's co-worker.

My parents would probably chastise me and cast me out. *Victoria* would definitely cast me out. Throw me to the curb and call me a disappointment for the *second* time in a year.

I already feel so much guilt about choosing myself over a career path I don't want. I couldn't keep up with those expectations that didn't make me truly happy.

Am I happy now? I'm not sure, but I'm allowed to continue finding what and where that happiness is.

I'm allowed to choose myself every time I feel like I have no choice in things.

There's a sound of the bells ringing on the door of the restaurant as I walk inside, allowing myself to focus on the *now*.

I've spent so much of my time in the past and my worries. I just need to get my damn tacos and enjoy the night. I head to the counter and put in my order with the kind waitress and then wait near the door.

There's another chime as the doors open for a customer and I look up and a smile spreads over my face.

"Hey, didn't think I'd see you here," I speak up, and Malcolm eyes me and flashes a big grin.

"Hey! You doing okay after last night? How's Lena?" He's wearing a nice suit with a black trench coat on top and his brunette hair swoops in nice waves. His eyes are kind and his smile is contagious. My cheeks are already hurting from how wide my lips are spreading.

"I'm okay, finally over the hump of the hangover and came for tacos. Lena's fine, she doesn't seem to get a hangover no matter how many shots she downs."

Malcolm laughs as he gets closer. "I wish I was like that. Kind of forgot I had an important meeting on campus and I was definitely stumbling through my words."

"Oh, no!" I laugh.

Malcolm shrugs. "It's alright, I did it to myself. My fault for forgetting I had to be on campus the next day after going out, but we wanted to celebrate Alex getting invited to a summit conference in the spring. I couldn't *not* go."

I widen my eyes. "Oh, wow! That's impressive. Kind of forget professors can get invited to those fancy events. My parents never really tell me about those."

Malcolm eyes me once I say *parents* and I immediately feel juvenile. I clear my throat and add, "My parents are professors as well at Yale."

"No shit! What department?"

I chew on the inside of my cheek for a moment before reply-ing. His eyes are waiting. "History and Egyptology."

His eyes widen and he chuckles, "Wow, small world. Is that why you and Julián were talking so much? I noticed how well you guys seemed to know each other."

My heart rate increases and heat rises to my neck and cheeks.

"What do you mean?"

Malcolm's eyes continue to stare and his brow raises as if he's surprised I don't know what he's talking about. "Julián is a professor there."

I press my lips firmly. "Yeah, you're all professors there." A laugh rumbles out of my chest just then and my mind goes into that same headspace from earlier. Of feeling like Julián and I don't know enough about each other yet. Why am I finding out about him through other people?

He shakes his head. "*No*, he's in the same department."

I cock my head up at him and my jaw falls slack. "What?"

"You didn't know?"

"He works with my mom or something?" I ask for clarity.

Malcolm shakes his head once more and I'm getting irritated by not knowing the full answer. He needs to just spill and tell me what he's talking about. I'm clueless and I feel like it's the most obvious thing in the world that I'm just not catching on.

"Eliana, he works under your father."

It feels like last night again, where my breathing gets stuck, and my lungs stop working. I have to remind myself how to work my lungs again and attempt to breathe in some kind of air. It's slow and harsh, but I get in a few breaths. I have my hands firmly placed on the seat of the chair I'm in and Malcolm makes a noise in his throat.

"Are you okay? You're as white as a sheet. I hope I didn't upset you. I thought your father would've mentioned him? Or that you met him with your parents at some function?"

I snap my head up to him, and that's when it *clicks*.

The Egypt Exhibit opening at the history museum. The event I went to with my parents where tons were invited from surrounding universities and *Yale* specifically.

The event where I met Julián for the first time.

•∙•‿ॐ•∘)◊(∘•ॐ‿•∙•

JULIÁN

Please answer your phone. I'm worried.

MY EYES STAY ON THE SCREEN, WATCHING IT SOON FADE FROM NO activity. It finally turns black and I click open the phone once more, looking at his text message.

It's late and I'm holed up in my bed, not wanting to talk to anyone. It seems like there's just so much going on that I can't figure it out. I was so set on making a new life for myself here and making the best of my circumstances by living at home again.

But I didn't think it would come to *this* where I am sleeping with my father's coworker.. Julián's boss, practically. I had to do a quick google search to make sure I wasn't freaking too much about it, but it confirmed my suspicions. My father isn't technically his boss, but he makes the big decisions for the department and can even revoke Juliàn's position if he wasn't doing his job.

That felt like a boss-position to me.

I don't want Julián's profession jeopardized. I don't want him to suffer or get disciplined for my dumb decisions. I should've known.

Julián has been trying to call me once I sent him a text once I came home from seeing Malcolm. That conversation with Malcolm didn't last long the moment I found out the news and connected the dots. I almost ran out of that taco place. I sent

Julián a quick *we need to talk* text and then got my tacos and left the restaurant.

I didn't pick up his three calls or his five texts asking if something happened or if I'm okay. I freaked out the moment I sent the text and couldn't handle talking to him just then. So, I've been sulking in my bedroom.

He doesn't know. He *can't* know.

My phone screen lights up and flashes his name as another call comes through. I look at the time and see that it's nearing eleven. Most students would be out partying in the city, but I'm here at home sulking about my life decisions.

I groan and finally pick up the phone. I take a deep breath before speaking.

"What?"

"Everything okay, Eliana?" His voice is full of worry and my heart is aching for him. We've barely known each other for a month, yet we spent so much time together. He deserves to know what's happening. This isn't high school where we're teens unsure what to do about our issues.

He's a much older adult and I'm still paving my way and trying to learn from my mistakes. I want to go about this the right way. No matter what it takes.

"No, I bumped into Malcolm," I confess through a shaky breath.

"Okay?" His voice sounds uneven and confused. "Did he say something to you? Upset you?" He clears his throat and his voice goes deeper. "Did he do something to you?"

God, he sounds so attractive when he's protective.

"No, he didn't do any of that. He just kind of told me something I wish I knew earlier."

"What did he say?" he urges.

I shake my head and breathe out heavily. "It's not something I can say over the phone or through text."

There's silence for a moment before Julián curses under his

breath and finally speaks up. "*Bueno, entonces ven*. Spend the night."

It comes out more demanding and like he's *telling* me what to do. And it's the sexiest thing ever.

Calm down, girl. I have to remind myself.

I shake my head again. "I can't."

"You can't, or you *won't*?" he asks slowly.

I sigh and push myself off my bed. I'm in comfy sweats and a long sleeve and I don't feel like changing into something else. I probably smell like tacos, too.

"*If* I go, I'm coming in my sweats. You will not get a dressed-up-me."

"*Corazón*, I don't care what you wear. I'll be ripping it off you the moment you step foot in this apartment. But I need you to come over."

And with that, he hangs up. Butterflies swarm my stomach and I can't lie that his words are getting to me. They're demanding and make my pussy ache even more for him and it's been a few days since doing anything with him.

The angel on my shoulder is nudging me to stay in and think about what to do next with what I know, but the devil on the other shoulder is much louder and much more convincing.

So, I get up and gather my things and head to Julián's.

Fourteen

ELIANA

I DON'T EVEN HAVE time to slip off my slippers that I stupidly wore to get to his place before he's pulling me in and crushing his lips to mine. He pins me against the closing door and my breath catches as my back is slammed against the wood.

"Hi to you too," I mumble in between kisses. His hands are all over me with fervor and my heart beats out of my chest like a firework ready to explode.

"Please," he moans through a kiss, causing the butterflies in me to erupt. The ache in my thighs grows and his beard moving harshly against my chin and cheeks is giving me flashbacks of when he ate me out.

I shudder for a moment with the thought, and I want him there again.

"Please, what?" I whisper, wedging my hands in between our bodies and grabbing his chest with both hands and pushing him a few inches away. Our lips separate and there's glistening saliva on his.

His eyes are dark and *hungry*. He moves his shoulders, flexing his chest underneath my palms, and it takes everything in me to not jump on him.

"I need you," he admits. So quiet that I barely catch it. But I do.

A smile spreads across my face and I nod slowly.

"I want the kitchen counter again," I tell him.

He nods before twisting the fabric of my long sleeve in his hands and pulling me to him. I squeal from the movement and crash my body into his. He guides us backwards to the kitchen before twisting us around so I'm backing into the table. The back of my thighs are pressed against the wood and I let out another sound.

His lips turn into a smirk before leaning down and sliding his hands under my knees and hoisting me up on the kitchen table. I could've easily done it, but I let him.

"You're here," he says in a quick breath. Like he can't believe it.

"I'm here."

His eyes find mine as his hands go back to my thighs. There's a hidden meaning beneath his irises, and I want to tell him that everything is okay. But that's when my mind goes back to the reason I'm here.

He works with my father. He works *for* my father. I shake my head and try to clear my thoughts.

"*Qué tienes, Corazón,*" he asks softly. His tone is low and not demanding.

"Nothing. I need you to go down on me." I push every thought away and reach out, encasing his neck in my hands. I attempt to push him down to my core and he obliges.

"Take these off then," he murmurs as his fingers play with the waistband of my sweats. I nod and lift my ass slowly so he can shimmy the fabric off my thighs and then my ankles. The sweats fall to the floor in a pile and he sighs as his eyes fall to my inner thighs.

I wore a pretty lace thong just for him. I don't mention I *definitely* wore big granny panties before I picked up the phone. I don't think he'd mind if I showed up in them, he said he'd rip my clothes off either way.

But I did think he'd look better with a lace thong between his teeth.

Julián wastes no time in dragging his hands up and down my thighs, finally settling one hand to my stomach and pushing down, causing me to lay back on the table. I keep myself propped up by my elbows.

"*Qué preciosa*," he murmurs to himself. *Precious*. I squeeze my thighs together and he glances up briefly, his lips twitching into a smirk. He licks his lips and I squeeze my thighs again and lean my head back.

"Fuck," I whine.

"I haven't even fucking touched you yet and you're a mess."

"Always."

Without notice, he moves his hands again to my knees and spreads my legs. The cool air captures my crotch and I suck in a deep breath. He leans in, nuzzling his nose in the thong's fabric. His nose pushes against the fabric right over my clit and I moan involuntarily.

My body squirms underneath his touch, and he grunts, shaking his head. He breathes heavily over my clothed pussy and I shudder. Goosebumps rise behind my neck, across my chest, over my arms, and even my god damn thighs.

It feels like my brain is mush and my eyes close halfway as I continue to focus on his movements. One of his hands keeps one of my legs stuck in the spread position while the other travels until his fingers push against the fabric.

"*Fuck, please*," I whine.

He shakes his head again and looks up before *slapping* my clothed pussy. I moan loudly and shut my eyes quickly. *Fuck, that felt so good.*

"Beg for it," he commands.

I shake my head. I don't mean to, but it just happens.

He raises a brow and slaps my pussy again. My knees try to close, but he keeps his hold on one of my legs strongly and he *tsks* under his breath.

Another slap, and I'm whining loudly.

"Please, fuck, Julián. *Please, I need it*."

"Do you?" he questions.

I raise my brows and I nod quickly. My breathing comes short the moment he slaps my pussy *again* and a groan falls from my lips. I want to close my legs so desperately, but he won't let me.

"Please, *please, please*!" I whine louder.

He's silent for a moment, watching my pleading face. His eyes remain dark, but his lips twitch in the corners and I know I've got him.

I need him, but I want him to *want* this as much as I'm craving him.

Because if I'm honest, I'm craving him in every way and it's like I've gone days, no months, without him.

"Please," I whisper one last time.

He nods swiftly, continuing to stay quiet before he leans closer and runs his palms over my thighs, causing my back to arch.

I breathe heavily as I watch him take his time with me. He moves his fingers up and up along my legs until they hook underneath the waistband of the thong and he pulls them down in a sudden movement. My body responds acquiescently and my back arches more and I lift my ass so he can get the fabric off.

He slides it off, slowly before they fall from my ankles, and he bunches it in his fist. His eyes stay on me as he leans closer. Flashbacks of the time I was here last time, and he stuffed it in my–

"*Abre la boca*," he demands and I obey.

There isn't a fight, never was with him.

My lips part, and he pushes the fabric into my mouth. He

resumes his position, but not before I see him adjust himself with one palm. I lay my eyes at the sight of the tented pants and know that I'm in it for the long haul tonight.

He will not let me get off easily.

And I don't want him to. My thoughts go rampant at the possibility that this might be the last time we can do this before I tell him who I really am. Who my father is.

Julián slaps my thighs with each palm before leaning down and rubbing his beard over my pussy. I shudder and my moans are muffled with the lace thong.

He exhales and it hits my pussy, causing my back to arch once more. I let out another moan, wiggling my hips for him to continue what he's doing. I need him to either taste me or fuck me. Or both.

He finally pushes his face into the crevice of my inner thighs, his beard scratching both sides of my legs as well as engulfing my pussy in his mouth. His tongue immediately latches onto my clit and I buck my hips forward, causing more pressure. I squeeze my eyes shut tightly as he devours me.

His tongue glides over my clit in slow motions before he sucks on it and then repeats the process. One of his hands glides up my body until he's underneath my long sleeve.

He lifts his chin up just enough to breathe and demands, "Take. This. Off."

I nod and quickly pull off the long sleeve and throw it on the ground next to the sweats. He focuses back on my pussy and wastes no time in sucking on my clit again, but softer this time. His hand resumes its position on my breast and his fingers pinch my nipple.

Goosebumps rise all over my body, and I let out another loud moan. He groans in response before I feel a long stripe of wetness go along my pussy. I can't hold myself up any longer and fall back on the table.

This allows him even more leverage as he eats me out with much more force, and I can't help but scream through the fabric.

"Fuck, so fucking sweet. Like *dulce*. I could eat you all fucking day," he breathes out before going back down. His fingers pinch my nipple again before working on the other breast. The sensations are too much that I close my eyes tightly until I see stars in my vision.

The moment I open my eyes, he moves his other hand toward my pussy and circles the tip of his finger over my hole before entering it slowly. His finger is thick and causing me to raise my hips again in pleasure. I groan louder and he curses under his breath.

"*Mi nena preciosa,* always so god damn *tight* for me."

His words.

He doesn't stop there. He continues to suck on my clit before moving his finger in and out of me, causing me to get even wetter than I already am. The orgasm is already rushing through me and I won't last long. But I know he'll want to make me come more than once tonight.

Because one orgasm from me is never enough, he needs to pleasure me for as long as he can until he breaks. *Then* he'll let himself get some in return.

I try to mumble words, but the thong catches the words. He looks up, his beard and nose drenched in my wetness before he chuckles and moves his hand that's on my nipple up to my mouth and takes the thong out.

"Please, faster," I beg and lick my lips.

He concedes by inserting not just another finger… but two. Three fingers are thrusting into me at a quicker pace and I scream, throwing my head back. My body can't take it and my thighs shake uncontrollably.

"Fuck, fuck, fuck!" I whine before the orgasm rips through me and the coil snaps. Julián doesn't stop thrusting his fingers into me as I come. It's wet and noisy as he thrusts through my orgasm.

"Fuck, you're like a waterfall, baby."

"Please, don't stop," I moan, leaning even more back onto the table and giving him a deeper angle to thrust into me.

He grunts before slapping my pussy and I jolt, but it brings me to another dimension as I feel another orgasm on the precipice. I look up briefly as I see him spit down where his fingers are and he continues his pace, but this time slower.

"I want you to come undone for me, baby," he whispers, locking eyes with me. I nod before he smirks and slaps my pussy again.

"Julián!" I scream, throwing my head back again.

"You're such a dirty whore," he pants. "You *like* it when I slap this pussy. You're on full display for me, baby. *Dame otro.*"

His pace increases and I shut my eyes tightly before the coil builds up and then *snaps*, but this time the orgasm is too much and I squirt even more alongside it. The noises are unearthly and make me even more needy.

"Fuck, so wet," he pants again.

"Please, inside me," I mumble. I reach my hand down to grab his wrist and pull his fingers. He slows his pace and pulls his fingers out of me slowly.

"Does my whore want more?"

I nod, locking eyes with his dark brown ones. There's a storm brewing in his irises, and I want to calm them.

I'd do anything for this man, and that scares me. To want to lay myself down for him with such a short time of knowing him. But everything feels right.

The angel on my shoulder is nudging me to listen to her, but I push past that voice and listen in on the devil on my shoulder. Because their words are more enticing and are exactly what I need at this moment.

"I want you inside me. Please, Julián. Tear me apart, ruin me. Destroy me until there's nothing left."

His lips curl at my words and he nods. His hands move to my hips and drag me closer to the edge of the table and I'm too cockdrunk to even squeal or make any sound.

He undoes his belt before letting his pants fall. I watch as he pushes his boxers down and his cock springs free. It's already leaking pre-cum at the tip and my tongue glides along my lips at the sight. His hand fists around his cock and he moves it in up and down motions. He moves his thumb over his tip and he shudders, moaning loudly.

I can't take it anymore. I'm already getting wet again from the sight and sounds of this man touching himself. "Please, *now*," I beg.

He chuckles under his breath as he nudges closer, moving his tip to glide over my entrance. The feeling is sensational.

"How are you already tight again? Oh, *baby*, you want me to stretch you open again?"

I nod rapidly before he groans as he enters his tip slowly. His cock stretches me inch by inch and he even leans down to spit where our bodies connect. It's the hottest thing and my pussy flutters around him. It feels like my chest is going to explode and I try to snap my thighs shut, but he's in the way.

He continues to stretch me out until he's fully seated. He takes a deep breath and lifts one hand to run his fingers through his hair and then his beard.

"You're so pretty like this. Spread out just for me, letting my cock *stuff* and *stretch* you," he grunts as he pulls out and slowly enters again.

The feeling is euphoric and I whine, attempting to grab him but he's too far unless I sit fully up.

"Stay down," he demands with a low voice.

He pulls out again, but this time he thrusts into me *harshly*, a scream leaving my lips. I'm sure the neighbors have the police on speed dial at this point from all the screaming. He chuckles before doing the motion again and again and *again*. I'm a blubbering mess as he destroys me with each thrust.

His grunts fill the room and my back lifts in an impossible height, giving him a new angle to thrust into. It almost feels better than when I'm on my stomach and he's pounding into me from behind. Almost.

"*Mírame*," he commands. I lock eyes with him as he leans his head down and puckers his lips before spitting slowly down where our bodies connect. The saliva hits my pussy and he moves a hand to rub my clit in gentle circles.

"*Ahh*, please," I whine, shutting my eyes closed.

His thumb lifts from my clit and I open my eyes, my breathing getting heavier.

"I told you to look at me. If you close your eyes, I'll fuck you in every corner of this place with no breaks. How many more orgasms can I bring out of you?"

Even though I would love to know the answer to that question, I don't think my body could handle that many orgasms. I'm already exhausted from two. This third one will be my last, I'm sure.

"Yes, *sir*," I grin. He presses his thumb against my clit once more and starts stroking it.

"I wonder, do you still like your pussy slapped while I'm fucking you relentlessly?" he whispers. I barely hear him and when his words finally become coherent for me, he lifts his thumb from my clit and flattens his hand. He slaps my pussy and I scream, throwing my head back.

He continues to thrust into me, his breathing heavy. "Look at me, Eliana."

I lift my head, and tears spring from my eyes. It's all too much, but not enough. I need more. "More," I beg, lips quivering.

He cocks an eyebrow before lifting his hand and slapping my

pussy again. I yelp again and he pulls out swiftly and thrusts *hard* into me.

He does this two more times before I scream out his name along with a string of gibberish. My thoughts are incoherent and all I can see is him and all I can hear is *him* and our bodies thrashing. It fills my ears and my body arches again, wanting to release once more.

"Come for me baby, *ándale*," he urges as he thrusts one more time. His thumb circles my clit a few more times and my whole body *shudders*.

Everything inside me *snaps*. I come, fluttering around his cock, and he grunts through it, not stopping his thrusts. It's becoming too sensitive and I cry out, lifting myself up on my elbows and attempting to reach with one hand to stop but he shakes his head before he grunts loudly and halts with his cock pulsating within me.

Heat swarms my insides and he leans down, collapsing on my shoulder and my arms wrap around him. I clench my pussy around his cock and he groans, lifting his head just enough to look at me.

"If you do that, I'm going to be ready for round four. Do you think you can last?"

I shake my head and laugh, causing a smile to twitch at the corners of his mouth before he rests his head on my shoulder again. My fingers go to his hair and twirl the curls.

We both stay like this for a while, in this exact position, before he pulls out and goes to grab a towel to clean up.

Once we're all cleaned up and I'm slipping on the sweats, he grabs my wrist.

"Shower with me and stay the night." His brown eyes are soft now and even showing pretty golden specks.

I nod slowly. "Okay."

He smiles before picking me up bridal style and walking us towards the bathroom.

Fifteen

JULIÁN

WE'RE cuddling on the bed while I play with the wet strands of her hair at her shoulder. She's burying her head in the crevice of my neck, comfortable and breathing softly. It feels *right* and I haven't felt this level of comfort before.

We're both naked, too tired to put on clothes after the shower. I took time to wash her hair and discover every inch of her. She did the same, and we were quiet the whole time. It felt intimate and more than what we were expecting for a shower together.

It terrifies me but also excites me at the same time.

My thoughts drift to the text message she sent me. I clear my throat and she shifts on the bed.

"Eliana," I say, dropping her strand of hair and rubbing her shoulder. She moves her head and mumbles something.

"Eliana, what did you want to talk to me about?"

She's quiet for a moment before she lifts herself from me. She rests on her elbows and her green eyes study me before she takes a deep breath. I shift myself up to sit against the pillow.

"I bumped into Malcolm and he told me something."

I raise a brow. "Yeah, I remember. You mentioned you couldn't say it over the phone?"

She nods, her eyes dropping to my chest and then the blanket covering our lower halves.

"Eliana," I push. Her green eyes rise to my face again and her cheeks are rosy. Her eyes look glossy and my chest cracks from the sight. "What did he say?"

"You work with my father."

Her words are rushed, and I take a moment to comprehend what she said. I scrunch my brows together.

"I work with your father? He's a professor at the University?"

She's hesitant as folds her hands together on top of the bedsheet and stays silent for a few beats. "Julián," she says louder. My ears perk up at her use of my name.

"What?"

"You work *for* him."

"I don't understand."

It feels like her words are clear as day, but then again, they aren't. Like they are drifting away the moment they leave her lips.

She continues to twist and twirl her fingers together, almost getting ready to pick at the cuticles. I instinctively raise my hand and smooth it over hers and she stops, studying me. She takes a deep breath and her eyes fill with mirth.

I quirk a brow and urge her with my eyes to continue.

She takes another breath. "My father is Carlos Haros."

There's silence. So silent, you could hear a pin drop. You could practically hear my heartbeat increase and beat erratically in my chest, on the precipice of breaking free. I'm frozen in place and Eliana takes another breath before lifting her hand and lacing her fingers through mine.

"Say something," she pleads in a whisper, her eyes asking–*begging*–me to say something. Anything.

But I'm not sure if I can be there for her in this shell-shocked state. It's like the words in my head are running a mile a minute and I can't stop them in time to form a complete sentence. I open my mouth to speak, but nothing comes out.

Her fingers squeeze my hand and I blink a few times before finally shaking my head. I attempt to calm my heart, but it continues to thump quickly.

"Eliana," I start. Her eyes get glossy and she bites her lip before looking up at the ceiling. "*Eliana.*"

"I didn't know!" she exclaims, a tear escaping her eye.

I watch her slowly lift her vacant hand to wipe the tear away. I want to be the one to wipe it away, but I'm still defrosting.

"Eliana," I repeat, more firm this time.

"What?" she scoffs. "You don't see the resemblance? No wonder I bumped into you that day in the hallway. I was on my way to see my *father* and there *you* were. In the same hallway. And it never clicked."

I continue to stay silent, still trying to grasp words to say besides her name. If I say it again, I'm sure she'll slap me and try to break me out of this trance.

"I can't believe this is happening. Of all the things that could happen to me," she babbles, sniffling and wiping more tears that escape her eyes. "Of *course*, the one good thing that comes into my life is just another—"

"Eliana, don't," I cut her off, finally.

She locks her eyes with me and gulps, watching me. She keeps her fingers laced with mine, but I can't think straight with her touching me. I wiggle my wrist until her grip loosens and I slip my hand away. Her brows scrunch before her lips tremble into a half frown.

I hate myself for pulling away, but I can't *think* with her touch. I need space. I need distance from this catastrophe. Because as much as I hate to admit how much this sucks, it does. It should've clicked for me too—when I saw her that day in the hallway and brought her into my office. I should've asked more about why she was in that *specific* hallway. There aren't that many departments on that floor, let alone that *hallway*, so I should've asked for clarity.

But I didn't and I have to take responsibility.

"It's my fault," I admit in a quick breath. I run my hand through my messy hair before sighing and leaning back against the headboard.

She moves beside me, sitting up and grabbing a pillow to cover her front. I watch her meticulously as she looks everywhere in the room but *me*. She continues to chew on the inside of her cheek and I know she's chewed it raw.

"I'm an adult. It was my fault too. I should've told you."

I shake my head. "This isn't right, Eliana. He's the department chair. Knowing that your father is Carlos Haros? That changes things."

Her head snaps to me and her eyes go glossy again and I curse under my breath. Her green eyes have flecks of yellow that I'm noticing more and more as I look at her. The freckles splayed on her face are even prettier today, for some reason. And the tan on her skin makes her skin glow in a way that makes me want to lick every inch of her.

Fuck, I can't think about that anymore.

I can't think about *her* anymore. It's too risky and too much. I can't be close to her—

She mumbles something under her breath before moving on the bed again to get in a different seating position, pillow still covering her chest.

"We can't do this anymore, I'm sorry," I whisper. I can't look at her and refuse to. It would hurt too much.

"What?"

Her voice breaks and it hits me like knives in the chest.

"You heard me, Eliana. This can't happen. It's too risky and—"

"So you just want me to forget about everything we did? How you make me feel? Because you can't just push that away."

My lips crack into a smile at her confession, but I refuse to look at her. I'm a coward and I know it. I'm proud of her for sticking up for what she wants and how she feels. I just can't give her the same energy. I have to protect her.

"Julián, please," her voice cracks.

I shake my head. I push myself off the bed and stand, grabbing some boxers on the floor and pulling them on. I hear shuffling behind me and before I know it, she's got one of my shirts draping over her naked body. Her brunette hair falls in waves all over and she pulls some strands behind her ear.

She crosses her arms over her chest and sizes me up. I want to laugh, but I can't alleviate the situation we're in.

"What happened to the man that is so *demanding* when I'm under him?"

I raise a brow and her brows scrunch in anger. Her eyes are fiery and I can't deny how adorable it looks on her.

"Julián!" she exclaims, taking a step towards me. She cranes her neck up and I take a deep breath.

"The University won't be kind if they find this out. They might think he's giving me favors because of the relationship I might have with his daughter... I don't even want to think about how your father would react if he found out his colleague, his much *older* colleague, is fucking his daughter. His very *young* daughter."

"I'm not young. I'm an adult. I've got my bachelor's degree. I'm twenty-three for fuck's sake."

This time, I finally crack a smile. "Baby, I'm almost two decades older than you. He would probably murder me and make it look like an accident. He'd probably—"

"So, we don't tell him."

I quirk a brow and she's smiling. She's got mischief in her eyes.

"Eliana…"

She smiles wider. "You can't tell me that you don't love the secrecy." She takes another step before her chest is flush with mine. She bites her bottom lip and raises a hand to my chest, pressing her fingers against the skin where my heart is. "You can't tell me that you don't like fucking me in your office. So close for my father to hear, yet you can shut me up with your *cock* stuffed in my mouth."

The mouth on this woman… She's learning from me and it makes me hard. It makes me want to flip her and toss her on the bed and fuck her until she can't think straight.

My breathing grows heavier and she notices, smirking. She gets on her tiptoes and brushes her lips over my beard before she reaches my lips. Her tongue glides over my lower lip and I hold back a groan.

Or I try to. The sound fills the air and she giggles under her breath. I grip her waist tightly. I don't care if my fingers leave imprints on her skin. That'll mean that she's *mine*.

"Eliana, if you keep talking like that, then we're going to have bigger problems," I warn her.

She pulls her head back and smiles. "Wouldn't that be better? Keeping it a secret… getting to find new places to fuck each other. Seems more fun than ending this. Also adds to the *excitement* of possibly getting caught. Maybe I *want* to see how you'd react if my father found out."

Her voice is distant as I think about the outcome. He'd kill me, that's for sure. But the feeling of finding secret hideaways around campus to fuck her is enticing. My mind flashes to the library, the rooftops of the buildings, and even the fucking *offices* near Laura.

Just the thought of fucking Eliana near my ex-wife and her possibly finding us gets me hard. I want her to hurt the way she hurt me and this would be the perfect way.

"Julián?"

I lock eyes with her and smile. "It's a dangerous game we're playing. But if you'll be a good girl then we can do it."

She shakes her head and I cock a brow.

"I don't think good girl is the right term for this. If you want me, you'll have to make me *beg* for it like a *naughty girl.*

"Fuck me," I breathe out, watching her eyes spark and her lips twitch into a smile. She sits back down on her heels.

"I'd like to, but I have places to go," she says swiftly, attempting to turn on her heels. But I catch my hands around her waist just in time. I pull her to me and she squeals.

I bury my face into her messy waves and she smells like my wildest dreams.

"You're not going anywhere, *Corazón.* I've got you until I say you can leave. Your pussy is going to be crying to be let go."

She laughs before twisting in my grip and faces me. She loops her arms around my neck and I breathe in her scent as she watches me closely.

"I'm all yours. Do what you want."

I nod and lean in, closing the gap between our lips. I devour her mouth and she moans into the kiss. I slip my tongue into her and she reciprocates.

I'm too far gone to think of the consequences of what we just agreed to. This might be a risky situation, but I'm all for the prize.

And she's the *tastiest* and most rewarding prize I've found.

••⋛•๑)✧(๑•⋚••

LAURA IS HUMMING A RANDOM TUNE AS SHE WALKS DOWN THE hall, almost colliding into me. I look up just in time to see her pursed lips and then her scoffing when I maneuver to not crash into her.

"Julián! You could've knocked me over," she exclaims.

I roll my eyes and sigh. "I didn't see you. It wouldn't be such a bad thing though, if I did."

She scoffs, following me as I get closer to my office door. I halt and turn my head back at her. She smiles and nods at my office.

"You can't come in here anymore."

Her eyes widen, and she laughs. "Honey, your office is my office. Now, let me in." She reaches her pale fingers up to the door handle and I cover it with my palm. I grip her hand over the door handle and she gasps.

"I said *no*, Laura. I've got a ton of assignments to grade and a long day ahead of me. I've got two night classes. Please don't start with me."

And to make my point, I tap with my other hand to the schedule taped to my office door. It has my office hours and my course schedule so students can know where I am at all times.

She rolls her eyes and pulls her hand out of my grip. "Fine, Julián. You can be rude all you want, but I know you'll be walking to my office later today. I'm free for dinner tomorrow night, thought you might want to know."

"Doubt it," I mumble. She smiles, as if pretending she didn't hear me, stuck in her delusional world. She nods and turns on her heels, leaving me in the hallway.

I sigh and twist the handle, pushing the door and getting inside the office. I shut it and lean my head back into the frosted glass. Thankfully, it's frosted enough that you can't see inside from the hallway.

"Hey, *professor*," a voice calls behind me and I whip around and almost have a heart attack.

Eliana is sitting, legs crossed over one another, on my desk. Her burgundy skirt is too short for her own good, but she's got black tights on covering any skin. Her collared shirt is layered by a sweater vest. Her hair is down, but has two clips on the sides of her head holding back some strands. She looks ethereal, and I lick my lips before I remember where I am.

"How'd you get in here?" I ask, stepping closer to her. She wiggles her ankles before laughing.

"The door was unlocked." She drums her fingers over her knee as I get closer to her. Her eyes fuck me as she takes in my outfit. I wore brown slacks and a nice beige sweater. I'm glad I put a little more effort into dressing this morning, especially with the reaction she's giving me.

But then I remember how close Laura was to entering the office. I close our distance and wrap my hand behind her neck, forcing her to look up at me.

"My ex-wife was right outside that door," I fume.

She searches my eyes with hers before she gasps. "She almost came in?"

I nod slowly, reaching my other hand along her thigh before sliding my fingers under the fabric of the skirt. Her breath hitches and I smirk.

"She could've seen my *whore* sitting on my desk looking like this. Ready to be fucked and clothes ripped to shreds."

Eliana closes her eyes briefly before letting out a shaky breath. I remove my hand from her neck and brush my thumb over her lips.

"*Abre,*" I demand. She opens her eyes and her lips part as I push my thumb into her mouth. Her tongue immediately flicks over it and then swirls around it.

My pants tighten as my erection grows, and I push my hip towards her legs. "Do you see what you do to me?" I ask her, pushing my thumb further into her mouth. She attempts to mumble something, but I shush her.

"I'm going to have fun with you. If you keep showing up in places you're not supposed to... We're going to find many places in this university where I can punish you–"

She lets out a moan before shutting her eyes tightly.

"You like the idea?" She nods. "Imagine stuffing my cock down your throat right next to Laura's office... Where she can hear your mumbles, but you're too stuffed that you can't even *breathe*. Oh, the places I can ruin you. You'll be my naughty girl?"

She nods incessantly before moaning again, and I pull my thumb from her mouth. A string of saliva follows from her lips to my thumb and she gasps, breathing heavier.

"Say it," I command.

She locks eyes with me. "I'm your naughty girl, professor."

"Uncross your legs, baby," I murmur and she listens, uncrossing her legs, and I immediately put myself in between them. She takes a deep breath.

I move my hand to rest under her chin and tilt it up, causing her to lock eyes with me. Her green eyes are the prettiest I've ever seen and those yellow specks just make me hypnotized.

My thumb rubs circles on her chin and her breathing staggers. I smirk, loving how she reacts to my touch; to *everything* I do to her. She blinks a few times before I lean in and kiss her. Her legs close in on my waist as the kiss deepens. I push my tongue into her mouth.

"I want to fuck you so bad," I breathe out after a few more seconds of kissing. "But I have things to do. Long day ahead of me."

She pouts and it does something to me. "It can be quick," she whispers.

"I can't, *Corazón*. What are you doing this weekend?"

Her eyes flutter around the room before landing back on me. "Essay, but I'm practically done with it."

"Come over if you'd like. You can stay the whole weekend," I offer.

A smile breaks out on her lips and she nods. "I'll text you. I won't be free Friday night though."

I raise a brow. "Girls night?"

She shakes her head. "My father's hosting a dinner with other faculty members–" her eyes enlarge.

That's when her words finally click. I completely forgot about that email. This morning, I got an email from Carlos about a faculty dinner Friday night. He likes to throw these dinners every semester to just keep us faculty members in good spirits. It's not always at his house, but this semester it is.

"Fuck." Eliana blinks a few times before sighing.

"I guess you're going?" she asks.

I nod. "I always go.. Location varies every semester, but I guess this time he wants it at his house."

"My house," she reminds me. I nod, cursing myself for the predicament we're in. Carlos has been nothing but kind to me. Victoria, on the other hand, has been a little more crass because of the divorce. She likes nothing interfering with her husband's work and thought the divorce between Laura and I would cause a rift between me and Carlos. I can't remember the last time I've had a one on one conversation with the woman.

Eliana watches me for a moment, as if she wants to see some kind of doubt in my face. But what I'm most worried about is her parents. It's easier to sneak around the University because we all have different class schedules and I do more night classes than Carlos. But her house? The Haros household?

That will be fucking difficult to hide anything. Especially if she's present.

I look at her and raise my brow. "Are you going to be there?"

A smirk fills her face and I want to punish her for even doing this to me. "I can be."

"Eliana," I start.

She sighs. "Of course I'm going to be there. My mother doesn't like me to hide from events. Why do you think I showed at the opening exhibit at the History Museum?"

She's got a point; she was there. I still can't believe Carlos

Haros didn't introduce me to her when we were all there. But I'm glad he didn't or else we wouldn't be here in my office.

I lower my hand to caress her shoulder before dropping lower to smooth over her arm and then her covered thigh. The tights aren't thick, so I can easily rip them if I wanted to fuck her. But I have so much to do today.

"Are you sure you can behave yourself?" I mumble, pressing my fingers into her thigh. She hitches her breath.

"Julián, I'll sit across the damn table and far away from you if I have to."

I pout. "What makes you think I don't *want* you to misbehave? We can even slip out of the dinner and I can–"

She shakes her head with widened eyes. "Now that is just asking for a death wish. You can't go *anywhere* in that house without them knowing. You'll have to stay where the party is."

I chuckle and her eyes stay big. It's cute the way she's so wound up over the idea that we can't sneak around her house. It excites me though, as fucked up as that sounds.

Visions of stuffing her panties in her mouth as I fuck her senseless somewhere in the house while the rest of the dinner continues. My cock gets hard at the thought and I sigh deeply.

"Eliana, I'm going to have trouble *not* pulling you away and fucking you until you can't speak."

Redness creeps up to her cheeks and nose before she shakes her head and coughs softly. "Now I don't even want to be there! You're making this too difficult. I can't."

A smile breaks through her tight lips and I smile as well. "I'll keep my hands to myself," I promise.

Eliana takes a deep breath before moving her hand to grasp mine that's placed on her thigh. Her fingers lace with mine and the gesture is soft and intimate. I smile and so does she.

"I'll see you Friday then," she whispers before I step back and let her hop off the desk. She adjusts her skirt to be a little lower and I watch her figure as she moves to gather her bag. She pulls it over her shoulder before stepping closer to me.

I look down, and she smiles. She gets up on her tiptoes and brushes her lips against mine quickly. Almost too quickly. I try to grab her waist to keep her here, but she's backing away.

"Bye, Eliana," I say.

She smiles widely before reaching for the doorknob. "Bye, *Professor*." Then she opens the door and slips out quietly and quickly.

Sixteen

ELIANA

"Your father actually invited me tonight."

I almost drop the croissant that's in my hand. I stare at Lena who is munching on her donut. We're at Crescent Cafe after her classes ended. Since I don't have classes on Fridays, I met up with her after my run. I got most of my essay done just in case I wanted to stay the weekend at Julián's.

"I'm sorry, what?" I ask baffled. Her eyes find mine, and she shrugs as she takes another bite of her donut. She then gracefully takes a sip of her steaming coffee.

My fingers tap the croissant before I tear off a piece and pop it in my mouth. I continue to watch her as she finishes her sip. Her black hair is pinned back with a clip and a few strands are falling out over her temples.

"He invited me since I'm his GA. I thought you knew? We were texting about your outfit last night!"

I shake my head and try to swallow this croissant. But it's very dry and I regret buying it almost immediately. I toss it back on the plate and brush the crumbs off my fingers.

"Yeah, I thought the outfit you sent *me* was the one you were going out in."

She raises a brow. "You really think I'm going to wear a turtleneck out to the bars?"

I give her a look before we both laugh. "Okay, you're right," I finally succumbed. Lena watches me for a moment as I take a sip of my iced coffee.

"They usually make the dinners at some fancy restaurant," Lena speaks up.

"Yeah, I heard," I slip out.

"It's nice. It'll be at your house. Though Professor Estrada will be there. I hope he doesn't make it awkward."

My cheeks burn at the thought of Julián and my heart stammers against my chest. *Act cool.*

"Why would it be awkward?" I almost squeak out.

Lena's eyes narrow before she laughs. "Because he was there when we got drunk. He saw me taking *shots* with Malcolm. I really hope he doesn't bring it up with your father. I don't want to lose my job."

I shake my head and wave my hand. "Don't worry about it. He won't spill the beans."

Lena sighs. "I don't know. Professor Estrada is nice, but I don't know him. Even at the bar, I was hesitant to keep drinking around him. His wife is a pain in the ass."

"Ex," I slip out, *once again*. I mentally slap myself and bite my lip from saying anything dumb.

She stills in her seat as her eyes lock with mine. Her brows scrunch before she nods. "Yeah, ex. How did you know? I thought that was the first time you met Professor Estrada?"

Shit.

"Uh y-yeah," I stammer out. "But when I went to see my parents during their free time in my mother's office, she was talking about the other Professor Estrada. It all clicked for me," I lie.

Lena nods, and it's as if she completely disregards her suspicions. Thank the gods.

"Well, yeah, she's his ex-wife. She's a pain and... wait, do you have classes with her?"

I nod my head. "Yeah, she's kind of my advisor, too. I met her privately once and classes have been okay."

"Does she talk about him?" Lena leans forward and plants her elbows on the table. I shake my head.

"No, but she still wears a wedding ring." Anger builds up at the thought. Why does she do that? I had class with her yesterday and she *still* had it on. Does Julián know? He must...

"That's weird. See? I told you. She's a mess and a pain in the ass. God, no wonder he divorced her," Lena chuckles before grabbing her coffee and taking a long sip.

My eyes travel around the cafe for a moment before locking back to Lena. I want to tell her so badly about Julián, but I can't risk anything. I love Lena, but she works for my father. She'd tell him.

But would she really? She can keep a secret, I'm sure, but this is just too big of one to force her to keep. It wouldn't be fair.

I take a sip of my coffee.

"Now, tell me about this weekend after the dinner. Are we going out?" Lena finally asks as she sets her coffee down.

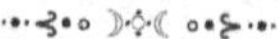

MY MOTHER RUNS HER HANDS OVER HER DRESS FOR THE FIFTH time in five minutes before I nudge her with my elbow. She yelps and gives me a glare before huffing her breath and taking a step away from me. We've been in the kitchen for over an hour, setting up the table for our guests.

Well, scratch that, *I was the one setting up the table*. My mother was drinking her second glass of wine and watching me with disapproving eyes. I had to keep myself from throwing the plates on the ground and stomping my ass upstairs.

With my blood pressure spiked, I'm pissed that she yet again chose my outfit. She bought me a really soft long sleeve, but it makes me look like I have a uni boob and goes way too long down my torso. I had it tucked into my pants, but the moment she saw it she pulled the fabric and cursed me out.

It took everything in me to not walk out the door and slam it in her face. But I didn't have anywhere to go. Lena is going to be here and so is Julián. I'd have to go find a cafe, restaurant, or a bar if I wanted some alone time. So, instead I stayed and here we are.

A knock comes to the door and my mother looks at me. "Well?"

Dad walks into the kitchen, clapping his hands. His eyes glance to the dining area where the table is and everything is set. "My girls set up the dinner table? How sweet."

I want to tell him I was the one who did it, but she just nods and walks up to him to give him a kiss. I almost throw up in my mouth at the sight and I roll my eyes. He steps away and gives me a hug before kissing my forehead. "You look nice, *Princesa*. Did mom pick out your outfit?"

"Yeah, sadly," I mumble. It's too low for him to hear. My mother walks to the front door and I look up at my dad. He smiles widely before wiggling his brows.

"Are you ready to meet the faculty? They're great and you'll love them. They're all younger than me, if you can imagine."

"Wow, that's shocking," I play along and he laughs, rubbing his hand over my shoulder.

"Come on, let's say hi to the first guest." We can hear chatter in the front as the first person comes into the house. My father grabs my arm and walks me down the hallway before we see it's Lena.

She looks up at me and smiles before running to me. "I'm here! Did the party start yet?"

"Lena! It's a dinner! Not a rave," my mother counters. Lena's lips twist into a frown before she barks out a laugh and turns to me.

It seems like my mother can only take Lena's backhanded comments, but with me she just makes it a living hell. I need to get out of here. Lena pulls me into a hug and I hold on to her tightly. My hands are shaking from nerves and I hope she doesn't notice.

Another knock is heard from the front door and my mother whips the door open for another professor and his wife. Professor Hall, Lena whispers in my ear. Alex Hall and his wife, Nicole Hall. They're sweet and I lead them to the dining room where we have a bar cart. Lena joins them so they're not alone as I keep greeting guests with my parents. As I return to the front door, my mother is laughing and waving her hand at the guest. I've never met them before.

"*¡Princesa*! Meet Harry!" My dad calls, waving me over. He laughs and then shakes his head. "Sorry, Harry. It's Professor Simmons."

The guy who I presume is Harry shakes his head and laughs. "That's alright." He lifts his hand as I near them and I take it. It's firm and cold.

"Nice to meet you, Mr. Simmons," I smile. He looks just a little older than me. Maybe in his thirties. My father is proudly smiling as we finally release hands.

"This is my daughter, Eliana. She moved back to town this summer. The medical career path wasn't for her, but I'm glad she's home. I've missed her so."

I roll my eyes and laugh. "Yeah, clearly that didn't work out."

Harry smiles widely before raising a brow. "So, what do you do now?"

I take a moment to think of an answer. I don't want to lie to him with my parents here, but I don't want to feel the pressure of my mother biting back with a response. I take a deep breath. "I'm getting a masters in creative writing."

There's a silent moment before Harry smiles and nods. "It's never too late to change careers."

"That's what I told her," my dad chimes in. My mother huffs from her place, but thankfully Harry doesn't acknowledge it.

Another knock comes to the door as I usher Harry to the dining area where Lena waves him over. When I'm back to the front door, I halt in my steps. I'm about twenty feet from the front door and my eyes lock with his dark brown ones.

Julián. His beard is trimmed to be more short and his curly salt and pepper hair is slightly gelled back with a few curls escaping. He's wearing brown slacks with a burgundy sweater. He looks completely appetizing and his eyes glance over my body as if he's eating every inch of me. I clench my thighs quickly and he smirks, as if noticing.

I gulp as my father is deep in conversation with my mother as Julián eye fucks me. I finally make my feet move and I'm walking towards them. My mother smiles, finally, and my dad does too.

"¡*Ah, Princesa*! This is Professor Estrada." He gestures between Julián and I and I nod my head, lifting my hand for him. Julián's lips twitch as he takes my hand in his for a moment longer than what's appropriate and I can feel the fire in my body rise and it feels like I'm going to explode. He's going to make me pass out with just his eyes, *dear Lord*.

"Nice to meet you," he plays along and I want to laugh, but my mother is watching me like a hawk. Not sure why, but I give him a curt nod before we let go. My father claps his hands again like an excited child and turns to me.

"You have the other Professor Estrada, Julián's ex-wife, as your advisor, right?"

I nod slowly as Julián's eyes turn dark and he rolls his shoulders, but my father doesn't notice. "Yeah, classes have been good so far."

"Great, Victoria has some news," my father says to Julián. He turns to look at my father. They're almost the same height, but Julián is slightly taller. He raises a brow but before he can ask what the news is, the door opens and my mother is embracing another woman.

A blonde who I know very well. My advisor.

Laura Estrada.

My jaw drops as I look at Julián, who is barely turning around to see what the commotion is about. Laura laughs and hugs my mother tightly.

"What are you doing here, Laura?" Julián speaks up and Laura narrows her eyes as she looks at him. My father tries to console Julián by placing his hand on his shoulder, but he moves and brushes him off. My father's lips turn into a tight line and he looks at me and I just stare back, unsure how to respond.

Who invited her? I want to ask my father, but he seems to be just as shocked. No wonder he didn't tell me or even Julián. He must've just found out right before guests started pouring in.

My mother finally waves to me and I do my best to smile as Laura gives me a once over.

"I invited her. I hope that's okay. Mary is great friends with her and we all went out for dinner the other night and we just clicked!" my mother says with a bright smile.

That's the first time I've seen her like this while I'm in the same room as her. I adjust my stance and Julián turns to glance at me and his jaw clenches. I don't keep an eye on him any longer and try to keep my gaze elsewhere.

"I hope that's okay. Julián, don't look so somber. I won't embarrass you," Laura jokes as she shrugs off her jacket and hands it to my mother, who takes it reluctantly.

The interaction is just so *odd* that I can't wrap my head

around it. I want to ask my mother why she is smiling so widely and *taking* her coat. She never does this for a guest. Hell, she made Alex and his wife walk inside with their coats.

"¿*Princesa?*" My father's words break my trance and I taste blood from how much I chewed on the inside of my cheek. I gulp and look at him and give him a small smile.

"Yeah?"

"Show Julián to the dining area while Laura, your mother, and I talk." He gives me a smile and I nod.

"Uh, this way," I gesture for Julián to follow me and he nods before glancing one more time at Laura, who is laughing at something my mother said.

We're further down the hall and almost to the kitchen and dining area before I feel Julián's body brush up closer to mine and his lips find my ear.

"Did you know she'd be here?"

"No!" I hiss, turning my head and stopping in my tracks. He bumps into me and he groans, his hands catching my waist from the impact. Butterflies instantly swarm my belly and I take a deep breath. We're still in sight of the front door, so I don't turn around.

"You look great, by the way," he whispers as one of his hands travels higher on my waist and my breath hitches.

"Julián, we can't," I whisper in a breathless tone.

He snickers before taking his hands off me. I muster up a deep breath and break our bubble, continuing to walk to the dining area. I hear his footsteps behind me and I can practically feel his gaze on my body.

This dinner is going to drive me insane, I just know it.

Seventeen

JULIÁN

LAURA KEEPS TOUCHING me in any way that she can. Sitting next to me at the dinner wasn't something I could control. I would've rather had Eliana next to me, but we knew the risks. Having Laura here only brings more tension than needed. And it's not the good kind.

Eliana's eyes continue to travel across the table to where Laura's hands caress my forearm. I try to make eye contact with her to see if I can communicate to her silently, but she doesn't dare to look up. Her gaze is fixated on Laura. And I hate it.

The blood boils within and I want to grab Laura's hand and push her off me, but that would only dramatize the situation. I want Eliana to know that I'll be on my best behavior during dinner for her.

Eliana clears her throat just loud enough for me to hear and she grabs her wine glass and takes a long sip of the red liquid. Her eyes finally cast on me and I gulp, watching as her eyes turn to slits and she places the wine glass a little too loud on the table. I look away just in time as Carlos and Victoria ask her if everything's okay. Laura smooths her hand again on my arm and I shudder.

"Laura," I whisper, turning my head slightly. She smiles from the corner of my eyes and if we weren't drowned in conversation around us then I'd say something louder. She seems to only hear me when I'm yelling at her or demanding her to stop acting preposterous.

"And how are things with you, Laura?" Carlos asks from a few seats away. Laura keeps her hand on my arm as she responds.

"Just *dashing*. This year is off to a great start." I keep myself from rolling my eyes at her response.

Carlos smiles widely before locking eyes with me and he raises a brow. "And you, Julián? Are classes alright? Any luck with the GA applications?"

"No GA yet, but I'll keep you posted on that position. Classes are going well." I haven't had the chance to let him know that I possibly wouldn't need one anymore. I've been able to handle my workload better than I thought.

Laura's hand moves from my arm so she can get her drink, so I take this time to adjust away from her. Carlos's eyes travel to where Laura was just touching me, and gives me a tight smile.

"Definitely think about it," Victoria speaks up as she cuts into her steak. I look at her as she bites into the piece and chews for a moment.

"I think I'm okay for now," I counter with a soft smile. Victoria shakes her head and Carlos half-laughs breathlessly as he looks at his wife.

"No, no, Julián. You're doing so much already, a GA would help ease the load. Laura has told me great things about what hers does. And Lena, you're my husband's and look how less stressed he seems!"

Lena looks up from her meal, next to Eliana, who is keeping her gaze locked on her plate, before she nods. "Y-yeah! Professor Haros seems less stressed with my help. I love my job!"

Eliana faintly smiles, but I catch it. She still doesn't look anywhere but her plate and Victoria continues. "Get a GA and see how better your life is."

I shrug. "It's not that big of a deal, Victoria. I can handle it."

Victoria scoffs before laughing and I raise a brow, watching her lock eyes behind me, and I know she's looking at Laura. *This* time, I rolled my eyes.

"You know–" Victoria starts, but she's disrupted by Eliana, who sighs loudly and slams her wine glass down harshly. The whole table is at her attention.

"*Mother*, please. We're having dinner. Stop trying to control his life and his decisions. Just because dad is doing great with having Lena as his GA doesn't mean Ju-Professor Estrada needs one."

My lips twitch as I catch her slip, but I hear Laura shift in her seat and I turn to see her looking at Eliana a little too closely. Eliana's cheeks are growing pink and it's absolutely adorable on her.

Victoria scoffs again and Alex and his wife continue to eat their meals at the end of the table to my left. Harry is next on the other side of Eliana and he nods, nudging his elbow into her and it lights a fire within. Jealousy? Possession? I'm not sure, but I don't like him touching what's mine.

Eliana turns to Harry and gives him a smile. "I think we're all here for a nice dinner and don't have to go into work stuff," he agrees. Laura murmurs something under her breath that I don't catch.

"I wasn't talking to you," Victoria snaps and everyone grows silent. Carlos clears his throat before smiling and bringing a hand to Victoria's that's nestled near her plate. Her eyes are blazing into Harry's, who just stares at her back.

Eliana is smiling awkwardly at the showdown, her cheeks and now neck growing pinker by the second out of what is obviously embarrassment. I hate seeing her like this.

"Don't ruin this dinner, *por favor*," Eliana finally musters.

Laura gasps beside me and I turn my gaze to her, shaking her head. The Halls are watching the scene unfold and I feel bad for them. They just wanted a nice faculty dinner and here we are, Victoria and Harry going at it.

And why the fuck is Harry defending Eliana? And why does she look like she's enjoying it? Is this not embarrassment on her face, but utter amusement? I peer my eyes back at Eliana and clear my throat, but she doesn't hear me. Lena, however, turns to look at me and gives me an apologetic frown as she picks up her glass of wine and takes a big chug.

Carlos sighs again and starts cutting his steak and taking a bite.

"I'm not the one ruining it," Victoria pouts. "I'm just trying to help structure things around here. It's doing so well with Carlos. I'd thought it'd be nice for Julián as well."

"I completely agree," Laura pipes up. I clench my fists at her words and my vision goes red as I feel Laura's hands find my back and she tries to soothe me when I haven't said a word.

"Excuse me," I finally say as I scrape back my chair and stand up. Laura looks up at me with expectant eyes, but I give her a glare. I give Carlos a smile before turning on my heel and heading back towards the hallway and the front of the house. The chatter continues as Victoria brings up another topic and Laura's laugh can be heard from the front door.

I take a few deep breaths as I try to recenter myself from that shitshow. This is going to be harder than I thought.

My fists continue to clench, nails digging into my palm. I walk around the foyer until I find a seating area to walk around. There's a large window that lets me look at the neighborhood, and it seems to calm me as I ignore the laughter and chatter in the dining room.

"You okay?" a voice speaks up and I twist on my heels and

see Eliana creeping toward me with a worried look on her face. I sigh and shake my head.

"Victoria–your mother–is a piece of work. Carlos never really introduced me to her. I've seen her around the University but we never really had a sit down conversation until tonight."

Eliana closes the distance and she peers up at me from underneath her lashes and bites her lip. Just that action alone causes all the blood to rush south and I want to push her into a closet somewhere and make her choke on my cock.

"Welcome to my life," she laughs, but her eyes say something else. Sadness. And I want to take that sadness out of her. I wrap my hand around her waist gently and pull her chest flush to mine. She gasps and that sound alone makes me go feral.

"Julián, we can't. Anyone can come and catch us. I told them I went to check on you in case you got lost."

That gives me an idea. I raise a brow. "Where would you look? If I did get lost…"

A genuine smile widens on her face, and my heart rate picks up at the sight. She thinks for a moment before she squeals, pushing herself off me and grabbing my hand. She lifts her vacant hand up to her mouth with her index finger in a *shush* motion, and I oblige. She pulls me into the hallway and then towards the stairs that are away from the dining room so they can't hear a thing. We walk up the stairs gently until we're on the second floor and head into a bathroom. It's tiny with a small sink, a standing shower in the corner and a toilet near a window. We barely fit inside and it's too clean that I assume it's more for decoration and never really used.

"Eliana," I murmur, but she locks the door and grabs me by my sweater. She gets on her tiptoes and moves her hands to clasp my cheeks. I peer down at her and she smiles wider.

"We can be quiet. They won't know."

"They'll definitely hear you with the way I'd fuck you."

Her eyes enlarge a smidge, and I lean in, kissing her. She moans through the kiss and I grab her waist, pushing her backside to the sink. I ease my hands to lift her up onto it, standing in between her legs.

"Julián," she moans, her eyes half lidded and her cheeks even more pink.

"Are you buzzed, baby?" I whisper, kissing her nose and then her forehead. She nods and giggles.

"Maybe, but that's what she makes me turn into. I like to drown her out and wine seemed like a good choice tonight."

I know she's referencing Victoria, and I don't want to push her right now. I'd rather she tell me when she's sober and can process her thoughts instead of saying something she might not mean. I might not know the full extent of their relationship and I want to give her time.

"Then are you sure you want to do something here? Given your state?" I ask.

She nods and pulls me closer and wraps her legs around my waist, locking her ankles behind me. I breathe deeper and she smirks. "Yes, *professor*, I want this. Please, stuff me with your cock. Make me moan your name."

My hands tighten around her legs and I smooth my palms over her thighs before running them up to her torso and then her breasts. Even though she's wearing a turtleneck, she looks damn delicious in it. My palms grasp her breasts and squeeze and she mumbles incoherently, closing her eyes and throwing her head back.

"I haven't even touched you beneath all these clothes," I tease.

She sucks in her cheeks and opens her eyes. "Please, Julián, I need you." She squeezes her legs around me tighter and I can't say no to *that*.

"Say that again," I whisper, leaning closer to her and our

noses brush. Her eyes look deeply into mine and my cock hardens, heart quickens, and everything that happens when you're infatuated with someone.

"I *need* you, Julián," she repeats.

I close our distance and kiss her, her hands instantly wrapping around my neck and pulling me in closer as if we're not already core to core, chest to chest, and tongue to tongue. Now we're heart to heart.

The fire within me is transformed into desire and I need to be fucking her soon before I come in my pants. She continues to kiss me slowly, her tongue tasting like the wine we had downstairs. One of her hands moves to my beard and her fingers comb through it before grasping my jaw and pulling me impossibly closer. I nibble on her lip and she giggles.

I pull back for a moment as we both look at the shut door before we laugh softly. "Be quiet, *Corazón*," I whisper before moving my hands between her legs and cupping my palm over her clothed pussy.

"Baby, please," she whines, kissing me once more as I move my hand in an up and down motion over her clothed pussy.

"You like that? Dry hump my hand, then. My whore," I whisper as she grinds her hips towards me, rubbing her pussy on my palm. I press my own tented erection against the sink counter for relief.

"No, I need you inside me, *please*," she whines once more. And I can't deny her, so I nod. I move my hands to her waistband and unbutton it before I pull her off the sink counter. She yelps before slapping her hand over her mouth. I grab the waistband and pull them down her legs, relishing in her black panties that face me. I'm now kneeling down, getting an idea.

"Take your pants and these off." I lean in and kiss her clothed pussy and she squirms before nodding and breathing heavily. Her hands are shaky as she leans down to kick off her shoes quickly before pulling off her pants and then slowly stripping her panties. She stands and peers down at me.

"What?" she asks after a moment, more pinkness rising in her cheeks.

"Sit on my face," I command. I see confusion cross her face before she watches me get even further down on my knees and grab her waist, pulling her closer to me.

"What?" she asks again, but before she can say anything else, I hike one of her legs over my shoulder and then pull her hips to my face before my lips touch her pussy. She yelps at the contact before a soft mewl escapes her lips and I chuckle.

"Now, be quiet while I have my dinner." I use my tongue to glide along her already wet folds. She tastes delectable, and I immediately suck on her clit. She whimpers from the contact. I move my tongue just enough to tease her entrance before dipping it inside her. Her leg that's keeping her balanced shakes and I move my chin, letting my beard brush against her skin, causing another sound to escape her mouth.

"Julián, I'm going to f-fall," she whimpers. I look up and see her with clenched eyes and biting her lip.

"Grab the wall," I demand as I shift myself back and then bring her standing leg over my shoulder so she's completely sitting on me. She instantly leans over, grasping the wall as best as she can. Her thighs clench around my head, but it only makes me want to eat her out even more.

I continue to glide my tongue over her folds and insert my tongue to tease her before adding more pressure on her clit and sucking it every so often. Her whines and moans are incoherent and it makes me so fucking hard to hear her like this.

That I can make her react this way. I don't care if the entire house hears. I want her to scream my name for all I care.

I hope Laura hears it.

"I'm so close," Eliana's whine cuts through my thoughts and I work overtime with my tongue and sucking her clit while also balancing her on top of me. Her thighs tighten around my neck, causing my breathing to falter, and it turns me on even more. I move my hands to her ass and press her closer to me, eating out her pussy like a man starved.

"*Ah,* so fucking close—Julián!" she whines before her legs shake uncontrollably and I taste her cum and I lick it all up as her hips grind against me. I suck on her clit one last time after I lick every drop of her release.

My lips are wet and so is my beard, and I'm pretty sure my nose, too. If I died tonight, I wouldn't be upset.

"Okay, please," she begs, tapping the walls with her hands and I nod, helping her get off my shoulders. She catches her balance by grabbing onto the sink and I get up slowly, stretching my legs from being in a kneeled position for too long.

"Are you okay, *Corazón*?" I ask, lifting her chin to look at me. Her green eyes are sparkling and dazed. She giggles and nods. I lean down and kiss her nose before kissing her lips.

She leans into the kiss and her hands go to my pants, cupping my cock but I pull back. I tsk under my breath and she whines.

"Why not? I want you to scream my name," she teases.

"Because we've been gone long enough that they might send someone else to look for us."

Her eyes widen and she gasps. "Fuck, if my mother came upstairs and found us I'd be dead. No, *you'd* be dead."

"Pretty sure Carlos would hang me by my balls before Victoria could even scold me."

This brings laughter to bubble out of her chest and she smacks my chest, but I clasp my hand over hers and pull her in for another kiss. We melt into it before we separate and she cleans herself up and pulls on her panties and pants.

"Let me go first and then you follow. We'll just pretend you got lost upstairs wandering the halls," she whispers.

I look at her dazed expression and her lightly smeared eye makeup. Her hair is even a little tousled and I know I'd have to adjust my pants and even my hair before I enter the dining room.

"They'll definitely believe that," I joke.

She smiles before pulling the bathroom door open and slipping out. I followed right after.

Eighteen

ELIANA

Lena is staring at me with worried eyes.

"What?" I ask, glancing at her once more before looking down at the magazine in my hands. There's an article about adding up points to see if he's really into you. I roll my eyes at the choices before Lena sighs.

"You've been quiet since Friday night. And that was like a week ago."

I look up at her again and tap my fingers against the magazine. "My mother is to blame. She can't keep taking over conversations and then telling *grown adults* how to do their job."

"She was just trying to help Professor Estrada."

"That's not the way you do it."

Lena watches me for a moment before shrugging. "Well, did you at least get his number?"

My heart thuds in my chest and I try to not be so obvious, but my mouth instantly turns dry. "Who's number?"

"Harry's!"

I raise a brow and try to think back to the dinner last week to see what would make her think that. After Julián and I had our fun in the bathroom upstairs, we finished our dinner with everyone and then the majority went home. Laura tried to drag Julián with her and my mother to the sitting room near the front of the house but he stayed in the dining room with my father, Harry, Lena, and I.

We talked about nonsense, and I didn't think Lena was studying me *or* Harry. There wasn't anything that I could remember about Harry and I that night. I was so fucked out and dazed by Julián that I kept smiling and giggling throughout the night. Was it that?

Just thinking about the bathroom, and how we tried a new move brings a smile to my face. Julián kept eyeing me all night, and I just wanted to grab him and pull him upstairs where he could fuck me properly on my bed.

"There, that smile. You were doing it all night!" Lena points at me and I try my best to wipe the dazed smile off my face.

"Come on, Len, don't be like that."

"So you *did* get his number!"

I think fast. "Sure." What harm can it do? Maybe then I can continue to sneak off with Julián and she thinks I'm with Harry. I don't have the guts yet to tell my best friend that I'm fucking my dad's coworker. I can't.

"Yay!" She claps her hands. "You know who I've been talking a lot lately?"

I raise a brow. "Who?"

"Malcolm."

"Who?"

"Malcolm! The guy from the bar."

A gasp escapes from me. "You mean the *professor*?"

"Yeah, yeah, so what? We're not in the same building or department. He's art and I'm Egyptology!"

"But you took his class."

Lena sticks out her tongue before *giggling*. "So? That was a while ago. Now I'm in my prospective courses and he can continue teaching in his."

I smile and watch her cheeks turn crimson at the confession. "So, have you been out with him yet?"

"No, that's what I wanted to ask you about…"

"I wouldn't care if you guys went out."

She shakes her head. "It's not that. I'd love for us to all go on a double date."

Double date.

"Wait, what?"

Lena nods quickly. "Wouldn't that be cute?! Me and Malcolm… You and Harry."

My jaw drops. She watches me for a moment and raises a brow, a confused look etched on her face.

"What?" she asks.

"I-I don't think that's necessary. Just go out with him and see if you like him just as much in person as you have texting," I offer.

She shakes her head and laughs. "Ana, you know you need to get out there! You've barely talked to me about your dating life and you just said you got Harry's number."

Shit, why did I do that. I can't take back my words without an explanation. A very awkward and inappropriate explanation.

I cock my head to the side and finally toss the magazine aside. My fingers lace together and I cursed myself for starting to pick at the sides of each nail. Bad habit, but everything about this has got me feeling stressed to the nines. "Len…"

"Come on! We need to put ourselves out there, and now we've got them. Why not go out and have fun?"

I feel stuck, like I'm in the middle of a tug of war. If I lean one way, it'll snap, and if I lean the other way… it'll still snap. There's no happy ending in sight. I have to stick it out by faking it with Harry and then seeing Julián when I can.

"I only just got his number. We haven't even hung out with just us two. I'll have to ask him."

She nods and smiles. "Of course! Just let me know what

Harry says and we can plan something. We should do something fun, especially with October around the corner. I heard there are some places that are doing apple picking and such. If not, we can do a nice dinner."

I slump in my chair, but she doesn't notice. "Sure, sounds fun."

Lena squeals and claps her hands before going back to her notebook she was writing in before she started asking me about Harry. I look down at the magazine and see a question.

Does he take you out on dates and pay for your half? Add five points.

I didn't have Harry's number, so I have to think of a way to get it by the time Lena asks me again about the double date. I have other things on my mind, though. Julián has been so busy with grading and teaching that I have seen little of him. I never got to spend the weekend with him as much as I wanted to.

It felt like I was getting *too attached* to him, but I didn't care. It felt like he was the same way with me. We can't keep our hands to ourselves whenever we're both in the same room, and I think that same rule applies with our thoughts about each other. I can't stop thinking about him as much as I try to concentrate on other things.

On Tuesday we got coffee, but that was brief and we didn't really talk. We tried to, but I had more assignments from Laura that I was working on while he graded papers. It felt nice though to just be around him while I worked. I think he liked it too, because he asked me out to coffee again the next day.

JULIÁN TEXTED ME HE'D BE AT A DIFFERENT BAR WITH HIS FRIEND Kane and wanted me to tag along. I remember him as the one who bought Lena and I shots when we collided with Julián and his professor friends. This could be fun if he has that same energy tonight.

But I'm not sure if I'm ready for Julián to tell his friend about us. Surely, he's told Kane something else—a lie. That I'm just joining because the last time was fun.

Lena hasn't reached out to me since our coffee date earlier when she mentioned the double date, so I immediately said yes to Julián. I missed him, sue me.

My phone buzzes as I ride in the Uber to the bar location that Julián sends me. I'm a block away as I glance at the screen and tap it, allowing the brightness of the screen to blind me for a moment.

JULIÁN

Almost here, corazón?

ME

A block away

JULIÁN

Kane bought you two shots already.

The car stops in front of the bar and I thank the driver before stepping out. The music is already loud for nine p.m. and I make my way to the doors, fishing out my ID from my purse. The bouncer lets me in and even though it's not that big of a bar, it's a similar layout to the other one I went to with Lena. The inside is structured like a house, with various rooms to adventure in.

There's a seating room with tons of people chatting with their drinks and then a bar in the next room where there are chairs to mingle. Even further back are more chairs and a seating area before there's a porch. It looks like a treehouse out there from what I can tell.

I push through some groups of people as I make my way to the second bar in the back of the 'house' before I spot Julián. I clench my thighs momentarily at the sight before waving at Kane, who spots me.

"She's here!" he bellows over the music and Julián turns

before traversing his eyes over my whole body. I thank past me for putting on this black dress that hits right at my thighs. It has long sleeves to keep me from being too cold from the weather, but I was anticipating drinking some to get warm.

My heels clack against the floor as Julián continues to drink me in and I do the same. He's wearing jeans and his *ass* looks good in them. He's wearing a canary colored sweater that defines his shoulders and arms as he moves about. He's even got a golden necklace that glistens under the lights above.

"Hey," I wave as I reach them. Julián gives me a wink before Kane is already passing me a shot glass with what looks like tequila and a quarter lime on the rim with some salt.

"Drink uppppp! You gotta catch up with us!" Kane hollers. He's handsome tonight, but I keep my eyes on Julián as I lick the rim, take the shot and then bite into the lime. My lips pucker, and I shake my head before squealing.

"That was so bad!" I yell at Kane who just throws his head back in laughter while Julián shakes his head and takes a sip of his own glass.

"You've got one more," Kane teases as he gestures to the other glass on the counter.

I look at Julián who continues to sip his drink and watch me. I nod and get closer to the counter, brushing my chest with Julián's arm as I lean over to grab the glass. Kane is on the other side of Julián and starts to whoop as I lick the rim, locking eyes with Julián and taking the shot before biting the lime. I squeeze my eyes shut as I take in the sour taste.

"Alright, now we can enjoy the night!" Kane says before slapping Julián's back. He jolts from the movement and chuckles.

"Don't scare her away, Kane."

"What? Eliana? You shouldn't have left last time, man. She was throwing back shots like there was no tomorrow."

"That hangover did last a whole day," I confess with a smile.

"You're not repeating that," Julián mutters as his hand reaches for my thigh under the counter and squeezes firmly.

I almost yelp but bite my lip instead to contain it. Kane doesn't seem to notice as he's looking around the bar.

"What's in your glass?" I nod towards his drink on the counter. Julián smiles before using his other hand to glide the glass closer to me. "Taste it."

I oblige and pick it up, taking a sniff before regretting it immediately. "Whiskey? No mixer or chaser?"

He shrugs before looking at Kane, who finally zeros in on our conversation. I lift the glass and take a sip before almost retching and I put it back on the counter. I shake my head and stick my tongue out.

"Nope! That is worse than the tequila. I'm going to need a mixed drink."

"I'll get it," Kane laughs as he flags down a bartender and I yell out a drink order.

Better tequila with pineapple Redbull. For energy and a buzz. I thank the bartender while they pass me the drink and Julián pulls his card out to pay and I thank him with a smile. Kane nudges Julián before ordering a drink for himself and Julián pays for it too.

"Have you ever been here?" Julián asks, leaning closer to me. I shake my head.

"Haven't had time to go to the bars around here yet," I say in his ear. My lips touch his skin and his grip on my thighs tightens and I clench my legs together. I can't help the noise that escapes my lips and Julián eyes me and smirks.

I busy myself with taking a long sip of the drink, and it doesn't taste as bad as the shots Kane gave me. Kane is waving down someone who happens to be a woman who looks a little older than me. She has pretty blonde hair and she's wearing a silver dress with matching boots.

"I'll be right back guys, found Rachel!" he calls to us as he grabs his drink from the bartender and makes a beeline for the blonde and wraps his arms around her.

I sigh and shift my balance on my heels. Julián turns to me and gestures to the side of the bar where there's a seating area. I nod and he leads the way. I can't stop looking at his ass as we walk and before I know it, he's sitting down and patting his knee for me to join him. There's a loveseat and a few bigger chairs that circle this side of the bar that seems more like a mini living room like what's in the front of the house. I look around for Kane, but he's too busy talking with Rachel as I take a seat on his lap, my dress riding up my thighs and I try to adjust it with one hand while my other is gripping my drink.

"*Te ves hermosa*," Julián whispers in my ear as one hand wraps around my waist to steady me on his lap and the other travels along my exposed thigh. My heart thuds faster and I can feel goosebumps rise along my legs.

"Julián, what if he sees us?" I ask, looking at where Kane disappeared.

"Let him," Julián whispers again as he travels his fingers even closer to the edge of the dress. I turn to look at him and he's smirking. He doesn't care that he's doing this to me in public and my body heat is rising to the point that I want to pull him into a restroom and have my way with him.

"You look good in this sweater," I tease, reaching over and laying my hand on his chest, smoothing my fingers over the fabric. I continue to travel my fingers up to the collar of the sweater before touching his neck. He gulps and my fingers glide against his Adam's apple. I clench my thighs and he catches it, pressing his own fingers firmly on my thighs. If he just moved his fingers a little more *up* then he can find my panties and tease my clit. Just the thought alone brings heat to my core and my insides flutter.

"You want me to fuck you," he says a little too matter-of-factly.

I nod. "Maybe." My fingers continue to crawl up his neck until I'm grasping his beard and running my thumb over his bottom lip. He moves a little in his chair and that's when I start to feel his erection underneath me.

A breath escapes my lips and he chuckles. "Come here, *Corazón.*"

I look around the room once more for Kane's prying eyes but I can't find him anymore. I lean into Julián and press my lips against his. He instantly opens his mouth more, pushing his tongue through my lips and a moan escapes.

"*Se oye tan bonito cuando gimes asi nena,*" he whispers as his hand travels further up my dress and slips in between my inner thighs.

We continue to kiss and it feels like I'm about to have a heart attack from the alcohol, the kissing, and the desire of wanting him. I break our kiss before looking around for the bathroom. I spot a door with a sign above indicating a bathroom.

"Follow me," I tell him and I push myself off him before he can say anything. He doesn't fight me though as he gets up, adjusts himself in his jeans and then grabs my drink that I've set on the nearby table.

I make a beeline for the bathroom door and before anyone can see that we're both entering it, we push past it and lock it. The bathroom is low lit and there's a stall in here with a sink next to it. Before I can spin around, I feel Julian's chest brush against my backside and he pushes us towards the sink where I watch our reflection.

He sets my drink down on the counter on top of the sink and grasps my throat with one hand and my hip with the other. He squeezes gently and I whimper, watching his eyes turn darker in the mirror. He presses his erection into my backside and I flutter my eyes.

"I haven't even flipped you over, baby," he mutters before moving his hand to the hem of my dress and pulling it up. The fabric bunches up at my waist, right over my ass as he breathes through his teeth and slaps my ass. I yelp and lean closer to the sink. I try to turn to look at him, but his hand on my throat keeps me looking at the mirror.

"I want you to look at yourself while I make you come undone."

"Please," I gasp as he slaps my ass again and plays with the waistband of my panties. He pulls it down my ass before leaning to the front and pulling it down. My panties fall to my ankles with ease as he smooths his palm over my thighs and my ass.

"Are you going to be my good girl?" he asks as I stare at him through the mirror. I nod and gulp, his fingers pressing lightly against my throat again. I take a deep breath and shut my eyes for a moment before he slaps my ass again and I yelp.

"Say it," he demands.

"I-I'm going to be your good girl," I whisper.

He glides his hand from my ass to my front and dips his hand low until he touches my pussy. I jump from the touch and he slips a finger through my folds. "So wet, baby," he whispers.

I nod before he presses his finger against my clit and I squirm, leaning closer to the sink. He slips another finger through my folds and then leans against me before he's inserting a finger inside while his thumb rubs circles along my clit. My walls clench around his finger instantly and the coil inside me tightens.

"Julián," I whimper as he thrusts his finger inside of me while simultaneously rubbing my clit.

"What?" he asks, pressing his fingers along my throat and making sure I'm looking at him in the mirror.

He licks his lips before adding a second finger inside of me and I gasp, throwing my head back and his fingers tighten along my throat, cutting off my oxygen for a few seconds. This brings the coil to tighten even more and I squirm under his touch as his thumb continues to rub circles until I'm seeing stars. I whimper and scream his name as everything snaps and I'm coming all over his fingers. I open my eyes and try to calm my breathing as I look back down and catch his eyes.

"*¿Cómo te sientes?*" He asks. I shudder and grab his wrist to pull out his fingers. He doesn't hesitate and I see him watching me as I lift his fingers to my mouth and lick the ones covered in my juices. He closes his eyes for a moment and presses his erection against me again before letting my throat go.

"I need more, please," I whisper, leaning over and pressing my ass against his jeans. He groans before I hear him pulling down his pants and I feel his cock press against my ass. I watch him in the mirror as he spits in his hand before the sound of him preparing himself fills the room. I wiggle my hips and he chuckles before slapping my ass with his free hand. I squeal and breathe harder, wanting more of him.

The head of his cock presses through my folds as he leans closer and grasps my hair with his hand, lifting me up to his chest. This movement causes his cock to slide right in and the angle is other worldly.

"Fuck," I whisper as he thrusts once and wraps his hand around my throat while his other hand goes to my clit.

"I could fuck you all day, if you'd let me. Tie you up and bring out as many orgasms as I could," he teases as he thrusts harder into me. Tears brim my eyes from the feeling.

I nod and whimper. "*Yes, please.*"

"Yes, what?"

"Yes, sir," I whine as his grip on my throat tightens and his thrusting increases. My gaze shifts to the ceiling as he continues to thrust into me. My core tightens once more and I know I'm close.

"I'm close, baby," he pants as he increases his speed and I scream his name as his thumb on my clit continues to rub circles and his grip on my throat tightens. Before we know it, we're both coming and screaming.

"Fuck," he grunts once last time as he stays still and lets his release fill me up. I lean my head back on his chest and he lets my throat go and kisses my neck gingerly. His beard tickles my skin and I giggle.

"Want round two?" he teases. I shake my head and pant, barely able to stand on my own. My legs feel like jello.

"No, I can't," I plead. He kisses my neck again before he slips out of me. He grabs paper towels from the counter and starts to clean me up. I lean down and pull my panties up once he's done. He just cleaned my thighs from the wetness, but I'm still full of him.

He pulls on his pants and buttons them. He sees me turn to watch him and he gives me a wink. My core flutters again and I can't believe I'm wanting *more* after we just did it.

"I like the idea that you're full of me while we're out here," he says.

I blush and laugh. "Of course, you do. It's like you're marking your territory with your cum."

"And you've had no complaints so far."

He's right, I'd let him mark me everyday if he could. In more ways than just this.

A knock breaks our thought and I'm surprised we haven't been interrupted earlier. Julián turns on the sink and we clean our hands quickly before I grab my drink and he opens the door for me. The girl waiting for the restroom widens her eyes as she watches us both walk out. Julián grabs my waist and we walk out of the bathroom and back into the bar to find Kane.

"Let's go, *Corazón*," he says before he moves his hand from my waist and he grabs my hand.

Our fingers intertwined together and it feels just right.

Nineteen

JULIÁN

SOMETHING IS wrong and I don't know what, yet. There's been so much silence and unread texts from Eliana that it's gotten me worried.

With it being Wednesday, I only have day classes. I've been holed up in the office the rest of my day grading papers when I finally pick up the phone and dial her number.

It rings three times before it goes to voicemail. Weird. I scrunch my brows as I stare at the screen and hang up, not wanting to bother leaving a message. If she ignored my texts, then she wouldn't listen to a voicemail.

Anxiety creeped in, making me wonder what's happening. Was she safe? What happened? I couldn't lie and say a feeling of rejection was starting to creep up into my chest and spread like a wildfire. My emotions were taking over and it was all because of her. I felt so much for her, finally realizing.

There's a knock at my office door and I whip my head towards it, wondering if it's her.

"Come in," I yell, watching the doorknob twist slowly; my heart rate is picking up speed as I watch intently for who's entering. I take a deep breath in and then exhale loudly when I realize it's not her.

"Hey, professor," Lena smiles as she walks inside. She's got a few papers in her hands as she strides over and gives me a once over.

"Hey, Lena. Everything okay?" I ask, sighing and dropping my phone to the desk.

She gives me a look before nodding her head. "Professor Haros wanted you to have these papers. Seems like there was a mixup at the printer and these are yours."

She sets the papers down on the desk, and I pick them up, nodding. I wondered where these copies went. I've been so busy with classes and needing to grade papers I completely forgot I printed these.

"Thanks," I tell her. She nods before turning on her heel. I remember then that she's good friends with Eliana. "Lena?"

She turns as she's almost near the door and she raises a brow. "Yeah?"

I try to think of a way to bring Eliana into conversation without bringing suspicion. "Kane wanted to know if you and Eliana were up for another night at the bar this weekend. I told him I'd ask you, if you don't mind."

Lena laughs and shakes her head. "Of course he did. But I can't. I have a date this weekend."

"Oh? Well then, pass on the information with Eliana," I smile. My heart thuds against my chest and I hope she can't hear it from there.

"Actually, it's a double date. Going out with Eliana and her date."

I almost fall out of my chair at her words and I take a deep breath, clear my throat, and try to maintain a poker face. My lips twitch into a half frown, half smile. She scrunches her brows for a moment, witnessing the scene before her.

"Oh, never mind then," I rush out, picking up my phone. She nods and opens the door, slipping out into the hallway.

I immediately open the text thread with Eliana and type out a message. Without thinking, I hit send.

A date? Since when? My blood boils and I need her to answer my texts. Call me back. I need her to do *something*.

I throw my phone down on the desk again, fuming. I try to busy myself for a few more minutes looking through assignments to grade, but I can't focus.

"Fuck!"

I huff out a huge breath before piling the papers together, tossing them in the file cabinet to worry about tomorrow. I need to get home and forget about what Lena just said. I gather my things, slipping on my coat and head for the door. The moment I'm out of the hallway, there's silence. It's almost four p.m., so I know most of the faculty in my department went home unless they have a night class to teach.

The hallways are dimly lit as I walk through them and head towards the elevators. I punch in the button and it arrives fast, entering and pressing for the main floor. Once the elevator beeps for the main floor, I rush out. I head straight to the lobby of the main floor before I almost collide with someone walking from another hallway heading the same way I was.

"Sorry," she squeaks. I stop in my tracks as I steady myself and see that it's Eliana.

"Hey," I say, watching her messy hair fall in front of her face as she balances herself from almost falling. She finally pushes a few strands behind her ear before she looks up.

That's when I get *angry*. Her eyes are red, like she's been crying, and she sniffles quickly.

"Eliana, what happened?"

She looks around the lobby where there's no one before taking a deep breath and shaking her head. "Nothing, it's nothing. I was just heading home."

"Did you get my texts?" I ask, watching her lip tremble as she composes herself. She shakes her head.

"No, I w-was busy. Had a meeting. I just really need to get home, Julián. I'm sorry." She sniffles again and tears brim her eyes before she brushes past me. But I don't let her get too far before I'm matching her pace and grabbing her elbow.

"*Eliana*, talk to me," I demand.

She whips around and pulls her elbow back so my hand falls. She takes a deep breath and looks everywhere but me. "I can't. Please let me go. I can't talk about it."

"Well, you had a meeting here. So was it with a professor? Do you want to talk about it? I might be able to help and can talk to them—"

Before I can even finish my sentence, she laughs and shakes her head once more. "I don't think that's going to do much. You were married to her."

"Wait, you spoke to Laura? What happened? Tell me."

She sniffles again before blinking a few tears away, but some cascade down her blotchy cheeks. "Julián, *please*."

"Eliana," I plead this time, reaching out for her elbow again. She doesn't move and lets me grasp her arm. I close the distance and reach my hand to her cheek, brushing my thumb along it before moving to her lips. They're still trembling and another tear falls from her eye, hitting my hand. "Please."

She takes a shaky breath before fluttering her eyes closed. "She gave me a horrendous grade on an assignment that is worth a lot. Said it wasn't what she expected from me. I've done nothing but succeed in her class and in all my other classes. I can't *fail*."

I search her green eyes that seem to lose their spark with every passing moment she's talking about her predicament. I want to hug her and pull her into my arms, but we're still in the building and there are students milling about, ready for their evening classes. I don't want to risk anything, but I want to be there for her.

"Come with me, let me take you home and you can feel all you need to feel. I can't change what she's done, but I can be here for you. You don't have to wallow alone."

Her eyes flutter again, teary still, before she takes another shaky breath. "I just want to lock myself somewhere and cry. The whole reason I'm here is because I couldn't find a job. I'm living with my parents because I couldn't afford to move out. That was their ultimatum. I'm not here because I want it. I'm here because I have no choice."

I stay quiet at her confession and my chest aches for her. To have her parents lay out that kind of choice for her, it's not fair. I've had my luck with great parents, but I can't imagine how she must feel. Especially knowing Carlos the way I do. Doesn't seem like something he'd do to his daughter.

It makes my blood boil. I want to go find him and corner him, force him to tell me why he's doing this to her. I want to protect her and fight for her—shield her from what's hurting her. I want to tell Laura to stop fucking with her grades. That's when a thought crosses my mind.

"Does Laura know about us?"

She scoffs and rips herself from my hold. "Oh my gods, Julián! Not everything is about you!"

"What?"

Her hair falls in front of her face as she stares at the ground before looking up at me again. "She didn't give me a failing grade on that assignment because of *you*."

"I had to ask," I say quickly, cursing myself for the way it came out. Of course I don't care about Laura. But if she's compromising Eliana's education, then I have to do something; I have to step in.

"You only care about yourself, *clearly*."

I wince at her words.

"I don't know what the fuck you're doing, but don't do that. Don't say that," I say defensively. If she wants to be mad, sure. But she can't try to pin this on me when I'm just trying to be here for her.

"It's true," she mumbles.

"Talk to me, *Corazón*. Please," I urge, taking another step closer to her. She's fuming, but I want her to talk.

Tears fall from her eyes again, and it suffocates me to see her like this. "Baby, if you need me to talk to Laura and fix this, then please let me. I know you said she's not doing it because of me, but it might be the reason. And she's just not telling you."

"Why do you think that is?" she questions with a raised brow, as if testing me to say the wrong answer.

I take a deep breath. "I've told you before that she's complicated. She might not know about us, but she might have suspicions of some sort with me and is taking it out on you. You didn't mention anything? Or your mother? They seem pretty cozy as friends as of late."

She gasps and shakes her head. "I can't believe you."

Fuck. It feels like I'm saying everything *wrong* I shouldn't be saying. I'm fumbling my words and I'm making it all worse. I just want her to feel safe with me no matter the circumstances. I'm so far gone with this woman that I'd do anything for her. I don't even know if she feels the same, but I don't care.

"Come home with me and let me take care of you. You shouldn't have to deal with this alone."

She huffs before her shoulders shake and her lips tremble again.

"Please," I command with a louder tone. Her eyes flick to me and she bites her lip to keep them from trembling.

"I just want this day to be over," she confesses.

I nod. "I know, baby. Let me take care of you and you can forget about it until tomorrow."

I take another step closer to her and she doesn't move back.

She lets me pull her in tight for a hug and I wrap my arms around her like a bear. She lets me envelope her and she slowly relaxes underneath me. I kiss the top of her head and she shakes for a moment and her head moves before I let her go. She takes a few deep breaths before gaining her composure.

"Okay, but only if you can order in tacos. From that place."

I nod, knowing exactly what place she's talking about. "Of course, *Corazón*. Let's go."

She turns on her heels, and we walk out of the building together. Once we're far enough from the building, our hands brush against another before our fingers intertwine together.

The walk back to my place is quiet and I even contemplate calling an Uber to bring us there faster, but she seems to need the fresh air. Even with it getting colder with the sun down and it being mid September, she seems content.

The moment we're inside my apartment, she immediately goes to the bedroom. I make sure to order enough tacos to last the night if she's extra hungry and I tidy up the place before I draw a bath for her. I don't have any fancy bath bombs or products, but the moment I let her know it's ready for her, she doesn't complain and strips down and slips into the tub.

I give her privacy as I answer the door for dinner.

"Julián?" her voice calls from the bathroom and I head in there, letting the food stay in the bag to keep hot.

"*¿Sí, Corazón?*" I ask, watching her create some waves in the tub with her fingers. She smiles softly, her face still puffy from crying. Her hair is only half wet where it touches the tub.

"Wash my hair?" she asks so softly I almost miss it. I nod quickly and bend down in front of the tub.

"Want me to wash from here… or do you want me to join you? I don't want you to just think I want to fuck you. I want to be here for you, like I said."

Her lips tremble again as she nods. "Yeah, it's big enough for the both of us."

Without hesitation, I strip from my work clothes and she makes room, scooting closer to the front of the tub. I enter the tub and the water is now a lukewarm temperature. She leans over to unplug the drain for a moment before she plugs it again and turns on the faucet, adding more hot water. She finally leans back as I'm seated with her in between my legs. Her back hits my chest and I try my best to not get too aroused by the feeling of her backside right on my cock.

She takes a deep breath, and I knead my hands through her hair before massaging her scalp. She gasps before leaning more back, head almost bumping into my chest.

"*Mmm*, feels so good," she whispers before going silent. I continue to massage her scalp as we stay in the tub. I make a mental note to get more lavish bath products so she can use the tub more often to decompress. I can't imagine living with Victoria. Carlos, I could handle. But her mother?

That's a whole other story.

"What are you thinking about?" she finally asks, breaking the silence. I pause the massaging as I lean over and kiss her cheek. She smiles before I pull back.

"*Nada importante, Corazón.*"

"Do you want to know what I'm thinking?"

I nod. "Of course. What are you thinking?"

"You," she breathes out. Her hands move from her sides to my knees and travel as much as she can upwards. My cock jolts to life and I can't hide it anymore with her touches.

"And what about me?" I whisper, getting closer to her ear. I remove one hand from her hair and trail it along her neck, arms, and then back up to her throat.

"Just being here for me and maybe more."

"Yeah?"

She nods before leaning her head back to watch me upside down. Her eyes are bright green again and it seems like some life is back in them. I lean in and kiss her forehead. She closes her eyes before taking a deep breath.

"You're too good for me," she whispers.

"Eliana, don't say that," I scold her.

"It's true. We shouldn't be doing this, yet here we are. And–"

"No, say nothing. It doesn't matter. We're adults. We can do what we want."

"But…" Her voice trails off. She lifts her head again and stares straight at the end of the tub. I take this time to knead my fingers through her hair before reaching for a shampoo bottle. I squirt some onto my palms and then massage her scalp again with the product.

She's silent, except for some groans of pleasure, as I clean her hair and hum a random tune. It's something that brings me back to when I was younger. The flashback seems to be at the forefront of my mind, with my mom doing this same thing for me as a child. My mom would hum a random tune and I'd ask what she was singing, and she'd just shrug and keep humming and washing my hair.

"Okay, lean back so I can wash the suds away."

She complies and scoots a little further to the front of the tub before leaning her body back until the crown of her head is flush with my chest and stomach. Her hair spreads like wildfire in the water and she looks like a goddess. The freckles on her nose are more prominent and when she opens her eyes, it's like I'm staring at a nymph. There's a sudden shift inside of me as I stare at her for a moment.

The clear infatuation that's been taking hold of me has transpired into more. My chest tightens at this realization and I know that I am deeply, *unequivocally* falling for this woman.

I wash her hair before she giggles, her chest moving with the sounds.

"What's so funny?" I ask, a smile spreading across my face.

She giggles some more. "I've never understood baths."

"How so?"

"We literally sit in water and then wash ourselves and then continue to sit in it. It's kind of disgusting."

A laugh bubbles out of my chest, and I shake my head. "You're not wrong about that, *Corazón*. But you need to relax and I'd rather your hair get washed right now than draining the tub and turning on the shower."

"I'd freeze just waiting for the shower to start," she nods. "I'll definitely do that for my body, though. I'm feeling better. Thank you, Julián."

"Yeah? No problem, *Corazón*."

She smiles and closes her eyes as I massage her scalp some more after rinsing her hair. My mind wanders to earlier today and what I completely forgot about.

After bumping into Eliana and seeing her needing my support, I forgot why I was fuming earlier. Lena mentioned a double date. I want to ask her what Lena might've meant by it, but I don't want to ruin this moment.

I want to comfort Eliana as much as I can and show her I can be there for her in more ways than one.

I'll wait until Eliana isn't in such a vulnerable state of mind to ask her what Lena meant.

Twenty

ELIANA

I GOT Harry's number earlier this week before the whole fiasco with Laura. And before the whole tub intimacy with Julián. It felt nice to be in his arms and be able to talk about my worries to him.

He listens so well and offers support when needed. He doesn't try to push too much and gives me space when I really need it. That night proved to me that what we had wasn't just all physical, but more.

I ended up spending the night with him, going to classes on Thursday and then holing myself in my room from Friday until Saturday night.

I didn't want to go on the double date tonight, but it's already said and done and I can't back out now. As much as I still want to tell Lena about Julián, I can't. I can't risk her knowing the truth.

I've already gotten myself in a metaphorical ditch with Laura. I can't afford to lose anything else. If I don't pass her class, then I'm not sure what I'll do. My living situation rides on the fact that I pass my courses and get this damn degree.

I'm not even sure if I want it anymore. I'm feeling the same way I did at the tail end of my pre-med degree. What if the same shit happens? I'm too far gone with college debt that I can't add *another* degree to the mix. I have to stick this one out.

As much as I love writing poems and short stories, it's not something I can completely see myself doing as a career in the future. Maybe I'll end up being a ghostwriter for a famous author and retire early.

A text comes through my phone, breaking me from my thoughts. I check it and see that Lena is here with the guys waiting for me. I've opted for a flowy black dress and some black, transparent tights that have fake crystal gems on it to reflect the light. I've got my black boots on.

An all black outfit to fit how I'm feeling towards this double date. I even contemplated making my makeup all dark, but that would be too much work.

I grab a purse and stuff the important things inside before running down the stairs and heading to the door. I can hear my parents in the kitchen talking, but I don't go to them. Ever since I had that meeting with Laura, my mother can't stop giving me an evil eye.

A disappointing eye, more like it.

I know Laura and her have been hanging out more and there's no doubt that Laura told her about my grades. I really hope my mother doesn't know about the assignment I failed, that would just be too far and I'm not sure if that's allowed to share between professors anyways.

I slip out of the house and see a nice black Mustang with Malcolm and Lena in the front.

She waves me over and squeals as I find my way to the car and open the back door, getting in. Harry is in the backseat and gives me a smile before I turn to Lena. I shut the door and throw on my seatbelt.

"Are you ready?" she asks, wiggling her eyebrows. I nod and chew on my cheek before turning to Harry.

Malcolm gives me a smile before turning on the music and driving away from my house. Harry leans in close, placing his palm on my knee. I jolt from the touch, but don't want to make a scene in the car.

"You look pretty tonight," he whispers. I give him a small smile before I look out the window and study the architecture of each passing building.

The ride isn't long as we pull up to a restaurant and Malcolm tells us to grab a table while he parks the car. Harry gets out, walking around the car and waiting for us. I don't *expect* him to open my door for me, but come on.

Lena gets out of the car and immediately latches her arm around mine before Malcolm drives off and Harry stuffs his hands in his pocket.

Once we're at the door, again, I notice how Harry walks in front of us and barely holds the door open for us. Lena is so caught up in waiting for Malcolm to finally rejoin us I'm sure she misses these things.

It brings me back to the magazine I was reading a few days ago… About how to tell if a guy is into you.

But this just seems like common decency that a gentleman should do. And he's getting 0 points so far. It's not something I truly care about, but I'd like this night to go smoothly and he's making it really hard to enjoy it.

And this is how the rest of the evening goes. Malcolm does everything right, even for me while Harry is so self-absorbed to where it feels like we're here at a dinner to watch Lena and Malcolm be on a date. He's nowhere like the same man that was at the faculty dinner.

It's weird and it turns into a point where I excuse myself as the waiter takes our food and we're waiting for the check. A check where Malcolm happily pays for Lena's food and Harry doesn't say a word and tells the waiter that he'll pay for his own. That's when Malcolm eyes me for a moment and gives me a pitiful look.

I am getting all the wrong vibes. I need to leave.

That was the last straw, I found some twenties in my purse and slapped them down. I told Lena I'd see her tomorrow and got up. I don't bother excusing myself to the restroom. I head straight out of the restaurant.

The Uber is on its way and I text Lena that it just wasn't working out and to not run after me. She sent me back an apology and a heart emoji.

As the Uber pulls up, they ask for my name and I confirm, getting inside. As they validate my address, I take a second and apologize and give them a new address.

It only takes us eleven minutes to reach the apartment building and I buzz the number for his unit.

Without hesitation, the building door unlocks, and I head inside toward the elevators. Once I'm up on his floor, I knock swiftly on the door.

We haven't been texting much since yesterday, but it's a weird feeling I can't explain. It's like I don't *need* to tell him I'm here. The door unlocks and swings open.

"Hi," I whisper. He's wearing gray sweats and a matching long sleeve. Just like the night I bumped into him at the Mexican restaurant when I went running.

A big smile spreads along my face, and he reaches his hand out. "You okay?"

I nod and take his calloused palm, letting him pull me inside as he shuts the door and I press myself against the other side. He lifts a hand to trace lines along my cheek. His brown eyes are boring into mine and I smile even bigger.

"What?" he asks, his own cheeks getting red.

"I just needed to see you," I admit.

Julián leans in for a kiss and I don't stop him. My erratic heart seems to almost calm at his kiss and comforting touch. Everything Harry wasn't tonight. I don't want to think about him, but it's making me feel better with my choice to run out of the restaurant.

"What happened?" he asks, finally separating us from the kiss. He takes a step back and finally eyes my outfit. I shift my weight before walking towards his couch, plopping down. I run my hand through my hair.

"Lena kind of forced me into a double date and it didn't go as planned."

He's quiet as he joins me on the couch. The long sleeve fits well on his biceps as he leans his elbows on his knees. He turns to look at me for a moment before staring at the TV in front of us. I watch our reflections as if time is still. He says nothing and neither do I.

We stay like this for a few more seconds before he sighs and leans back on the couch. His arm reaches out though and he places his palm on my knee. It feels much more different than when Harry did it. Sparks almost hit my skin instantly.

The chemistry between Julián and I is something I'll never be able to understand. Not even science could interpret it.

"What happened?" he pushes again, this time his tone is firmer, more commanding.

I take a deep breath and place my hand over his. I squeeze until he looks at me with worry beginning to form on his features. "Nothing went right and I didn't *feel* right."

"Who was it?" His voice is low.

Our eyes lock and I can't look away. "Harry."

"Harry?"

I nod.

"Harry who?"

"Harry Simmons."

His eyes go dark and his jaw clenches. I squeeze his hand again, and he shakes his head. "*¿Corazón, te hizo algo?*"

I almost laugh, but the air is thick with tension that I don't think it would help. "He did nothing. That's the problem."

He cocks his head to the side and tries to read me, but I've got a steel trap mind. I nibble on my lip before he huffs and leans in close. He moves his hand from my knee and grasps my chin.

"Tell me what he did."

"He didn't *do* anything, Julián."

"Then why did you come here?"

I roll my eyes and try to pull my head away, but his grip tightens on my chin, almost squeezing my cheeks together until my lips pucker like a fish.

"No one can touch you without your consent."

I reach my hands to his wrist, and his grip loosens. I pull my chin out of his grasp and he takes a few deep breaths. "He didn't touch me. He just wasn't what I was expecting on a date."

"So if he did all the right things, you wouldn't be here tonight?"

I contemplate my answer, but I know I fucked up. He takes my silence as an answer and takes a deep breath before pushing himself off the couch. He heads to the other side of the living room, near the hallway that leads to his bedroom. His shoulders sink and my chest aches.

I fucked up.

"Julián, I didn't mean it like that. You know that."

"If you really did, then you would've told me about this double date. I already knew about it?"

"What?"

He nods and my jaw drops. "Baby, Lena slipped it out the other morning. Told me she was taking you on a double date, but I didn't think it was with *Harry*. And now that you've mentioned how he treated you. It all makes sense, but it doesn't make fucking sense the way you answered that question."

"I didn't even answer it, though."

"You hesitated, which is an answer in itself."

I stand up from the couch and cross my arms. "Julián! What the fuck?"

He scoffs and heads into the hallway. I follow him immediately and enter the bedroom. He pulls off his long sleeve and tosses it to the ground. He's not facing me, but I can see his broad shoulders and back muscles tense under his emotions.

"Julián, please."

He finally turns, walking towards me. "You don't get that when I said we shouldn't do this, I meant it."

"You don't mean that," I gulp, feeling the tears start. I came over for his consolation not to be lectured.

But why did I really come? And why did I say those things about Harry? I want Julián to be wrong about the fact that if Harry treated me better tonight that I'd still be at dinner. Would I go home with him? Absolutely not. But he didn't give me the time to explain that.

"We wouldn't be arguing about these kinds of things. You'd be having a nice night out with your friend and I'd be here grading papers or some shit. Hell, I'd be slamming the door on the ex trying to get into my life again."

His eyes search mine as I take a step closer and reach for his arms, gliding up until I wrap my hands around his neck. He takes a deep breath and closes his eyes as he attempts to calm his breathing.

"Julián, I came here for a reason. Even if dinner went well, I would've still come over. I know we never really explicitly stated this, but I like you. It seems like the odds are always against us, but I'm willing to fight them if you are."

"Are you sure about that? Because that means telling your best friend. And eventually your parents."

I take a deep breath and nod, knowing I have to tell him the truth no matter what. "Those are things *I* have to do, though. Those are bridges I have to cross on my own. I don't want you to have to do it with me. It's asking too much of you."

"I'm going to talk with Harry, though," he breathes out. I furrow my brows and shake my head.

"Absolutely not."

"*Corazón*," he starts.

"No!"

"He has to know how to treat women, even if it's not with you. Save the next girl from that shit he pulled with you. Whatever it was."

I give him a small smile before one splits his face as well. He leans in and kisses my forehead before wrapping his hands around my waist. I squeal as he squeezes me into a bear hug.

"You're suffocating me!" I scream, but he only squeezes me harder before loosening his grip.

"I like you too," he finally says.

I giggle, because I can't fucking help it. It feels nice to just be in this bubble of just us. It helps me feel better about our decisions. But I know I'll have to eventually face the reality of it all. I don't want to, but for him it's so fucking worth it.

"What are you thinking about?"

I shrug and nuzzle my nose with his chest. "You're worth it."

His muscles seem to relax with those words and I know I hit a deep spot in him. Whether it's an insecurity or doubt, I've hit something. I hold him tighter by the neck and he breathes even deeper.

"You're worth more than anything I've ever had in my life," he responds.

"Can I stay the night?"

He grabs my arms and unlocks my hands behind his neck. He pulls me toward the bed and he sits down, letting me climb his lap and straddle him. With our cores touching, I can feel his erection grow and I start to circle my hips, already gone for this man.

"Eliana," he warns.

"What?" I giggle.

"You're so fucking worth this," he states before pulling me back on the bed. I squeal and tighten my thighs around him as he attaches his lips to mine.

We both moan through the kiss. His hands find my thighs and then my hips. "You're so fucking beautiful. Never let a man treat you the way you don't deserve."

"I just kept thinking about you and how you'd probably dig your own grave before you repeated any of those things he did."

"I'd dig two graves, happily."

I laugh and he smiles brightly. He kisses my nose before kissing my lips and I melt into it. I could do this forever.

"I have one request, since we're talking."

"Hmm?" I ask through our kisses.

"What are you doing for fall break?"

This catches me off guard and I lift myself, resting my chin on his chest. He bends his face to look at me and I smile. "Not sure. My parents always leave for their beach house in Florida."

"Spend it with me."

I watch his eyes sparkle at the question. "I'd love to. Anywhere you want to go?"

"I've got a few places in mind I'd love to fuck you," he says as his hands move to my hips and squeeze firmly. Heat pools in my lower belly and he winks.

"*Professor*," I tease.

"Now that we've got that covered… Sit on my face, *Corazón*."

I concede as he squeezes my hips again. He helps me with the zipper of the dress so I can throw it off. I then take my time to take off the tights and lace thong. He sees my matching lace bra and immediately cups my breasts.

"You wore this for me?"

I nod. "Kinda knew I'd always come over tonight."

"Fuck."

His fingers glide over my pebbled nipples, and I moan, circling my hips on him. My bare pussy presses against his clothed erection and I almost come right there.

"Please," I beg.

"Come and sit on me," he commands. I move my legs until I'm hovering over his face. He takes no time to grab my hips and slam me down on his mouth. His tongue attaches to my clit instantly and I scream his name.

I grind my hips down on him and he doesn't stop licking my pussy and eating me out. He's like a man starved, and I let him take everything from me.

"Fuck, *Corazón*," he finally breathes out as he lifts my hips. I whimper at the loss and he chuckles before going back to lapping my juices. He adds a finger into my pussy and I almost come right there.

"Oh my gods!" I scream, feeling the coil tighten inside me, begging to snap.

"So fucking delicious. And you're all mine."

"I'm yours," I whimper as he inserts a *second* finger and continues to suck on my clit. The feeling is overwhelming in the best way and within seconds of him sucking and thrusting his finger inside me I come violently on him. I continue to grind and circle my hips against him and I come a second time within minutes.

He licks up every drop of me before I fall over, flipping on the bed. He joins me and pulls me close. My thighs shake from the intensity of my orgasms and he smooths his palms over them. He kisses my neck before kissing my cheek and then lips.

"You're perfect, *Corazón*," he whispers.

"You don't want to finish tonight?" I ask, nodding to his erection.

He shakes his head. "You needed me. I'll fuck you all day tomorrow. How about that?"

I laugh and he pulls me closer. I wrap my arms around him and throw a leg over his hip.

"That sounds like the perfect Saturday," I respond as he kisses me again and I drift off into a calming sleep.

Twenty-One

ELIANA

LAURA'S EYES narrow as she watches me fidget in my seat. Everything about this meeting is *awkward*.

It's Tuesday evening, the first week of October. The cuticles on my thumbs are being ripped to shreds and sure to bleed soon if she keeps staring at me without saying anything. I gulp and feel my heart quicken its pace.

She takes a deep breath before looking down at the paper on her desk. *My paper*. The one that I was positive would get me an A. I got a C and there were red ink corrections on almost every line. It was disappointing to see so many errors on something I worked two weeks on. Some classmates bragged about writing it the day before and got an A.

"It's distant," she finally says.

I furrow my brow and my nail digs into my thumb's cuticle and I wince from the pain. "Distant? How so?"

"It lacks a connection between the tone and mood. I'm not sure where you're trying to go the more I read it. The assignment was pretty thorough." Her eyes go back to me as she watches me basically hyperventilate in my seat.

"I-I really tried," I insist.

"It doesn't seem like it. That other paper? Horrendous. I thought you'd learn from it."

I fight back tears as I listen to her criticism. The number one thing I had to learn growing up with my mother was to not take her criticism to heart, but it's hard to hear it from a professor. Someone who is supposed to give criticism constructively. Not tearing me down and making me want to give up.

There was a time I even contemplated meeting her during office hours to talk about the assignment, but she was never available. I really tried to do my best, so this grade has truly shocked me.

"I did," I whisper. My eyes fall to my thighs and I cross my ankles.

"Doesn't seem like it. I'll give you another week to work on this, but I won't extend the other assignments. You'll have to turn those in on time."

The silence is deafening as I take in her words and slowly nod. I swallow the knot in my throat as I keep down the tears that are begging to escape. She doesn't seem to care at all though, and it makes me wonder why she's acting like this suddenly. She was so nice when I first had an advisor's meeting and now.... Even at the faculty dinner, she seemed fine and chatty with my mother.

But since then, it feels like I've been fighting tooth and nail with her to give me a good grade on assignments. My other classes are going better than hers, which makes me confused why I'm sucking so badly.

"Does that sound good?" she asks, raising a brow.

"Yes, thank you," I respond. I blink tears away before getting up. She picks up the paper and extends it to me and I take it. As I try to pull it back, her grip is still on it. I look at her and she's narrowing her eyes yet again.

"Your mother told me some things."

This causes me to pause in my actions and stare at her.

"Wh-what do you mean?"

She smirks for a moment before drawing back to her poker face. "I wonder if you haven't been putting as much focus into your masters program as you've let on."

My brows furrow. "I take it seriously."

"Is that why you're never home? Out on weekends? With how often I see you around this building, I'd expect better grades from you. I'm not just your professor, Eliana. I'm your advisor as well. I need to keep track of these things so I know you're going to graduate on time. You don't want to disappoint your mother."

It's like a knife is piercing through my lungs and taking away all the air to breathe. I stare at her, attempting to calm my breathing, but there's no use. I swallow the lump in my throat, but it's stationary.

"That's none of your concern," I remark.

She smiles, but it doesn't reach her eyes. "It is, when you're close to failing a class."

I widen my eyes. "I'm not failing! I'm going to work on this paper and get the rest of these assignments done."

"You do that, Eliana. And please try to take your academics more seriously. You've got watchful eyes on you."

My chest tightens and it's getting harder to breathe in this small office. I want to throw my paper back at her and scream at her. Tell her I'm doing my best and that it shouldn't feel like she's threatening me. Because it feels like she is! Is that even ethical? To bring my mother into this?

"Okay," I chirp. She nods before I pull the paper into my hands and her grip falls. I turn on my heel and stomp away, throwing her door back as hard as I can. The slam echoes throughout the hall and a few passing faculty members give me a look, but I just throw a small smile before walking away.

I'm not sure what my mother told Laura specifically, but now it's ruining my only way out of this situation. Without a passing grade, I'm going to get kicked out and have to find a place and a job. I can't afford that right now.

Thankfully, fall break is in less than two weeks and I can spend that time focusing on assignments and reworking this paper.

As I head down the stairs to the lobby of the building, I think about marching into my mother's office to yell at her, but I decide against it. I'm not sure if she's there or if that would help my cause. Laura seemed pretty bent that she's on my mother's side. And my mother is never on my side. It was clear the moment she gave me an ultimatum, no less through my dad, this summer.

I pull out my phone and think of the one person I'd rather curl up with and cry about this paper. I send him a text. Almost immediately I get a reply that I can come over tonight.

Instead of waiting at home to meet up with him after he's off work, I hang out at Crescent Cafe until closing time. I mostly drink hot chocolate and wallow over the grade before finally starting a new draft and working on the corrections Laura wrote in red judgmental ink. To be honest, her feedback wasn't as bad as I was expecting, but it seemed so *specific*. Things that wouldn't have been highlighted by other professors.

I understood where she was coming from with my voice and how I wasn't explaining mood and tone effectively, but that was about half of the corrections throughout the paper. The rest of the corrections were for minimal things that didn't change the base of the paper.

By the time nine rolls around, I head out of the closing cafe and get an Uber to Julián's place. Since seeing Julián after the double date two weeks ago, things have been better for us. We're actually talking whenever we see each other instead of just fucking. At first, I didn't really mind either, but now it's something I also crave.

I want to know that he can protect me from other things in

my life and not just offer me a good time intimately. And with the way he seems to comfort me when needed, in more ways than one, it makes me believe he feels the same way. As much as we've been doing everything in secret, I really like it.

We both know that eventually the bubble will pop and someone will either see us or we make it public, but we're just enjoying this. We even planned a little getaway for fall break, but now I have to break the news to him of what happened with Laura.

I thank the driver before I step out of the car and hitch my bag over my shoulder and buzz his apartment. He buzzes me inside and I head to his door, which he leaves unlocked.

The moment I step inside, I smell something lemony and garlic. I put my bag down near the door and kick off my boots before I see him with his back to me, stirring something at the stove.

I tiptoe just enough to get behind him and wrap my arms around his waist. He jolts for a moment at the sudden hug, but then I feel him take a deep breath and relax. I squeeze him tighter, locking my fingers together to keep him in this hug forever.

"Hey," I whisper and he turns slightly to look down at me and gives me a bright smile. He's wearing glasses I've never seen before and his hair is a bit tousled. He looks so handsome. I can't help but push away today's thoughts and just focus on *him*.

"How's my baby?" he asks, stirring the pan once more before he wipes his hands on a kitchen towel on the counter and grabbing my hands.

I release the hold I have on him and he twists, this time pulling me into one of his bear hugs. I wrap my arms around his neck, burying my nose in his chest and taking in his scent. He smells like laundry, some kind of mountain spice body wash and *Julián*. If I could bottle up this scent and spray it on my pillows every night, I would.

"I'm okay, just want to forget today," I admit. He kisses the top of my head before squeezing me tightly and swaying our bodies for a few seconds. I lift my head to look at him and his brown eyes search mine.

"Everything okay?" he whispers, rubbing my back soothingly. I take a deep breath and shake my head.

I don't want to lie to him and I came over because he makes me feel safe and calm. I want him to know I'm struggling, because I have no one else. Lena would just encourage me to try my hardest and keep showing Laura that I'm doing what I can. But Julián will let me *cry*, *scream*, *yell*, and whatever else I'd need to do to cope.

"No, I–" my voice cracks and he squeezes me more before I finally let the tears fall. I swallow the heaviness in my throat, but I don't care. I know I'll feel better once I confide in him.

"*Dime, Corazón*," he whispers.

"I got another poor grade on my paper. It was for Laura's class and I had a meeting with her today."

He continues to look at me, his brows pinching together slowly. "*¿Qué pasó?*"

"She didn't have nice things to say about the paper. And then mentioned that my *mother* even told her how I'm not around anymore and how they don't think I'm taking my graduate program seriously."

He says nothing, just continues to smooth his hands over my body. I take another deep breath. "Julián, I wrote that paper for two weeks and made sure it was perfect after I failed that last paper. I swear I've been focusing. But they think otherwise."

He finally breaks his silence. "Do you want me to talk to her?"

I shake my head. "No, you know that wouldn't end well. They would be suspicious about why you're standing up for a student that isn't taking your class."

He takes a step back, causing my hands to fall from his neck.

Instead of walking away timidly, he grabs my hand and laces our fingers together. He turns off the stove and checks on the pasta that's been slowly simmering in the pan.

Julián works in silence as he uses one hand to grab a pair of tongs and places the pasta noodles on two plates. Once he's done, he lets go of my hand to place the plates on the kitchen table. He comes back to me, grabbing both of my hands this time and dragging them up to his face, kissing them one at a time, each knuckle and then the palms.

"I've been thinking," he starts, analyzing me before he continues. "It's already October… We've been trying to keep this secret for a while and it doesn't seem to do us any good in the outside world. Do you think we really need to keep this secret any longer?"

I look at him for a moment before I let my lips part. "Are you kidding?"

He shakes his head. "Seems like people notice that you're not around and I don't need people prying. Especially Laura. She wouldn't rest until her hunch was proven, if there even was one."

"That wouldn't change the way she treats me, though. She'd probably immediately fail me," I counter.

Julián's gaze turns dark before he shakes his head. "I'd handle her then, if she ever did something to you."

"She already has," I whisper, looking down and pulling my hands out of his grasp. I sigh and walk to the vacant table, pulling out a chair and sitting down. The food looks amazing, but with today's events I can feel my appetite dwindling.

Julián finally follows suit as he takes the chair diagonally from me and scoots close to the table, our knee touching. He grabs the pitcher of water in the center of the table and pours me a glass before doing so for himself.

"Are you sure she has any suspicions? As much as I love to bash on her, she's an excellent educator."

I shrug. "I think my mother's getting to her. They've been

hanging out more and my mother loves to talk trash about me whenever she can."

Julián is quiet for a moment before he rests his hand on top of mine. "I'm sorry, *Corazón*. If I can do anything, let me know. I don't want to push you if you think you can figure it out."

He lifts his hand and I grab a fork, twirling it around some of the pasta. "Can I stay here for the night? I want to get a head start on revisions tomorrow morning, but I can't even think about going home tonight."

"Of course. Stay any night you'd like, even if I'm not here."

"Yeah? Where would you be if that happened?"

He gives me a look before smirking. "Probably talking some sense into your mother or lecturing Laura."

"You wouldn't!"

He laughs. "Eliana, you have to know by now that I'd do anything for you."

Butterflies swarm in my stomach from his confession and my body goes warmer. "Really?"

He nods before twirling some pasta and taking a bite. "All you have to do is ask, *Corazón*."

My cheeks warm at the nickname he's been calling me lately. *Corazón*. My mother refused to talk much Spanish at home, so I never became fluent. As much as I want to talk to my dad in Spanish, it seems like we don't converse well. He still calls me his *Princesa*, but that's about it. Sometimes I hear him in his office talking fluently to his relatives.

It feels like all of the problems centering my life and my family have to do with one common denominator: my mother. But there's nothing I can do. Dad *loves* her. He'd never leave her and she treats him right. Me? Not so much. It's like she just wanted the marriage and had to *tolerate* a child.

I swallow the thickness of this revelation and attempt to get out of my headspace. Julián seems to notice, but says nothing. I silently thank him for that as we finish our dinner and then he cleans up even after I offer. He ushers me to the bathroom and draws a bath like last time. But this time I don't call for him to join me, I let myself sink in the tub until I'm completely covered up to my neck in the steaming water.

Since the last time I did this, Julián's upped his bathroom inventory and filled the bath with some bubbles as well as a pink shimmery bath bomb. My body feels silky smooth and even glitters every time I lift my hand out of the water. I'm at full relaxation for about half an hour until I'm ready to get out.

"I've got a warm towel for you," Julián says as I drain the tub. The door to the bathroom is open, but Julián stays at the entrance and I look at him, seeing him in his sweats and a baggy shirt. I wave him over and he complies, stepping inside the bathroom and waiting for me to stand up from the tub before wrapping me in the towel. I step out slowly before he rubs my arms up and down, attempting to dry me off.

The motion is so childish, yet so endearing, I can't help but laugh. This brings a smile to his face and the flutters come back to my stomach at the sight of him.

"What?" he asks, after I laugh again.

"I–thank you, Julián. For always being here when I feel like a damsel in distress."

He leans in and kisses my nose before he pulls me in for a hug and rubs my back. "You don't have to thank me. And you're not a damsel in distress. It's just a lot going on, but we're going to figure it out. I promise."

"Yeah?" I whisper, feeling my throat get thick again and tears brimming my eyes. *God, stop crying!*

"Yeah. I promise."

I take a deep breath and then feel him unlatch himself from the hug before helping me dry my body and slipping on some of his pajamas. They're a little big on me, but they're so comfy. I cross my arms and bury my nose in the crook of my elbow, smelling him.

"Come on," he says as he leads me to the bedroom. He wastes no time to draw back the sheets and pick me up, bridal style, and set me down. Before he can pull away and step back, I wrap my arms around his neck and pull him close to me, until he's forced to climb the bed to lay on top of me. He doesn't lay his entire weight on me, but he lays his head on my chest. I run my fingers through his hair.

"I wish we could stay like this forever," I whisper.

His hands move to my hips and he takes a deep breath, his movement reverberating throughout my body as well. "We can, baby. We go at whatever pace you want. I'm not going anywhere."

And his words cut like a knife to the chest because I know he's not lying. I'm falling for this man more than I ever thought, and it scares me to death.

Twenty-Two

· JULIÁN ·

I'M LOOKING up some hotels for fall break when the office door opens abruptly. I look up in time to see Laura striding inside, decked out in a tight red dress with matching heels.

"Julián," she calls out as she nears the desk. She dramatically plops down on the chair in front of it and I slowly close the laptop before peering at her.

"Yes?"

"What are you doing for fall break? Victoria and Carlos will be at their beach house, and I have nowhere to go."

I want to ask her how that's any of my problem, but I just continue to glare at her. In moments, her brows scrunch and she sighs, leaning her head back.

"Well, I can book us a hotel of sorts," she mumbles.

I almost choke on my spit at her suggestion. "Absolutely not, Laura. I think it's time you cut the act of thinking we're still together," she gives me a look before I add, "*or* act like we can get back together. And for fall break, as much as I'd like to hang out with *you*… I have plans."

Her eyes narrow before she huffs. "Oh, you do? What are they?"

I clasp my fingers together before pressing my lips into a tight line. She waits for me to spill my plans, but I keep my lips shut.

"Julián, you don't have to lie to me. If you don't have fall break plans, that's fine. We can grab dinner that first night and then–"

"No, Laura. I really have plans. I'm going out of town. A trip," I confess.

She raises a brow. "Julián… You can't just say that and then drop it."

I shrug.

"My plans and business are none of your concern."

She huffs one last breath and sits straight. She crosses her legs, one over another, and glares at me. Her eyes are trying to get information out of me, but I put on my best poker face. I tap my fingers against the laptop.

"Did you ever get a GA yet?" she asks randomly. I know she's just pulling at strings, attempting to get conversation to stay in my office. The last thing I want to do is have a simple conversation with my ex, but here I am.

"Never got the time, but I'm handling it. I've got my de-stressors." I can't *help* but slip that one out. It's like I love the way she reacts so vividly to what I say. I know it's horrible to say, but seeing her suffer the way she's made me over the last few years makes me smile. My lips twitch into an almost smile when I see her eyes cast down and then her body almost deflates at the shoulders.

"Oh, of course you do," she stutters. I nod and lean back into my leather chair, spreading my legs out comfortably. I study the desk for a moment, letting my thoughts go elsewhere.

To Eliana. I want to fuck her on this desk. And anywhere I can around this place. Laura clears her throat and I glance up at her, smirking.

"*¿Necesitas algo más?*" I ask her. She shakes her head before standing up and smoothing out her dress. Before she turns on her heels, she gives me a look.

"I don't know what's gotten into you this school year, but I don't like it. You're cocky, rude, and just not the same Julián I married."

Her words take me back, but I don't let her see it. She spins on her heels and marches to the door. Before she can slip out, I say loudly enough, "That's a good thing then, Laura."

She closes the door much louder than necessary and I let out a chuckle before opening the laptop and checking out the hotel I was previously looking at. It's got a gorgeous view of New York City. I've never been. Laura hated the city.

I really want my first time in that city to be with someone I really care about. *Her*. It'll be nice to do something *I* want for a change instead of abiding by the copious rules Laura laid out during our marriage.

Once I complete my last class and grade all the papers, I get out of the office and enter the hallway. I hear footsteps and see Lena walking with a stack of papers. I give her a small wave and she smiles widely.

"Professor Estrada! It feels like I haven't seen you in weeks!"

"It feels like it, huh? This always seems to happen right before big breaks," I tell her. She laughs.

"Any big plans?"

I shake my head. "For now, no. I might try to go to New York City for a small vacation, but it'll be to relax and sightsee some. How about you? Malcolm told me he's been seeing you more frequently."

This is a lie, of course. I barely talk to Malcolm outside of the bar scene, but I care for Lena just because she matters to Eliana. All the information I have on Lena is through the grapevine of Eliana.

Lena nods quickly and her cheeks grow crimson as she answers.

"Yes! He's been the best. We might do a staycation thing where we rent out a hotel room nearby and just relax. I've been so busy with GA duties, I don't even remember the last time I cooked an actual meal."

"Definitely cherish the break then. It'll only get more rumbustious with finals and then prepping for winter break."

"I can't wait for winter break, though. It'll keep me going, I think! Six weeks to just do *nothing*?" She smiles brightly.

"Well, good luck with the rest of the week and Monday."

"Thank you, you too!"

I give her a smile as she adjusts the papers in her hands. She finally waves as she turns and starts heading towards Carlos' office. I lock up my office before I head out of the building and make my way home.

••᛫᛫)◊(᛫᛫᛫••

"I HAVE GOOD NEWS," ELIANA WHISPERS AS SHE KISSES MY chest and then drags her lips up to my neck. She's circling her pussy on me as my grip on her hips tightens. I want to flip her over and fuck her until she can't speak, but her excited eyes make me push those thoughts away.

"Yeah? What is it?" I grunt as I pick her hips up with ease and slam her down on my cock. Her eyes flutter at this and a whine slips out of her.

Her palms fly to my pecs and she tightens her grip. "I got an 'A' on my revised paper."

"Really? We should celebrate," I murmur. She giggles before circling her hips again and she lets out a shaky breath.

"We kinda are," she whimpers as I move my thumb to circle her clit slowly.

"I thought we were just fucking in general. If you want to celebrate, I have a few ideas."

"Oh? Like what?"

My thumb presses a little harder on her clit and her pussy tightens around my cock. I'm so close to coming, but I want her to continue enjoying riding me.

"Get either handcuffs or rope and tie you to the bed, edge you until you can't fucking think," I tease.

Her gaze falls down to me and a smile spreads on her lips as her cheeks grow scarlet. "What? I've never done that kind of thing before."

I lift my thumb from her clit and she mewls, circling her hips in a faster motion. "Me neither, doesn't mean we can't try new things."

"Fuck, Julián." I feel her walls start to tighten even more around me. I place my thumb back on her clit and pinch her nipple with my other hand. She gasps and curses my name under her breath, but I catch it.

"Say my name louder, baby," I urge.

"Julián!" she screams, stilling her movements and her thighs are shaking uncontrollably as she comes. The pressure of her pussy on mine makes it easy to finally let myself come inside of her.

"I love it when you scream my name." I stay inside of her as she leans down, laying her head on my chest. I wrap my arms around her body and hold her tightly.

"I love it when you fuck me senseless," she giggles. I tickle her side for a moment and she squirms, before her pussy starts to clench down on me again. I gasp and groan, leaning down to bite her shoulder.

"If you keep doing that, I'm going to really tie you up."

She's silent for a moment before she lifts her head and kisses my cheek. I look down at her and her green eyes are bright.

"What?" I ask with a smile.

"What other ideas besides tying me up do you have in mind?"

I turn to look at the ceiling, contemplating my next answer. I've never done those kinds of things, but I've definitely thought about it. I even had a vulnerable moment with Laura years ago about those ideas, but she shut them down.

With Eliana, it seemed so easy to just slip it out while talking. And her reaction didn't disappoint me, it made me want to think of all the other ideas I've fantasized about.

"I'd love to not just edge you with oral or fucking you, but maybe get some toys as well."

"Hmm, that sounds like that would be the death of me," she giggles. "You already make me come so easily. I'm not sure if I'd last with a vibrator."

"Then I'll just have to learn how to edge you with one," I say in a husky tone. She giggles again and nuzzles her head into my neck. I take in a deep breath and smooth my hands over her soft skin and then her plush thighs. I'll never get tired of touching her.

"Do you know what I want to try?" she finally asks.

"Hmm? Tell me."

"So, this just came to my mind. Don't even know why, but since you brought it up…" her voice trails off and I rub her back and look at her.

"Tell me," I whisper. She sucks in her cheeks and I know she's chewing at it in nerves. I lift one hand and brush my fingers along her cheekbone.

"What if *you* were tied up, and I edged you," she finally says. I see her eyes studying me, waiting for rejection. But I smile and chuckle.

"I think that'd be something unique to try," I confirm.

She lets out a shaky breath and nods. "Plus, if we didn't enjoy doing these things, we already know we love fucking like rabid animals on the kitchen table and any other surface. We don't need those ropes and handcuffs to have fun. We make enough of that on our own."

I rub her back again, enjoying her rambling. "I agree," I murmur.

She smiles brightly and lays her head on my chest again. My heart beat continues to thump loudly and I know that's all she can hear right now. My hand smooths over her soft skin again and I think back to what she said the other night. How she wants to just stay like this forever.

I feel the same way and it's terrifying. It feels like there's not just one emotion or one thought when it comes to Eliana. I feel so much for her in every way and sometimes it's all that consumes me.

It's scary sometimes. I think about her daily, get hard just from flashbacks of fucking her, and now planning to hopefully spend fall break with her. She's got me wrapped around her finger and I don't think she realizes it.

"What are you thinking about?" She breaks my thoughts and I take a deep breath before exhaling.

"How much I care about you, Eliana," I admit.

She's silent for a moment, save for our breathing. "I care about you too, Julián," she whispers.

"I'm serious," I say, squeezing her. "I actually found a place I'd like to take you next week."

"Where?" She lifts her head.

"New York City. I've always wanted to go. Laura never went on those kinds of trips with me. Even when I went to Egypt either for spring break or a month in the summertime. I always went solo."

"I've only been there a few times as a kid, but I think it'll be fun to go with someone that isn't my parents."

I give her a look and laugh, "Please don't make me think of your parents at a time like this. I literally have my cock stuffed inside you still."

"Hey! You started talking about Laura," she giggles. I play-fully roll my eyes, but she's right.

"Sorry," I pout.

"It's okay," she smiles before playfully slapping my chest. She then makes eye contact with me before I feel her pussy clench around me. I groan and my cock hardens at that.

"Eliana," I warn, but she giggles and lifts herself so she can get back into a riding position. She places her palms on my chest and my hands move to her hips. My fingers are digging into her skin and I hope I leave marks; claiming her.

"Would we get a hotel with a view?" She asks, circling her hips and causing me to grit my teeth.

I nod. "I'd get enormous windows. So I can slam you against them and fuck you for the entire city to see."

She whimpers at that, and I glide my thumb over her clit. She shudders from the feeling before she grinds her pussy around my cock faster. I can already feel her tightening around my cock, and I know we're both close to our second orgasm of the night.

"*Fuck*," she mutters through shaky breaths.

"Say that you're mine," I grunt as I slam my hips upward and she screams.

"I'm yours, Julián," she concedes.

I slam my hips into her one last time and she circles around my cock a few more rotations before we're both coming at full force. We both groan and she collapses on top of me. This time she moves up so I slip out of her and I'm thankful. I can't last another round with this position. I'd have to flip her over and have more control of the movements.

"You're mine, *Corazón*," I whisper as I get up and head to the bathroom to grab a towel to clean her up.

Once I'm done, I hop back in bed and she's quick to cuddle me, burying her face in my chest. I wrap my arms around her and kiss her shoulder before kissing her head.

We stay like this for a while, calming our breathing, before we finally get up and shower. I book the hotel for Tuesday once we're out. I can't wait for our first trip together. Even if we're still doing everything in secret, it'll help going to a city as big as NYC.

We can truly be ourselves and not be afraid of watchful eyes.

Twenty-Three

ELIANA

LENA'S PEN drags along her planner as she crosses out the rest of this week for break. We're at Crescent Cafe catching some lunch before I leave tomorrow morning with Julián. We bought train tickets since that was something I always wanted to experience.

"You're staring," Lena says as she writes in her loopy cursive handwriting 'fall break' along the days of Tuesday to Friday. She even adds a smiley face to one day. She finally looks up, her eyes scanning mine.

"I'm just watching you, Len," I laugh.

"You've barely touched your sandwich. It's Monday, so I know it's a good one."

Lena usually spends her weekdays all day on campus and eats here for lunch, so she's got the lunch specials down to heart. Today is a ham grilled cheese sandwich and it's yummy, but my mind is elsewhere.

I shrug, picking apart the sandwich and seeing the cheese pull before I pop it in my mouth. "I'm going to the city tomorrow."

Lena places her pen down before raising a brow. "Like the

complete break? I thought you had to focus on your assignments."

"Not the whole time," I tell her. " Just until Friday. I'll be able to focus the entire weekend on those assignments. I've got a good streak going, Len. The ones that I've already turned in have been graded and I've gotten A's so far."

She purses her lips before nodding. "And your parents are the ones bringing you? I thought they always went to their beach house. That's what your dad was telling me earlier."

I nod, pulling another piece of the sandwich apart. "They are going, I'm not joining them. I'm going alone." The lie slips out of my mouth easier than I expected.

"And what city are you specifically talking about?" Lena inquires.

"New York City, where else?"

"I don't know!" she defends. "You could be talking about some other big city closeby."

We stare at each other for a moment before laughing.

"You're funny, Len."

"Thank you," she smiles before picking up her pen again. "How are you getting there?"

"Train. It's about two and a half hours. I just got a basic hotel room. It helps that it wasn't too expensive."

"So you're going to be in the city all alone this week and your mother is fine with it?"

I look at Lena before scoffing, throwing the piece of the sandwich I tore off back on the plate. I slap my hands together, brushing off the crumbs. "Lena, I'm an adult, you know. Way past the age to worry about what my *mother* thinks."

"I know, but we know how she gets. I don't want you getting hounded down by her while you're trying to enjoy your break. "

"Yeah, but I'm allowed to do whatever I want," I counter.

"Yes, but just don't get into anything messy. If you need me to rescue you, I'm a call and a train ride away."

I give her a warm smile. "Thanks, Len, but I'll be fine. It'll be good for me to just explore the city and have a break from home."

She continues to draw on her planner, her brows scrunched and her face deep in thought. I watch her for a while as she doodles, but then she looks up as if a lightbulb just flipped on in her head.

"What?" I ask.

"You know who else told me they'll be in the city?"

My heart thuds at the possibility, and I try to tame the panic in my body. *Don't be obvious.*

"Who?" I ask, my throat thick with guilt.

"Professor Estrada. Did you know? Maybe you can get his number in case you need someone closer. I'm sure your dad wouldn't mind that. He'd appreciate someone like *him* being around if something happened."

Lena keeps her eyes on me for a moment as I take in her words. Julián told her?! What did he specifically say? I can't stop the sweat that slides down the back of my neck. I clear my throat and squirm in my seat.

"I-I didn't know. I'll definitely mention it to my dad. Seems like a good idea, to know he'd be around."

She smiles and nods her head, her curls bouncing every way. "Great! Maybe you'll bump into each other or get lunch or something!"

I nod and pick up the abandoned piece of bread I threw in haste before chewing on it slowly. Lena doesn't pay any mind to me and I'm thankful for that. I can breathe and focus on not showing any more obvious signs that I'm lying to her.

"How are you and Malcolm?"

She snaps her head up from her planner and her cheeks grow rosy. "We're good. He actually wants me to spend this week with him and just see how it goes without the pressure of academics and work."

226

"Woah, are you guys serious?" Lena and I haven't had the time to really discuss her relationship since the last time we were together; the double date from hell. I don't even think I've seen Malcolm on campus since then.

"No, but I think I'm going to ask him this weekend if he doesn't. We're having fun and doing so well."

"You're not scared that making it official will ruin the spark?"

She pinches her brows. "Why would you think that?"

I bite my tongue to keep from saying anything dumb. *Stop projecting, Ana.* "I just heard that somewhere," I lied.

Lena glares at me for a moment before her features soften. "Well, you can tell those sources to suck it. I don't think making it official will ruin anything. Besides, it's just dating. We're not committing to marriage or anything ."

I sigh, wishing I said nothing. It makes me happy to see Lena going out with Malcolm, with no need for secrecy. My lips part, wanting to tell her about Julián, but I can't. Maybe by next semester.

It's presumptuous to think we'll last, but with what we're confessing to another makes me believe that we'll stick it out for as long as we can.

"Have you talked to Harry since that night?" Lena asks, breaking my thoughts.

I shake my head and laugh, "God, no. He was horrible!"

"Yeah, Malcolm wouldn't stop berating him after you left. I know we talked little about that night, but I do wanna say that I'm sorry I set you up with him. Well, more like pressured you into it. I truly do want to apologize, Ana."

I wave her off. "It's okay. He's an ass and it would've happened regardless if I pursued him on my own. He just isn't date material, to be honest–he's a lost cause. But thanks anyway, Len. I appreciate it."

"He didn't even want to pay for his meal," Lena adds. "Malcolm thankfully paid for it, but we just couldn't figure out what the hell his problem was. We haven't really seen him since. Unless Malcolm has and is just choosing to save me the stress of talking about him."

"Yeah, he teaches undergrad, right?"

Lena nods. "Yeah, but I rarely see him on campus"

"It's a good thing for all of us."

"Agreed," Lena laughs. She then locks eyes with me and cocks her head. "So, who *are* you seeing then?"

"What do you mean?" I ask, my voice raising a decimal.

Lena smirks. "This whole time I thought you were talking with Harry and flirting with him, but then that dinner happened. It got me thinking who was making you act that way."

I chew on my lip before glancing around the cafe; it's not crowded but there are a few students studying and some locals just getting their daily coffee. I turn back to my best friend and take a deep breath.

"It's not serious. Downloaded a dating app and found someone to talk with." I hate how easily it's become for me to lie about this. My heart hammers against my chest in the fear of my lies crashing down on me.

"Really? Why didn't you tell me?"

"Didn't seem *that* important. Besides, it's nice keeping this part of my life a bit private. No unnecessary lectures from my mother. After that whole Harry debacle I didn't want to jinx anything."

"Well, I'm glad you're telling me the truth now."

My heart pangs at that and I sink in my chair a few inches. She stares at me, studying. My body gets hotter by the second and I huff my breath. "Stop staring at me, Len! You're making me feel like a criminal under a spotlight."

"Are you telling me the truth, Ana?" Her brows pinch together and her lips are drawn to the side in curiosity.

I push myself back into a normal seating position and nod

my head. I try to make eye contact with her, but her stare is too intimidating. I stare outside the window and nod my head again. "Yeah, I am."

"Okay," she murmurs. I turn to look back at her and she's back to picking up her pen and doodling on her planner. My throat gets thicker and my stomach churns.

Lena refuses to look at me as I finish my sandwich. She's going to wear down that page in her planner with how much she's scribbling, but she still doesn't look up. She doesn't even hum or make any noise. And that terrifies me.

Shit, she knows.

••·⋛•○)✧(○•⋚·••

MY PARENTS ARE ALREADY GONE BY THE MORNING AND I'M OFF to the train station to meet Julián. I've got a small duffle bag packed to the brim with my necessities.

Julián gets to the train station just a few minutes after me and we make sure we have our tickets as we wait for the train. We huddle in a small corner of the station, trying not to be seen by too many people. We don't really see anyone we recognize, but since it's the start of fall break, we need to make sure no one catches us.

I wanted to let Julián know we could've gotten the train on Wednesday, but he *insisted* on having as much time as we could to be spent in the city. It was heartwarming to see how much he cared for us and how much this week means to him.

By the time the train comes, Julián doesn't let me lift a finger and carries our luggage. We make it to our seats and he easily hauls the bags up top in the storage sections before plopping down in the seat next to me. I had to shed a few layers in order to not sweat profusely and even made Julián ball up the big jacket I had and throw it up top with the rest of our luggage.

The train ride is quick as we listen to music, read, and even talk about nonsense. It feels comfortable to just do mundane things with him. It became my favorite part of the ride when his fingers would catch my hand and draw invisible shapes while I leaned my head on his shoulder and drifted off for a while.

We get to Grand Central Terminal within two and a half hours and the noise envelopes us as we get off the train to find another to take us closer to where our hotel is.

Once we're out of the subway, I almost gasp at how it feels to be in the city. It shocks me to my core that I've never experienced the city like this. My mother always got us plane tickets and then a driver to take us from the airport to our hotel. I've always wanted to just be in the city like this as if I lived here.

"Let's go get our hotel, baby," Julián murmurs beside me as we walk. He continues to carry our bags and walks on the side of the street where there's traffic. He pulls out his phone to get navigation, and he tells me he found the prettiest hotel in the Upper East Side and I bug my eyes out, wondering how the hell he found that and could *afford* it. Although my mother was very picky about places to stay in when I was little, she never chose that neighborhood. She'd rather do Chelsea or even West Village. But that was years ago.

"You didn't have to," I remind him as we get closer to the hotel, according to his map.

He smiles brightly as he continues to carry my duffle and his. I kept telling him I could carry my own, but he insisted. "When you're with me, *Corazón*, never worry about that kind of stuff."

"Julián," I start, but he shakes his head.

"*En serio*, Eliana. Don't even bat a pretty eye of yours when I hand you my card, either. Just ask and you shall receive."

This brings the biggest smile to my lips as we finally round a corner and see the hotel he's got for us. It's a skyscraper with vast windows, so I know he's going to keep up his end of the deal with fucking me pressed up against it and it brings flutters to my core.

"We're here," he announces as we walk inside the lobby and head to the check-in counter. I keep my eyes wandering around the pretty sculptures and accents around the lobby as he talks with the worker and finally gets our keys.

The elevator is even prettier as we make it to the 25th floor and he scans our door, pushing it open for me to slip inside. The hotel room is *huge* and I almost scream at the beauty of it. It's got a hallway entrance, a nice kitchen, living area with a couch, king-size bed in the bedroom with a master suite bathroom. There are two massive windows that look out onto Central Park. Once I shed off the layers of my jacket and sweaters, I find myself stuck on looking down at the ant-size people while Julián drops our bags on the ground behind me.

I feel strong arms wrap around me and his face nuzzling into my neck. I giggle and grab his hands, holding him close.

"Thank you for coming with me," he says into my neck. I nod and rub my hand over his.

"Thank you for this. I really needed it."

"Anything for you, *Corazón*," he says before kissing my neck. His beard tickles me in the best way and I twist in his arms, wrapping my hands around his neck this time.

His brown eyes are bright and I notice some flecks of golden. I move my hands to grasp the sides of his face and I let my fingers glide over his features. His temples, eyebrows, cheekbones, and then his lips.

"I'm glad I'm here," I finally say, seeing his eyes light up even more at my words. I mean them.

"Yeah?"

I nod before getting on my tiptoes to kiss him. His arms around my waist tighten and we lose ourselves in the kiss. He presses his tongue into my mouth and I kiss him with fervor.

He moans into the kiss and it sends shivers down my spine.

His hand moves slowly down until he cups my ass and squeezes hard. I gasp and our lips separate, but not before he leans in again and bites my bottom lip.

"*Julián*, don't do that," I whimper. He presses me into his body even more if that's possible, and I feel his erection pressing up against my stomach.

"How about we christen this place?" he whispers, leaning in to litter my neck with kisses.

I groan before nodding and pushing him backward toward the bed. He doesn't hesitate to fall back on it and I climb on top of him like a saddle. He licks his lips as he watches me pull off my long sleeve and then my bra. His large hands immediately go to my breasts and he pinches each peaked nipple.

"Fuck," I whine as he continues and I circle my hips, pressing my clothed pussy over his erection.

"Take these off," he says, nodding toward my yoga pants. I nod before shimmying off the bed and slipping the pants and my panties off. He takes no time to unbuckle his belt and pull down his pants along with his boxers and then tossing them to the ground. I giggle as I hop back on the bed, eyes on him as I crawl to him. I quickly notice how erect his cock is, already glistening from pre-cum and I lick my lips.

His brown eyes glide over my breasts and then my face as I position myself on top of him. His cock sits tall right behind my ass and I circle my hips once more, causing us both to lose our breath. My clit rubs against his growing hair right on his pelvic bone.

"Fuck, baby, you're already getting me wet just rubbing your pussy on me," he murmurs through shaky breaths. His hands go straight to my hips and his fingers dig in, for sure going to leave bruises, but I don't care.

"Did you bring the handcuffs?" I tease, rubbing my clit again on him and moaning through the feeling. I can't help but close my eyes and then he chuckles.

"No, but now I wish I did."

I look down at him before getting an idea. But not for *me*. I smirk. Julián raises his brow before he watches me lean over the bed to where his pants are and I fish the belt out of the loops he kept them in. I hoist myself back on the bed with his help before I show him the belt.

"So you want me to tie your wrists in that? I can do that, baby," he smiles.

I shake my head, and his brow raises again.

"First, take your shirt off. Then, give me *your* wrists, Julián."

He's fast to take off his shirt that falls silently off the bed. He then presents his wrists to me acquiescently before I wrap the belt around them and looping it to be tight enough. I give them a tug for good measure and he grunts, moving his hips until I feel his cock brushing against my ass.

"Fuck, baby," he shudders, looking at me with a darker stare. I take his wrists and push them over his head. I lean my body over so my breasts dangle in his face and he has no choice but to suffer through this moment. "God dammit, Eliana. Such a fucking tease."

"I know," I giggle, leaning back to my normal position and placing my hands on his chest. His breathing grows ragged as he keeps his arms above him and his eyes ignite a fire with how desperately he wants to touch me. I circle my hips once more, letting my clit brush up against him and I swear I see goose-bumps travel along his chest, stomach and arms.

"Please, baby," he groans, moving his hips so his cock can continue to brush against the backside of my ass. I tsk under my breath and shake my head, leaning closer to him so his cock has no contact with me. He groans and rolls his eyes back, his jaw clenching.

"Ask me one more time, *nicely*," I urge him.

I lay a finger on his neck, gliding it lower. He gulps before attempting to move his arms down but I shake my head. "If you move your arms down, then you're breaking the rules. I can leave you here like this…"

"Eliana," he warns, his eyes growing darker and his breathing grow even more rapid. I know his warning is that if I don't let him fuck me soon he's going to make me pay for it. Flashbacks to all the times he's edged me come to the forefront of my mind.

"Say it," I press, gliding my finger down his stomach as I move my hips back, lifting myself so his cock is now in front of my pussy. He hisses through his teeth before submitting.

"Fine, baby. I will beg, but just know that the moment you let me switch and take control, I will not go easy on you. You'll be begging me for mercy I won't give. Are you ready for that?"

I stay quiet for a moment. My hand moves to his cock and I lean down, maintaining eye contact with him before pursing my lips and gathering enough spit in my mouth. The spit falls like slow motion over his pulsating, leaking cock and he moans. My fingers slowly wrap around his cock and move up and down. His hips buck up and I giggle, watching how this dominating man can become putty in my hands.

But I know it'll all change the moment I let him take over, so I'm enjoying this while I can.

"You can't come once you're inside my mouth," I warn him before leaning even further and wrapping my lips around his tip.

He curses under his breath before I twirl my tongue. His hips thrust up again and it makes his cock move a few inches inside my mouth. A moan escapes my lips as I lean further, letting his cock press deep into my mouth and hitting the back of my throat. My other hand goes to hold his thick thigh as I continue sucking him.

"Fuck, Eliana, please more," he groans from above. I smile before humming a 'yes' and pushing down the tears springing my eyes from the motion. My hand that's still wrapped around his cock continues to twist and pump in quicker motions as I thrust my mouth up and down over him. His cock stiffens and before he can come, I lift my hand and mouth from him. I sit up and see his features darken and his breathing change to something more desperate.

"Eliana," he warns, moving his hips as if to help fight the friction he's feeling right now.

"What?"

I move up on the bed so I'm hovering right over his cock to my entrance. I glance up at him and he watches me slowly. His hands are *red* from how much he's been trying to get out of the belt, but I know he won't slip out of them without me saying so. I trust him to only do so when I say the words.

"Please," he whimpers.

It's like music to my ears and I spit in my hand before reaching down and rubbing my pussy. I moan through the action before sitting down, holding his cock just enough to align himself with my entrance. His girth is thick and practically splits me open as I continue to lower down on him inch by inch. We both curse from the feeling and my pussy clenches around him instantly.

"Fuck, fuck," he curses as I get fully seated.

"Yeah?" I tease as I circle my hips and grind my clit against his pelvic bone. He mumbles under his breath as his hands try to break through the belt.

"Move *faster*," he orders, but I take my sweet time, even though it's killing me. I'm so close to coming myself that it's pure torture taking it slow right now. I speed up just a little for my own enjoyment before I stop and try to even my breathing.

"Do you really want to come?" I ask him through loud breaths. He nods as he shifts his hips forward, causing me to fall forward and steady myself with my palms on his chest. The angle is pure torture as he has more control with the thrusts and his cock is hitting my G-spot perfectly. But he doesn't move. He just stares at me.

"If you want me to take over, just say so."

As much as I enjoyed being the 'top', I love it when he takes over and wrecks me. He knows exactly how to take me apart and put me back together again.

"Yes, Julián. *Please*," I tell him.

And without another word he smiles before lowering his arms until they're around my neck, his wrists still tied up. In a quick breath, he twirls us so he's positioned on top of me and my back hits the mattress. My hands immediately go to his back. My legs wrap around his waist.

He doesn't move, just stares at me for a moment and I raise a brow. I clench my pussy around his cock and he groans, shaking his head. "*Corazón*, you make me fucking crazy. I could drown in what you make me feel."

Before I can respond, he's pulling himself out of me before thrusting *hard* back into me and I scream from the intensity. He doesn't stop the thrusting, causing the headboard to slam against the wall. My legs shake as my mind turns to goo.

The orgasm comes in no time and my body responds so well to him. He curses and yells my name while I do the same, our bodies dripping in sweat. He continues to have his hands around my neck. His muscles flex as he continues to thrust inside me. I move my hand to press my fingers against my clit to add more friction.

"Fuck, Julián, I'm going to come," I whine, rubbing my clit at a faster pace. He doesn't let up his thrusting as he leans in closer, his curls tickling my forehead. He kisses me for a moment before moving his lips to my ear and nibbling on my earlobe.

"Yeah, baby? Come for me, milk my fucking cock."

And I do. I scream his name again, as loud as I can, as I feel the rush of pleasure in my core and I'm coming. His cock stiffens inside of me as I feel warmth and his orgasm comes right after mine.

He continues to thrust into me until I'm begging him to stop and he finally slows down until he can slip out of me. He collapses on the bed and I reach for his wrists, unwrapping the belt. His skin is red from the tightness and from his pulling, but he doesn't hesitate to pull me close to him in the aftercare.

"Fuck. Did you like that? Being my beautiful dominatrix?"

I laugh and bury my head in my chest. "I was not! I just tied up your wrists. That was barely anything. Plus, I liked it better when you took over."

"Yeah? I like it too. I love hearing you scream my name like that. Like there's no other thought in your mind, but me."

I lift my head to look at him and he's looking at the ceiling before he glances down at me. "It's because it is."

It takes a moment for him, but his lips curl into a smile before he pulls me tighter and kisses me.

We stay like that, listening to the honking and loud noises of the city just outside the window as we cuddle each other.

I wouldn't trade this moment for the world.

Twenty-Four

JULIÁN

AFTER WE *CHRISTENED* the hotel room on Tuesday, we decided to venture into the city. We walked around Central Park and even ice skated. I haven't done that for years, so it was comical to try while Eliana skated almost gracefully. Her legs looked *good* in those yoga pants and skates. I wanted to drag her somewhere and fuck her, but there wasn't a place secluded enough to do it.

So, I did it once we got back to the hotel room. We then walked around the neighborhood, Eliana pointing out all the pretty buildings before we found an Italian restaurant to try.

On Wednesday, we ventured out to Times Square to sightsee and take some more pictures. It felt nice to be with her in public and not have to worry about prying eyes. With how many people there are in the city, it would be almost *cosmic* if there was someone who saw us.

After Times Square, we even checked out the box offices for the plays they had on Broadway and chose one to watch that same night.

We've spent two days in the city so far and she's already begging for more of the New York pizza that costs a dollar. I gladly buy her some every time she asks for it, I love the way her green eyes brightens at the sight of those pizza shops and sees that damn sign.

Now, it's Thursday, and she's munching on some mochi donuts after having the best Korean dishes for lunch. We're in K-town and taking in the nice weather that's not too cold. The sun is bright as we walk along the streets and dodge people walking faster around us. The noises are loud and I've come to really enjoy it.

I could see myself visiting the city more often with her by my side. The views are incredible from the tops of buildings and the food is amazing. We've tried so many places so far that she found on a blog that she read up on. We even tried some places she's previously been with her parents when she was younger.

My favorite part about this trip is just having her here and being able to hold her hand while we walk down the streets. It's nice and I never want to give up this feeling. The dreadful feeling of knowing we go back to reality tomorrow night doesn't help. My stomach churns just at the thought.

Eliana finishes her donut and wipes her fingers before looking up at me. We've been walking for a few blocks out of K-town and we can see the Empire State Building. Her green eyes glow and I can't tell if it's because of the food I've been getting her whenever she points at a place, or because she's staring at *me*.

"*¿Qué?*" I ask with a laugh.

She shrugs and grabs my hand, pulling me away from the busy sidewalk until we're past a crosswalk and in an area where there are chairs and tables. It's a vast space for people to hang out in between the two driving streets, and it seems like a place where people can just eat their lunch before returning to work. Some pigeons fly around us trying to eat the crumbs people have dropped.

"Nothing, I just don't want this week to stop," she sighs.

I pull her close to me before rubbing my nose against hers. We both take in a deep breath before I kiss her.

"We can run to this city whenever you feel like it gets too hard, *Corazón*. Just say the word and our bags are packed and the hotel is booked."

She keeps her beautiful gaze on me for a moment, her lip turning into a half frown. I ponder what she might be thinking.

"Eliana," I press.

She looks up at the sky before tightening her grip on my coat's collar. "I just don't want to go back to secrecy. It's fun, yes, but eventually we need to tell people. I want to. Do you?"

"Of course," I say without missing a beat. Her eyes light up at that. "But we have to think about the *after* parts. There will be a lot of things that we have to discuss and maneuver once it's out."

"I can handle my parents," she confidently says.

I shake my head. "*We'd* have to handle them. We're adults, Eliana. If I'm going to make this public with you, then I'd have to talk to your parents just like any 'boyfriend' would. You will not do it alone."

Her lips curl into a big smile. "You said 'boyfriend'."

"I did," I smile back. My heart beats faster in my chest and I wait for her to say anything else.

"I like it," she confesses.

"Me too."

She gets on her tippy toes and kisses me again. I hear the flock of more pigeons around us and I have to remember that we're in the middle of the city on a random street. I can't help but laugh through the kiss.

"What's so funny, *boyfriend*?" she asks, pulling away. She moves her hand to grasp mine and continues to drag us closer to where the Empire State Building is.

"Nothing, you just make me happy. Very happy, baby."

"Good, because you might hate me. I want to see the Empire State Building again. It's been a while since I've been up there!"

She continues to pull us through the crowds and I let her. If my baby wants to see the Empire State Building, then she's going to see it.

I'd give her the damn world if she asked.

··⊰•∘)✧(∘•⊱··

WE SPENT OUR MORNING IN BED BEFORE CHECK OUT AND WE DID the most that we could. I was already looking forward to the next trip we'd make back to the city. This would be our new 'thing' I think. Escaping to the city whenever we needed it or simply wanted to. I even suggested it to Eliana, and she agreed. She enjoyed it much more this week than any time in the past, and that made me happy.

The train ride back home is quick and we both nap most of the way. There were times where I'd check my phone for messages and notice Eliana already on her phone, texting away like a madwoman. I didn't want to budge and ask her who it was, but the moment I would lean into her, she'd turn it the other way.

If she wanted me to know who she was texting, then she'd tell me. We all deserve our privacy, but I couldn't forget the way her brows scrunched and she chewed on her cheek and started to pick at her nails.

It's dark outside once we get off and head to my place. I invited her to stay the rest of the weekend with me and she agreed. She was quiet the entire way home and I know it has to be because of whoever was texting her. I didn't want to pry and I won't until absolutely needed.

"Want me to get a bath ready?" I ask her, dropping our bags

off into the bedroom. She stalls and doesn't follow me. I hear her though, kicking off her shoes and sighing in the other room.

I head towards the bathroom, lifting the handle to the drain stopper before turning on the water and making sure it's not too hot. As the tub fills I turn to look out into the hallway, waiting to see if she'll walk near. After a few seconds, I stand up and make my way to the living room.

Eliana is sitting on the couch, her face in her hands and crouched over. I head to her and sit down gently, placing my hand on her back and rubbing in smooth circles.

"Baby? Everything okay?"

She's quiet for a moment before she shakes her head and sniffles, lifting her head. When she finally looks at me her green eyes are glossy. I pinch my brows and continue to rub circles on her back.

"She knows."

"Who knows what?"

She shakes her head again before taking a deep breath and exhaling loudly. "Lena. She knows about us."

My hand stops with the movements on her back and I retract it back to my lap. "Oh. How?"

She nods at her phone that's on the coffee table. The screen is face down. I look back at her and her lips quiver. I bring my hands to either side of her jaw and lift her head to look at me.

"Eliana. What did she say? Was that who you were texting with on the train?"

She tries to look away, but my grip on her jaw won't let her. She's forced to look at me and she blinks, a few tears spilling from her pretty eyes. I wipe them with my thumbs.

"She didn't tell me, but she wants to talk to me tomorrow. She's angry, Julián. I know it."

"Are you sure?"

She nods.

"Yes, I'm sure. She knows and now she hates me. I can't see her tomorrow. I don't want to."

I let my hands drop and she takes another deep breath. "Why don't you take that bath and try not to think too much about it? She can't hate you. She's your best friend. Lena cares about you. She's also very smart, so I'm not surprised if she caught on."

There's a small smile that paints her face and it makes me smile as well. *There she is*. I stand up and extend my hand out, wiggling my fingers at her. She hesitates for a moment, a million thoughts crossing through her mind before she nods and takes my hand. Her touch is light, but it still sends sparks throughout my body.

It always has.

I walk us to the bathroom and help her strip, making sure we do it all at her pace. She gingerly dips into the water that is still running. I add some soap and a bath bomb to make the water pretty. She's silent the whole time, lost in her thoughts as I shut the water off just in time before it leaks over the rim of the tub.

She leans her head back and closes her eyes. Some tears still fall and cascade down her cheeks. She's so beautiful, it hurts me to see her like this. It brings me back to the last time she came over and I drew a bath for her. I tried my best to make her feel better.

I lean over and brush a strand of hair behind her ear and her eyes flutter open before a small smile etches on her face.

"Thank you," she whispers.

I nod, not wanting to say anything to ruin the moment. She seems to thrive the most when she can be alone in her head and process things that way. I'm more of the type to talk it out and find a solution, but I know we're all different. She likes this way and really being in tune with her emotions before she makes decisions.

It's what I admire about her. She likes to take the time to think of things before acting on them. My heart swells at the thought of her wanting to find a solution to this situation. It's not a problem to be fixed, but we need to get through it.

Together.

That's when I realize that this woman makes me want to do whatever I can to make her feel better. If she needs to think alone, then I'll leave her alone. If she wants to talk about it, I'll be her listening ear. If she wants to end things, then I'll painfully go. Even if it hurts me in the end, I don't care. As long as she gets what she wants and ultimately needs. And if I'm not what she ultimately needs, then I won't stand in her way. I won't cause destruction. She deserves better than that.

"Hey," she mumbles, breaking me out of my thoughts. I've been staring at the bathroom walls for a while, deep in my thoughts. I catch her eyes.

"Is everything okay?"

I nod, brushing my hand over my beard. "Yeah, baby. Everything is okay. I just want you to be okay. I won't stand in your way, okay?"

"You-" she starts before shaking her head. "You're not standing in the way of anything. Why do you think that?" She lifts herself into a more comfortable sitting position in the tub, the water sloshing around her in the tub and her hair gliding over her wet body. Her breasts are only halfway covered by the water and I focus my eyes back on hers.

"Eliana, our bubble is about to burst. Seems like it already has with Lena. She knows and it's not long before she tells someone. Or someone else finds out."

She shakes her head. "She wouldn't do that to me."

"So why haven't you told her about us then? There has to be a reason."

There's silence that stretches between us. I want her to say something, *anything*, but instead, she looks anywhere but at me. She lifts her hands out of the water and picks at her nails. I reach over and press my palm over her hands, so she stops. I look at her with more ferocity, and she gulps. Her eyes wells up with tears and my chest cracks.

"I trust her, but there's just so much at stake. My living situation, the fact that you're almost two decades older than me, my relationship with my dad, my grades with Laura, and *your job*." She makes sure to point out that last fact.

I smirk. "I like how you made the most prominent point being about my job and not that I'm almost two decades older than you."

She huffs and sighs but I don't miss the hint of a smile that curls at the tips of her lips. I squeeze her hands under mine and she takes a few deep breaths.

"Meet with her tomorrow and figure out what happened. How she found out and then talk to her. She'll understand. We'll figure the rest out together."

She watches me for a long time before nodding. "Okay, together."

"*Juntos*," I repeat, squeezing her hands three times.

I don't know why I do it, but maybe it's my own way of telling her I'm always going to be here for her.

Three times.

Three words.

But I won't say them. Not yet.

Twenty-Five

ELIANA

My hands are shaking as I reach the cafe doors. I've walked this entrance millions of times, yet this morning my gut is twisted and I'm so close to throwing up.

Once I'm inside, I immediately find the mass of curls that belong to my best friend. She's sipping on a mug of coffee before she looks up and smiles, waving me over.

I take a deep breath before heading to her, skipping the register line completely. My stomach is in knots and I know I won't be able to hold down anything even if I tried. I'm too nervous to know the outcome of this conversation.

"How was your trip?!" She gleams as she stands up and pulls me into a hug. Her sweet perfume fills my senses and I want to cry. If today is the last time I get to hug my best friend, then I'm going to cherish every moment.

"It was okay," I mumble before we both sit down. She's smiling and twirling a strand of curly hair between her fingers.

"Yeah? Well, how is *you know who*?"

I clear my throat. "Okay. But Lena, you never told me how–"

She waves her hand and scoffs playfully. "Malcom told me."

"What?"

She nods.

"Yeah, he told me… On Wednesday? I just got wrapped up in what we were doing and forgot to text you until yesterday."

"Wait, I'm confused. How did Malcom know?"

"Well, that's what I mainly wanted to talk to you about… Have you talked to your parents yet?"

My jaw falls. "My parents *know*?! Fuck, why didn't you tell me? I haven't had time to go home. They're going to ki–"

"Relax!" Lena raises her hands and her eyes widen. "I was just trying to fit in some catch-up conversation. I realize that wasn't the best way to do it. The parent question was entirely separate from how Malcolm heard."

"So, tell me before I have a heart attack," I press. My anxiety is sky high and I don't know how much longer I can last with this conversation or with anything right now. I just want to curl up into a ball and sleep until everything fades away. Maybe wake up in a different century.

"Okay, so Malcolm was going to get some bagels for us one morning when he bumped into Harry."

"Harry Simmons?" I cut her off. She nods.

"Do you know any other Harry's? Yes, that one." She visibly shudders. "Anyway, he started blabbing about you and how he was so confused why you left the double date so early. Ya da, ya da." She rolls her eyes. "Malcolm had to remind him how much of a *dick* he is before Harry finally slips out that he saw you and Professor Estrada at the Amtrak station."

"Fuck," I spit out.

She looks at me apologetically before continuing. "Malcolm came racing home, without my bagel *mind you*, and started telling me how *you're* with Professor Estrada. And I had to get over the fact that I was hungry with no bagel before I realized that my *best friend* lied to me about her trip. I should've connected the dots. I'm so stupid."

"No, you're not. I honestly thought you knew this whole time but tried to pray those thoughts away and hoped you'd get mild amnesia just for this."

She laughs. "Jeez, thanks, Ana. You really love me."

"Carry on, Len," I look at her pointedly.

"Right," she nods. "So then I force Malcolm to get my bagel again and he comes back with it and more news. He tried to call Professor Estrada, but it seems like he turned off his phone or something while he was with you. How *attentive*. I hate how great Julián is, by the way. It'd be easier to hate him if he was a jerk, babe."

"Lena," I scold.

A smile grows on her face and on mine as well.

"So then he called Kane. He wasn't budging *at all* about you two. Malcolm tried every way to make the conversation into something where he can get information on you guys. He wouldn't say a peep."

"Good," I laugh.

"We tried. So yeah, I'm not sure where Harry is or what he's going to do. But just know that you've got my full support. Even if you lied to me. I respect Professor Estrada–"

"Please, call him Julián," I beg her.

I feel my body cave into itself every time she says *professor*. It doesn't help that we're inside Crescent Cafe where students are milling around.

"It doesn't stick as well for me. I'm sorry. Maybe if I get to know him more, then sure," she laughs.

I roll my eyes jovially. "Lena."

"Right, back to the point. Professor Estrada just needs to talk to Harry, honestly. I doubt he told anyone else. He wouldn't ruin someone's life over this."

I try to think of all plausible scenarios. I'm not convinced that Harry would take the high road. He doesn't seem like the type.

My phone buzzes in my pocket, and I pull it out, seeing a

text from dad. I haven't heard from either of my parents this entire break even after I texted them a couple of times. I didn't want to be a bother since they like to spend their vacations unplugged from everything.

PAPÁ

Come home as soon as you can. We need to talk

Oh shit. My eyes bug out.

"What?!" Lena asks, leaning over the table to look at my screen, but I don't let her see it.

"It's just my dad. He wants to talk to me about something."

"Do you think he knows?"

I shake my head. "No, but it is strange that they're home today. They usually leave the last day of their break. They try to enjoy the full time they're off."

"I wish I could go with you, Ana."

I wave her off. "It's okay. It's a good sign if he's the one texting me, not my mother."

She gulps and nods. "Yep, I'd already be booking a flight and trying to change my identity if your mother was the one texting you that."

I take a deep breath and stand up, not wanting to waste anymore time and get home.

My mind quickly goes back to Julián and when he squeezed my hands three times in the tub last night. Like he was telling me something that he didn't want to verbalize just yet. I've thought about it too, but it's too soon. I think.

I don't want to say something and then have him not say it back. Everything is just so up in the air right now with so much on the line that I can't *think* of those three words until I know it's safe.

But will it ever be?

··₃•₀)◇(₀•₃··

I WALK INTO MY DAD'S STUDY AND HALT IN MY TRACKS WHEN I see my mother's black hair before she turns to look at me. Her eyes are almost dagger-like as she pierces into my soul with just one look. I gulp and know I'm in deep shit.

Harry fucking told them.

I look at my dad who is giving me a small smile before he gestures for me to sit down in the vacant chair next to my mother. She moves her hair delicately behind her ear and she watches me sit down slowly. I sink into the leather chair and I take a deep breath before looking up at my dad.

"You wanted to talk?" I squeak out.

My mother nods and clicks her tongue before my dad nods as well. "Yeah, *Princesa*. It's about… Professor Simmons called me today."

Fuck.

I try to keep my cool, but my body is almost vibrating from the predicament.

"And what did he say?" I attempt to say through gritted teeth. My mother shifts in her chair, crossing one leg over the other.

Dad is twisting in his chair before he places his elbows on the table and leans in. "Do you have anything you'd like to tell me?"

I gulp and go from my dad's gaze to my mother's. Hers isn't welcoming, and I can almost hear her thoughts. They're not nice.

"I-I don't know. Do I?" I try to act dumb, but they can see right through me. I won't say anything until they do.

"Are you sure, *Princesa*?" he asks, leaning even more towards me. I chew on the inside of my cheek until I taste iron.

"Mhm," I nod.

My mother huffs before pointing at me. "Carlos! Just say it!

We know what's going on. She's just waiting until we say it first. I know my daughter."

I look up at my dad and he looks *pained*. It breaks my fucking heart seeing him like this. Conflicted, but also wanting to talk. I hate my mother. Not letting me talk to him alone.

"I'm giving you this chance, *Princesa*," he says, looking at me with pleading eyes.

He doesn't want it to be true. He wants me to tell him it's not what Harry said.

I'm already feeling the world collapsing on me. I can't take it much longer. Tears brim my eyes and I take a shaky breath.

My mother laughs. "See? She'd rather tear up than confess what we know, Carlos. I can't believe it. I didn't think we'd have a whore as a daughter–"

"Victoria!" my dad yells, making me stop mid-sniffle. Her brows pinch together before a scowl fills her face. She rubs her temples and an exasperated sigh leaves her lips.

"You can't even admit it yourself. Pathetic, I'm sorry." She stands up and turns to me with a hand on her hip and the other pointing at me in an accusatory way. "I won't have a whore under my roof. Your father might, but that's not what I live by. You can go sleep with anyone you'd like, but sleeping with a professor? Your father's *subordinate*? That is unbelievable, and I can't believe you kept this from us."

I open my mouth to say something, *anything*, but nothing comes out. Tears spill down my cheeks and dad sighs. He looks guilty and like he's being in the middle of a tug of war. He wants to comfort his daughter, but he wants to stand by his wife.

"Say something!" she screams, taking a step closer to me. I sink further into the chair and close my eyes for a moment. She's never hit me before, but I wouldn't blame her if she does now.

"Victoria, get out. I'll talk to her," dad says loudly.

Laughter bubbles out of her. "I can't believe you, Carlos. You're defending her actions?"

"No, but we need to go about this some other way. We won't get anywhere like this."

She clicks her tongue before turning back to me, letting her hand fall to her side.

"Get out of my house." I finally look up at her in horror.

"What?" I squeak out. Dad is about to say something when she raises her hand to silence him.

"Get out of this house. I won't have you under this roof, not after what you've done. I don't care where you go. Your father can fund you enough for a hotel. But I don't want to see your face anymore around here. That's final."

Before I can protest and before dad can say anything, she strides out of the office and slams the door. That's when the tears fall and don't stop. My chest constricts, and it gets harder to breathe. I can't even blink the tears away fast enough. My nose gets clogged and I try to sniff it away, but it's no use.

I'm a slobbery mess and dad just sits there in silence. It's a few minutes of me trying to gain my composure before he finally speaks.

"*Princesa*," he starts. I look up at him and wipe my eyes with the backs of my hands. "Why didn't you tell me? Did he... force you or anything?"

I shake my head. "No, no. He didn't."

My voice is meek, and it's hard to even swallow.

"Then what is it? I'm confused, honey. Why *him*? He's my colleague and he's much older than you. He might be younger than your mother and I, but that still doesn't make it okay."

I'm silent for a moment; I know the answer to everything. It's three words. But that would be ridiculous to confess in front of my dad. Let alone say it to my mother, who just cast me out and called me a whore.

It's like no matter what I did to please her, it's never enough. I'm never enough and never will be. This just confirmed it.

"Honey?" he asks, standing up and rounding the corner of his desk before he's kneeling down in front of me. He lifts his hands to my face and wipes my tears. One of his hands moves to my back and tries to soothe me.

"It's complicated. I didn't meet him at Yale." I finally let out. I don't know if that would make things better, but it's something.

I take another struggling breath, attempting to clear my nostrils, but they're still stuffy.

"Where did you meet him?"

Here goes nothing. "That Egyptian Exhibit opening back in August."

His hands pause on me before he takes a deep breath. "Oh."

That's all he says for a while as we sit there. I nod and he leans over toward his desk where he's got some tissues and hands me some. I take them graciously and blow my nose before using another to wipe my eyes. They hurt from all the crying and my throat is dry and is starting to hurt.

"We didn't know. Not until a few weeks later. We just kept bumping into each other in every place. There's just something about him, I won't go into detail. I know you don't want to know that. But I'm an adult."

He nods. "You are an adult, I won't deny that. But that doesn't negate the fact that you're still young. Honey, you're twenty-three."

"Almost twenty-four," I remind him. He smiles.

"Yes, but you're still twenty-three right now. And that is just too *young* for him. Don't you think? He was married, remember?"

"Oh, I remember. He told me about her. Well, as much as he could."

"Yeah, but don't you think that might be a warning sign of some sorts? Laura Estrada is your advisor, Eliana." He pauses with intent before continuing, "A divorced man? I just want you to experience dating with people your own age! Or at the very least, someone younger than him."

"Like Harry?" I scoff. My dad looks at me with worry etched onto his face.

"Not exactly, but that's not a bad idea."

"Too late, I went on a double date with him and Lena and–" I stop myself before I spill the beans about Lena and Malcolm.

"And how was it? Better than Julián?"

"No," I laugh half-heartedly. "He wouldn't even open the door for me. Or pay for his dinner. He wasn't a gentleman at all."

He presses his lips together firmly before asking, "And Julián is?"

I nod finally. "He really is. He makes me feel–" I ponder for a moment before continuing. "He makes me feel safe. Makes me realize that age doesn't matter when it comes to a relationship. He has a kind heart and cares about me. He opens the door for me, walks on the side of the street where there's traffic. He gives me the larger portions of food whenever we go out. He makes sure that I'm happy."

My father watches me for a moment as I confess everything about Julián. My heart swarms with butterflies and warms at the thought of everything that Julián has done for me. He really cares for me. I picture his hands squeezing mine three times last night. I want to tell him the same. My lips twitch into a smile.

"Funny," my dad starts as he stands up, resting a hand on my shoulder. "Laura never said those things about him. She was very self-centered and put the blame for her divorce on him. She can be bitter."

"You think? She almost failed me."

He looks down at me and raises a brow. "She what?"

I nod. "I thought you knew. I was close to failing, but I redid my assignments and passed so far. Now, I'm not so sure since mother is obviously going to tell her about me and Julián. Laura mentioned that they talk about me quite frequently."

"I didn't know, *Princesa*, I'm sorry. That's not okay and I'll definitely be talking to Victoria about it. Regardless of that, I know you're not lying about how you feel about him. I just hope he feels the same about you, or else. I've got a lot of power at work and I won't hesitate to lift a finger if you tell me to."

I shake my head vigorously. "No, please don't. I know he feels the same way. We've talked about it to some extent, but I think he's terrified of the same things you're terrified of. Losing me and his job."

"And you're positive about that?" He quirks a brow with a sly smile on his face.

I smile and nod. "I'm sure."

He drops his hand from my shoulder and walks back to his desk. He plops down on the chair and clears his throat. "I'll handle your mother, but I can't stop her if she's already told Laura. You'll have to deal with that with Julián. If you guys can do that and if you guys can really show me and everyone else that this isn't just some *phase,* then I won't bat an eye. I love you, *Princesa,* but I just want the best for you. I won't tell you no, but I want to make sure this is what you want and that he's got his head on straight. I won't let my daughter's heart break over a man I see every day. It won't be pretty."

His words don't appear threatening as they sound, but I appreciate him still. I smile and nod my head before shakily standing up. "Thanks, *papá.* I won't disappoint you. If it's fine, I might stay with him then. I don't want to push *her* anymore than I already have."

His eyes are back to the kindness I'm used to. "Do what you have to. I'll talk to Victoria. She'll come around, eventually."

I head towards the door before turning around once more. He looks at me expectantly, and I give him a big smile before running over to him and wrapping my arms around him.

"Thank you," I whisper.

"Anything for you, *Princesa.*"

I run back to the door and whip it open before heading upstairs, dodging my mother in her bedroom. I pack a few things and text Julián that I'm going to spend a little longer at his place if he doesn't mind.

He immediately texts back that it's okay and for me to tell him if there's anything he can do.

I smile at his response and almost cry. He's perfect.

He's already doing everything.

Twenty-Six

JULIÁN

Eliana drops a few duffle bags on the floor once she comes inside and I envelope her into a hug. "I thought you were just staying 'til Monday?"

She looks exhausted and her eyes look puffy. My chest aches at the sight. "She kicked me out, but my dad is cool with us."

Her words jumble out of her mouth at lightning speed. "Wait, they know? Eliana, we were going to do that together."

She smiles. "Harry did that for us," her words are laced with venom but she continues to smile.

"Why are you smiling?" I ask, looking her up from head to toe to make sure she's not bruised from whatever fall she obviously has been through.

"Because," she says before closing the distance and wrapping her arms around my neck, pulling to her and smashing her lips on mine. I lean into the kiss and she pushes her tongue into my mouth, causing a moan to escape from me. It doesn't surprise me how easily my whole being caves when it comes to her.

I grab her cheeks before pushing her away gently. I laugh. "That's—wow, okay. Are you going to tell me why?"

She shakes her head. "You're perfect and I just need you to

know that Julián." Her words fall from her lips and I search her eyes for any falsities, but there are none.

"Eliana, baby," I whisper, caressing her cheek with my thumb. She breathes deeply before smiling wider.

"Julián, there's no one else I'd want to do this with. It's difficult, *complicated*, messy and something not everyone will accept or like."

I wait for her to continue.

"Tell me you want me," she whispers. Her eyes search mine and I take a deep breath. Her green eyes are shining bright for me and I want to hold onto them forever. The specks in her eyes are like stars in the sky and I want to be under them for all my days.

"I want you, Eliana. I want *this*." I rub my thumb over her lip and she hitches her breath.

"Tell me you–" her voice cracks and when she closes her eyes, my heart falters. She opens them and they're glossy. "Tell me you love me."

There's silence that could crack open the Earth, but I waste no more time to answer. Because it's not like when I confessed my love to my ex-wife. This is different. Not only is my body in this, but so is my heart and soul.

My whole being is in this and she has all of me. She has my soul and there isn't anyone else. There never was. Our paths crossed for a reason in that exhibit and I have to thank all of the gods for that divine timing.

"Eliana." I brush some hair behind her ear. "I don't think it's enough. There will never be a word sufficient enough for the way I feel about you. I *love* you, but I–"

"But?" she whispers, tears escaping her eyes. I smile, hoping she doesn't fixate on the 'but'.

"*But*," I start. "I love you, but not just in this lifetime, *Corazón*. In every lifetime I will ever live. Even if you're not destined to be mine, my soul is yours. My heart is yours and yours alone. I love you, *Corazón. Eres mi cielo, mi sol, y mi luna. Tienes mi alma, mi amor. Tienes todo mi corazón.*"

"Translate, please," she begs with a laugh.

I smile. "You're my sky, my sun, and my moon. You have my soul, my love. You have my whole heart."

She takes a deep breath and shakily exhales with my confession. "Julián, I'm supposed to be the one with the well thought out confession."

I laugh. "Just tell me you love me too, *mi corazón.*"

"I love you," she whispers, getting on her tippy toes again and crashing her lips against mine.

And it feels like my world is complete.

•••≈••)◊◊(••≈•••

SHE'S SLEEPING PEACEFULLY ON THE BED AS I GRADE SOME assignments at the small desk in my bedroom. Her eyes are still a little red and puffy from the crying, but I put some cold water on a towel and had her hold it up on her eyes for a while as she rested.

Although we confessed our love, we ended up unpacking her bags and I ordered take out. I didn't want to feel like just because we confessed and bared our soul to each other that it had to result in intimacy. She was exhausted anyways with the conversation she had with her parents.

She finally told me what Victoria said while I drew her a bath. I made sure to put extra soap in the bath as she spoke, wishing I could take her pain away. I know Eliana seems to be used to and almost *numb* to how Victoria treats her, but this crossed the line. She never should've said the things she did to Eliana.

I don't want to see her hurt and it made me want to go over to her parents' home and talk some sense into Victoria. Her father seemed okay once Eliana told him how she felt about me, but I'd still like to talk to him as well.

Man to man.

Victoria will just have to be another time. We need to give her space and enough time to process this.

Elaina stirs in her sleep and she mumbles some incoherent words, and I get lost in it. She's so beautiful, in every way, and I hope one day she can truly see herself the way I do. I never want someone else's words to tarnish her self love.

I take my time grading papers until my body feels completely exhausted. The moment I get in bed beside her, she immediately curls up next to me and wraps her body tight around me like a koala. I breathe her in before closing my eyes and knowing the next few days will be tough, but we'll make it through.

She's worth it and more.

•·•⋛•◦)◦✧◦(◦•⋚•·•

I LIFT MY HAND AND GENTLY KNOCK ON THE WOODEN DOOR. After a few seconds, I hear a gentle '*come in*' and I twist the doorknob, pushing myself through.

Eliana didn't want me to speak with her father just yet, but we already waited for a few days. I even took Monday and Tuesday off to be with her. I had to make sure she'd be okay after everything that happened.

She was on the verge of calling the provost office and dropping out, so I had to encourage her to know that she can't let other people's opinions ruin her life choices.

The moment Carlos lifts his head, his face turns from excited to see who's entering to a saddened expression that I know too well.

It's the face of disappointment. I could point it out in a millisecond from anyone. Laura gave me that face for so many years, it became almost a trademark expression of hers. I'm surprised she doesn't have more wrinkles from all the frowning she did.

"Julián, what brings you here?"

The door slowly closes and I walk towards his desk before taking a seat, his eyes never once leaving mine. His stare doesn't waver even when I clear my throat and look around his office for a little. It's different from the last time I was here.

Some more photos are around the place as well as a plant in one corner.

"Well?" he speaks up, crossing his arms over his chest and leaning back in his chair. I run my hands through my hair and take a deep breath.

He's a decade older than me, but I feel like a kid in front of a scolding parent. His stare starts to turn cold and calculated as he watches my eyes. Like watching a kid reaching their hand into the cookie jar.

"I want to apologize, Carlos," I start. He doesn't say anything, so I take this as a cue to continue. I take a deep breath and wipe my sweaty palms against my slacks.

"I should've told you. I want to apologize for that. I'm taking full responsibility for everything. I shouldn't have kept pursuing her the moment I knew who she was; her last name. I should've put together some of those pieces, but I never did. I was too caught up in it all."

Carlos is silent still, but his icy stare falters and I catch it. I take another encouraging breath before speaking more. From the heart, this time.

"It's been a while since I've felt like this in my life. To be honest... I never felt this way with Laura. I feel like I've gotten my spark back, like I can look forward to the days ahead of me instead of dreading it. I love my job here, but being so close to the things that once hurt me was taking a toll. I don't want to sound so bleak, but it's true. It was getting too much, and then I met her that night."

Carlos listens attentively, and I silently thank him for it. He takes in my words before he takes a deep breath and uncrosses his arms, placing them on the desk and leaning forward. He takes another few deep breaths before locking eyes with me.

"You say you're taking full responsibility, but what for?"

He catches me there. "I want to take full responsibility for making the relationship drag on without you knowing. It wasn't respectful to anyone. I'm the older one," Carlos clears his throat with this, and I take a shaky breath. "I'm the older one, yes, we have to get over that elephant in the room. I realize that is a huge disparity when you look at things, but that doesn't take away the feelings I get with her and–"

"I don't need to know the extent of these things. Never did care for that with previous boyfriends of hers," Carlos waves his hand, as if batting a fly away. I want to laugh, but I know he means it.

"Of course, my apologies."

"You're not asking for permission to date my daughter, because you're both adults. And I won't chastise her for finding someone who she really cares for. It's just very *complicated* when it's a coworker of mine. Let alone someone that works under me due to my position."

I nod. "Believe me, that thought alone made me want to call it quits, but your daughter is very persistent."

There's a hint of a smile on his lips and I'll take it. "She knows what her *heart* wants. Does it ever agree with her mother and I's thoughts? Absolutely not. She never really was a fan of our input. Victoria and her clash every second and sometimes I wonder if there was something I did wrong in the process. But it's just their personalities, I guess."

I want to tell him that he's wrong about that and how it is all Victoria's doing. She puts Eliana into a box full of expectations and taped every inch of it shut, not letting her breathe or escape. But what Victoria forgot was that Eliana has been clawing her way out this whole time. And I'm so proud of her for her strength to even do that.

No one can stop her from what her heart really wants.

"So tell me, Julián," he starts. "Why do you want to continue things with my daughter? She's 23 years old and she can make her own decisions in her life, but I *am* her father. I want to make sure that her best interests are at heart. That you won't hurt her. The result won't look pretty on your end, I might add."

I nod, knowing that he'd do anything for Eliana. But he has to know that I'd do anything for her as well. I'm not well versed in all of the boyfriends that she's had, but I don't need to. What matters is right now and what we feel for each other. How much we care for each other.

"Carlos, there are sometimes things that you just can't explain, but I hope with the way I treat her you can see it. She works hard to make everyone around her happy even if she's struggling. I see it and I try to understand and help her find some of that happy for herself. If I make her happy, then that's great. But if her happiness relies on me leaving then that is something I've also considered."

Carlos raises a brow. "You'd leave Eliana just to keep her happy?"

I nod curtly. "I would."

He takes a moment to process everything.

"To be honest, I've never heard anyone say that about my daughter before. And that's all I care about. The rest, I don't need to know or worry about. But her happiness? That is the most important. Her mother might go to extreme lengths to keep our daughter safe but in the end we just want what's best for her. And if it's you, then I can't stop that. I don't want a daughter that hates me because I pulled you away from her. That would just absolutely wreck me and this is coming straight from the depths of my soul, Julián."

"I understand," I hum out in response. He smiles and lifts his arms off from the desk and leans back in his chair.

"She's had nothing but great things to say about you, by the way. When I drilled her about why she had to choose my *coworker*, of all people."

I smile at this. "Yeah?"

"Yes, Julián. Her eyes lit up like I've never seen it. So you take care of her heart. Please."

"I will, Carlos. Thank you," I say before standing up. He does the same and rounds his desk before reaching his palm out. I clasp mine around his and we shake for a good second before he smiles and pulls me in for a side hug and pats my back.

Once we release, the world isn't collapsing on me anymore. I can breathe better and my body isn't sweating bullets.

"I do have one more thing, though," he says while walking back to his desk.

I raise a brow. "What's that?"

"Wait a while for Victoria to come to Eliana. Don't meddle. They need to really work out what's going on between them. I think this is the ultimate breaking point and Eliana will need you by her side. My wife is very adamant about her opinions. She doesn't sway. But she might if she realizes what you two feel is a once in a lifetime. That is something you just have to let the universe decide to take the reins of. We can't control it."

"Thank you," I say.

He gives me a curt nod before I head out of his office. Once I'm in the hallway and take a deep breath and my heart starts to calm down. I'm alive and well, I have a woman back in my apartment that loves me and that's all I could need right now.

I don't need anything else.

Twenty-Seven

ELIANA

Time has flown since that day in my father's office. Part of me can't believe it's been a month since I last spoke with my mother. While I've been able to call and even chat with my dad in his office, it's like a dark cloud is hanging over us. We both make an effort to avoid bringing her up in conversation.

It's all really complicated, I want to repair the relationship but I can breathe for the first time, free of her expectations.

Julián and I have been doing better than ever, despite the circumstances. The moment he went and spoke to my dad about everything it felt like a weight was lifted from both of our shoulders. We could breathe just a little better.

We still had to deal with the reality of my mother, but it felt nice to be able to not be scared of the outcome of us wanting to go out in public around town. We were able to see Lena and Malcolm a few times at the bars and even for some double dates. Those went exceptionally better than my last experience.

Lena is spending her Thanksgiving with her family and then going to spend the rest of her weekend with Malcolm and meeting his family. They're completely smitten for one another.

I've never seen my best friend like this for anyone and it warms my heart to know she found someone just like I have.

I look at my phone and see a text from my mother, taking me away from my thoughts.

DIABLA

Thanksgiving dinner. 6pm sharp.

I almost gawk at the text and look around me for cameras and a crew to jump out and yell at me I've been Punk'd. But no one jumps out of any bushes and I'm still alone. I look down at the text and type out a quick reply.

ME

I'll be there. Thanks.

I take a deep breath and try to center myself. I'm sure she expects me to bring Julián, so I don't even bother calling or texting her for permission. But… it would've been nice for her to actually invite him instead of just assuming.

If she can't handle him being there, then she shouldn't have invited me.

She had an entire month to reach out. I left her some texts here and there, but dad advised me to not bother her too much. He wanted me to tread lightly.

My grades were still doing well, so even with Laura knowing about us I know she's not trying to sabotage my academic career.

That was something I was super wary about as well, when Julián told me two weeks ago he was going to tell Laura about us. I didn't think it'd matter until we were at least official a little while longer but he was persistent. He wanted nothing impeding us and that included Laura. I couldn't lie and say it made me super anxious and worried when he told me his plan, but I trusted Julián.

As I walk back home from a cafe nearby, I think back to

when Julián met up with Laura and how he told me later that night. I was deep in drafting my final paper when he came home and dropped his things at the door and crawled onto the bed, still with his outside clothes on. I had to brush all the papers away from the bed that consumed the space to let him freely curl up against my body.

He didn't speak for a while as I typed on my laptop and hummed a few songs while he took some deep breaths. It wasn't until a little after that he told me she didn't take it well, but she'd have to eventually. There was a lot of screaming, she even threw a glass at the wall. It gave him flashbacks to their marriage and it made me so angry.

To think she treated him like that for years and he couldn't do anything about it. It's hard to leave someone you have so much history with. It reminded me of my mother and how you just become *numb* to their actions. But since he was gone from it for a while, seeing her act that way he could really see it clearer.

Some tears were shed, but I held him close and let him talk it all out. I knew I had to be there for him—for us. We started off so physically the moment we met, but we're growing to be there for each other in more serious and intimate times. Just like this moment and when I ran to him when my mother kicked me out.

My phone buzzes again and it's Julián asking what we're doing this weekend. I brush away the thoughts of two weeks ago and try to remain in the present. We did what we could and Laura isn't biting back anymore, which I have to be very thankful for. I submitted most of my final papers before break started so I could focus on studying for the in-person exams I'd have in two weeks.

I let him know that he'll be joining me for Thanksgiving at my house and I'm almost to his apartment.

Home.

Once I'm up the steps and unlocking the door, he's sitting on the kitchen table sorting through some mail. He lifts his gaze to me and gives me a small smile. I take off my coat and hang it on the hook before strolling to him.

He instantly wraps his arms around my waist, pulling me in. "You sure you want to go to your parents tonight?"

I nod.

"We have to face her eventually. And she seems to have made the first move."

He watches me for a moment before conceding. "Just tread lightly. I'm here for you, *Corazón*."

"I know," I breathe, closing my eyes and leaning my head against his chest. His hold around me tightens and I relish the moment. I'm safe and warm and I could be wrapped up in his arms forever.

"What are you thinking about?" he asks after a few beats.

"You," I smile.

"Yeah?" His heart thuds a little quicker.

"You make me feel safe, Julián. You make me feel like I can conquer anything as long as you can wrap me up in your arms when I need it."

He moves back and forth a little, making me sway with him. "I'll always be here, *Corazón*."

"I love you," I whisper. I don't intend for him to hear it, but he does.

"I love you too," he murmurs.

I lift my head and get on my tippy toes to kiss his cheek. He smiles before shifting us closer to the bedroom.

"We've got some time," he teases, leaning in to kiss my nose and then my neck before traveling his hands lower to my hips.

"Since when has time ever stopped you, Mr. Estrada," I giggle.

He pulls away slowly to look at me and his lips twitch into a smile. "You've never called me that."

"I think it's better than *Professor*." I lick my lips and his eyes fall to them. "Don't you?"

Without even hesitating, he nods. "Definitely, baby. I like how you say it."

Before I can say anything else, he's pulling us to the bedroom and we're fast to strip our clothes before our lips are on another. This time it's not a slow and steady moment, we're touching each other like it's the last.

His touch ignites goosebumps along every inch where he inhabits.

He consumes me like he's going to lose me. And I do the same.

I study every movement, every smile, every glance and take mental pictures every second to never forget him.

"You're so fucking beautiful, *Corazón. No puedo creer que eres mía,*" he whispers as he pumps his cock and spits on it for more lubrication. His other hand is slowly pressing against my clit before he glides the tip over my entrance.

I lift my hips in anticipation and he wastes no time to press himself into me before he's fully seated. We moan at the sensation and take deep breaths as we mold our bodies to another.

Like two broken pieces finding themselves perfectly fitting into one another. It wasn't something we expected, but found.

"Julián," I whimper as he thrusts into me at a faster pace, shaking the bed with the motions. He sits up on his knees, tall, his chest puffed up as he continues his rhythm. He runs one hand through his hair before running it down his face and beard and it's the hottest thing.

He licks his lips before leaning down where our bodies are connected and he spits and I shudder from the feeling.

"Fuck," I whine. He continues to thrust even faster as we both feel the intensity forming within us and I can't hold back. I scream his name as my orgasm washes over me and his follows mine shortly after.

"Baby," he coos, as he slows his thrusts and then collapses on top of me, breathing hard. I wrap my body around him like a koala and we stay like this for a moment. Our breathing is almost in sync and I smile, kissing his forehead before his nose.

"If tonight doesn't go well, promise me," I start, tears brimming my eyes. He knits his brows together before kissing my chin then my lips.

"Don't even finish that sentence, Eliana. Whatever you need tonight, tell me. Don't think whatever you'll ask will be too much. You're never too much. I'm sorry she made you feel that way for so long."

I gulp, attempting to push the knot in my throat, but it stays. "I know, but it's still hard. It just doesn't go away."

"I understand. I really do," he whispers.

He's not lying. We come from different places, yet they're so similar. We can understand each other better because of it.

"Alright, wipe those tears, *Corazón*," he says, pulling out of me and sitting up. "We gotta get ready before I keep seeing you like this. I might not let us leave the apartment tonight."

"Is that a threat?" I tease, flipping over on my stomach and lifting my hips ever so slightly so he has a full view of my ass and pussy. He groans before hopping off the bed.

"Join me in the shower then," he calls out before turning and heading out of the bedroom, almost walking into the doorframe.

I giggle and hop off the bed and follow him.

•••⋛•◦)❖•◦(◦•⋚•••

"¡*PRINCESA*! AND JULIÁN! COME IN." DAD WAVES US INSIDE THE house. He's wearing a cute sweater vest over a button-down shirt and his hair is slicked back with some gel.

Julián reaches his hand out as I slip through the door and my dad shakes it. I silently breathe a sigh of relief at the exchange and take off my coat. Dad wraps me in his warm hug before we wait for Julián to take off his coat.

We decided to match as I wore a long-sleeve beige dress and he wore a matching beige sweater and some brown slacks. His beard is neatly trimmed and he added some volume to his curls so it's even fluffier than normal and I love it.

I reach for his hand and he pauses for a moment before lacing his fingers in mine. My dad notices, but he gives us a warm smile.

"Your mother is taking the turkey out of the oven, but I have to warn you–" he starts as we walk down the hallway toward the kitchen. That's when we hear a gasp and a flit of blonde hair fill our visions.

"Julián! Wha-What are you doing here?!" Laura asks with a high-pitched voice. Her eyes slowly lower to our laced hands and my heart thuds against my chest. She hasn't seen us *together* since he told her.

I try to give her a small smile, but she doesn't even focus on me. It looks like a million emotions flash across her face before she settles for a friendly smile.

"Just here for Eliana," he responds, squeezing my hand three times. I look back at him and his eyes are soft, his smile warm and comforting. I return it and want to almost melt into his arms, but I remember we have people watching us.

"What are you doing here?" I ask her as we get closer and she laughs.

"Victoria invited me! Wanted some help with preparing the meals. Told me how much you love stuffing, so she made me in charge of that. I hope that's okay?"

I nod and we reach the kitchen to see my mother basting the turkey. She looks up at all of us and she smiles at my dad before it falters as she notices Julián. I try to give her a smile, but it doesn't ease the tension.

"I'm going to get some wine. Care to join me, Laura?" my dad speaks up and Laura nods quickly before following him out of the kitchen. It's quiet and Julián takes a step toward the kitchen island and I follow, our hands still entwined.

"Thank you for hosting tonight. It means a lot to her," he says softly. He's treading lightly and even though I'm scared shitless, he looks confident and unwavering. Like he could go into raging waters and not be knocked down. My mother takes notice and raises a brow.

And then she *smiles*. Victoria Haros *smiles* at him.

"You're welcome. I have to admit… I had a feeling you'd come, so I set an extra plate."

"Thanks," I say, catching her eyes.

"Of course, I hope we can talk after dinner? Don't want to spoil anyone's appetite with all of this food ready to eat." She motions to the island full of dishes ready to be served.

We both nod and we're about to turn to head to the dining table when my mother speaks up.

"Actually, Julián, do you mind carrying the turkey to the table?"

"I'd love to," he smiles and he leans in to kiss my cheek before our hands separate and I make my way to the dining table to join dad and Laura. They're chatting about finals and their winter break plans. She mentions going to the mountains in Colorado for a getaway and to learn how to ski, something she always wanted to try.

I take a seat and my dad gives me a bright smile as he fills my glass with wine. I thank him and Laura and I catch each other's eyes.

"So, do you have any winter break plans?"

I shake my head. "No, nothing set in stone. You said you were going to try to ski?"

She nods and laughs, her eyes shining brightly. "It's something on my bucket list! Ever since–" she stops herself as she picks up her glass of wine. I crane my neck but give her a reassuring smile to continue. "Ever since the divorce, I made a list of things I'd like to do. Skiing just happens to be one of them. I was stuck in a trance of not being able to do anything for years after the divorce was final. But now, I'm doing it!"

My dad claps his hands in glee and I raise my glass, hoping this can ease any worries she or I might have about each other. She smiles and raises hers, clinking it with mine. We clink ours with my dad's and we all laugh.

"What's going on? Everyone's *smiling*." Julián hollers as he brings in the turkey on a huge platter. We scoot our chairs to let him have enough room to lean over the table and place the plate down.

"We're cheering to her finally following her bucket list," my dad mentions. Julián looks at Laura for a moment before his hand falls behind my chair and his fingers lightly touch my neck. I shudder at the soft touch and I try to focus on where we are.

"Oh? A bucket list?"

Laura rolls her eyes, but laughs. "Don't sound so surprised, Julián. I can have fun! Took me a while," she pauses before taking a deep breath. "Took a *damn* while, but I'm finally there and have my list. I'm going to start off with skiing."

"You?" he laughs, throwing his head back. "You on skis? Please have someone record that because I *cannot* for the life of me envision that."

"Yeah, yeah, you're going to have a good time laughing at all the pictures I'll take. But just remember, it won't be as bad as that time you showed me photos of you on the camel in Egypt and fell face first."

A gasp leaves my lips and Laura nods, pointing her glass to Julián. "Honey, he may love Egypt, but he can't ride a camel to save his life."

"That was *one* time and they insisted I take photos to share with everyone back home," Julián defends himself. I throw my head back to look at him and he winks, pressing his fingers into my neck and rubbing small circles.

"I'd love to see those photos," I chime in.

"I'll find them, I'm sure he tried to delete them the moment I saw them and made fun of him," Laura teases before giving me a smile.

My heart couldn't be happier. Having us all here and acting *civil* under one roof. My mother walks in, her heels loud enough to announce her entrance into the dining room as she sets down two side dishes.

"I'm breaking my neck and back over there and all I hear is laughing! Honey, please help me with the rest of the dishes."

My dad looks up at her and nods, getting up quickly. Julián speaks up that he'll help too and they both disappear into the kitchen. My mother takes a deep breath and flips her hair over her shoulder. She's wearing a nice black dress with some maroon detailing. She matches the table spread.

Laura pats the chair next to her and my mother smiles brightly, walking over and taking a seat. She lifts her glass of wine that my dad had set out for her and she takes a long sip. The guys are back, filling the table with all the yummy dishes before they sit down.

We look around the table and Julián places his hand on my lap. I place my hand over his and squeeze three times. He glances at me for a split second, his eyes lighting up and it brings flutters throughout my whole body.

After a few minutes of sharing things we're grateful for, my dad is eager to carve the turkey.

"Let's dig in!" My dad bellows out and we do.

WITH OUR BELLIES FULL OF GOOD FOOD, WE MIGRATE TO THE sitting room at the front of the house. My dad's got on a football game to watch with Julián as Laura fiddles with the piano in the corner. One I haven't touched since I quit lessons as a kid. She looks like she's enjoying it and is even playing really well to my surprise.

My mother walks to me. "Mind if we talk?"

I nod, seeing Julián crane his neck from the couch, and I give him a reassuring smile before we slip out of the sitting area and into the hallway. She laces her fingers together near her midsection. I lean against the wall, ready to take on whatever she's been wanting to say since I walked in.

She locks eyes with me. "He makes you happy?"

Her question catches me off guard. I'm silent for a second before I nod. "Immensely."

She presses her lips into a thin line before she takes a deep breath. "I don't ever want to push you away from your true happiness, Eliana. I've always wanted the best for you."

I hold myself from rolling my eyes. "Not necessarily… You've only wanted what you *thought* was the best for me. What *you* really wanted."

Her eyes narrow for a moment before they return to normal. "That's not true–"

"It is!" I counter. I try to keep my voice leveled and we both look down the hall to the archway that leads to the sitting room. No one's heard us yet.

I sigh. "I don't want to fight. Not anymore."

"I don't want to either. I didn't drag you out here for a screaming match. It hasn't done us much good in the past, has it?"

I shake my head.

"I've wanted a lot for my life, I will admit that," she finally says. "Before I met your father, I had big dreams. Dreams bigger than either one of us really could handle. They were just *dreams*. My own mother wanted that for me so it became something I wanted to strive for."

I watch with cautious eyes and it starts to click. Her mother wanted to control her and in the process, she did the same to me.

It's not an excuse, but it helps me understand some of the things she's tried to push me to do.

"Your father helped me see a different path. Was it something I wanted? No, but it became things I ultimately chose for *myself*. He just showed me what I could do and I was able to make choices on my own. My mother had no say in them. That's when we had you and I spiraled. I didn't want to become her, and look at what happened. I admit I wasn't the best, always wanting you to follow my rules. It wasn't fair. I know it's long overdue, but I'm sorry."

She reaches her hand and smooths it over my shoulder before she rests her fingers on my hair. As if she's trying to keep me here for a moment longer to hear her out. Not run away like I always have.

"It'll take some time," I whisper.

"I know. I don't expect you to forgive me today or even next week. I just want you to know that I messed up and I shouldn't have done or even said those things. They weren't fair and you are *none* of those names that I called you."

Tears brim my eyes from the memory of what she called me. I believed those words for a while until Julián kissed them all away. Without his love, I wouldn't have been able to get over her venomous words.

"I'm not," I agree.

"You're such a strong woman and I see it, Eliana. I see it all and I hope you can start to forgive me and let me into your life. Julián is a great man. He always has been. It did shock me for a moment hearing about you two, but love has no rules."

"It really doesn't."

"I mean look at your father and I! We've got a few years between us as well and it was quite hypocritical on my part to be so crass toward you and Julián."

My chest constricts at her words. "Mom," I whisper.

She smiles and moves her hand to brush a strand of hair

behind my ear. "You've become the woman I always wished to be, honey. Your father and I love you. I see how Julián looks at you. That's not something that happens everyday. That's a once in a lifetime kind of love and you deserve it."

"Dad looks at you just the same," I reassure her. She laughs.

"He does, doesn't he? I won't ever deserve him, but I love him."

Without thinking, I pull her into a hug and we hold on tight. Her breathing is rapid, but it soon calms down. My own erratic heart starts to slow.

"Thanks for this," I whisper.

"Always, honey. I love you."

I close my eyes and a tear slips down my cheek. "I love you too."

Twenty-Eight

JULIÁN

I'M STUCK at the office grading finals when a knock comes at the door and I murmur for them to come in. There are tons of papers scattered all over my desk. I can't even see the surface.

Eliana pops her head in with a bag of food. She raises a brow. "Care to have lunch with me?"

I smile and wave her in. She closes the door and locks it, making me pause. "Are you wanting more than just lunch, baby?"

She gives me a wink as she makes her way to the desk and places the bag of food on the desk, not caring for the papers. But neither do I as I watch her round the corner of the desk. She's wearing a cute skirt that hits just above her knees. She's not wearing tights underneath, which makes me worry that she's cold.

"What's going on, *Corazón*?" I ask, pushing my chair back and she instantly straddles me. My hands go to her hips before moving lower to her bare thighs. I run my hands underneath her skirt and she circles her hips over my growing erection. I take a deep breath and she squeaks out a moan as my fingertips find her bare hips.

278

"You're not wearing anything?" I ask with a raised brow.

"Mhm," she mumbles, a smile catching at her lips. She leans in and kisses me as she continues to grind her hips and I glide my hands to her inner thighs. I let my finger rest right over her pussy and she takes a deep breath.

"You want me to fuck you right here, baby? Where people might hear us in the hallway?"

She nods, mischief glazing over her eyes. "I've been a *bad girl,* Professor." She lifts her hips just enough so my fingers can slide in between her legs and glide against her lips. She's wet and I press firmly on her clit.

"Oh fuck," I groan. My cock is rock hard and the only thing stopped me from fucking her right here are my pants.

"Mmmm, I love it when you do that," she whines, circling her hips some more.

I take my time to slip my fingers inside her pussy and she constricts around me. She's so wet, it's not hard to pump my fingers in and out of her. She moans and whimpers at the sensation as I add my thumb to her clit for more friction.

"You gonna come all over my fingers? Like my needy whore?" I whisper in her ear as she kisses my neck and even bites down on the skin. It just makes me press my cock further into her and she gasps.

"Yes! Please, fuck me faster, Professor," she whines and I oblige.

My fingers are at a faster pace until she's whining and whimpering. She's a mess as her pussy tightens around my fingers. I hook them at an angle to hit her G-spot and she breaks down in my arms, stilling and convulsing underneath my touch. She rides out her orgasm for a moment before I pull my fingers out of her and lick them each slowly.

She's attempting to even her breathing before she moves her hands down to my tented pants. "I need you, Julián," she whines.

I don't hesitate to work fast to unbuckle my belt and she lifts her hips just enough so I can shimmy the pants down to my thighs. My cock springs free from the boxers and she licks her lips before spitting in her hand and wrapping around my cock.

"Fuck, Eliana. Please," I beg as she pumps my cock and my release builds quickly. Before I can come, she moves her hands away and aligns herself with my tip. She lowers herself and we both gasp at the feeling. I grab her hips tightly.

"You're so tight for me, baby."

"You're so big," she counters as she circles her hips that make me roll my eyes to the back of my head.

"Please, move," I beg her, attempting to lift her hips so she can thrust down on me. She giggles before she accedes.

We work together to lift her up and down on my cock as my own hips grind against her to provide the right friction against her clit. Her movements grow rapidly as she gets closer to her release. I grunt as I almost reach my own. We're silent save for our moans and grunts as we get closer and closer to our climax.

"Julián!" she whisper shouts, constricting her pussy on me and I'm done for. One more thrust and my cock twitches and I'm coming inside her.

"Milk my fucking cock," I grunt as she continues to thrust onto me. She whimpers at the sensitivity and I slow my pace before we're a sweaty mess attempting to calm our breathing. She leans down, pressing her forehead to mine.

"I love you," she whispers.

I kiss her before humming. "I love you too, *mi reina*."

She lifts her head for a moment as she's deep in thought. "Queen?"

I nod. "You'll always be my queen, *Corazón*."

"I like the sound of that," she smiles before leaning in to close the distance. She kisses me passionately, and I almost melt into her touch.

··⋛·o)·✧·(o·⋚·· ··

"Ana!" Lena screams from across the bar, catching both of our gazes. Eliana waves her and Malcolm over to the table we're sitting at. We found a round booth in the back of the bar to hang out.

Eliana stands up to give Lena a hug while Malcolm gives her a side hug right after. He slips into the booth to my left and we give each other a nod and a smile. Lena eyes me for a moment, looking at Eliana before a huge smile spreads across her face. She takes a seat next to Malcolm while Eliana settles back to her seat to my right. Her hand finds mine and I give her three squeezes. She leans into my body at that and I can see the ever growing smile on her face.

"So, how's your winter break going?" Lena asks, eyeing us. Eliana and I look at each other for a split second.

"I moved in!" Eliana squeals, leaning her head on my shoulder for a moment.

"Seriously?! That's amazing!" Lena screams while Malcolm nods his head and tells us congrats.

"I'm not going to be fully moving in until this summer, but for now I've got the majority of my things there," Eliana explained.

"And how are you feeling about Ana now taking up your space?" Lena asks me with a wink.

I look at Eliana and lean in to kiss her forehead. "I don't mind at all. She can rearrange whatever, as long as she likes it."

"Right on," Malcolm laughs.

Lena nods. "I haven't moved in *yet*, we've got time. But I already know what painting I want to put up. Oh and the plants I want to hang! And–"

"Is that so?" Eliana cuts her off with a giggle. Lena nods her head again and a smile appears on her lips.

"Well, we're happy that you guys are happy," I chime in, wrapping my arm around Eliana's shoulders and she sinks into my hold.

"Now, I get that we're all catching up, but it is a Saturday night. Are we going to get some drinks? Maybe to celebrate a great semester ending?" Lena speaks up.

Eliana gasps and we all look at her. "I forgot to tell you, Len. I passed all my classes!"

"No fucking way!" Lena squeals, clapping. I kiss Eliana on the top of her head.

"Sounds like that's a really good reason to celebrate!" Malcolm bellows. Lena and him get up and head to the bar while Eliana lifts her head to look at me. I watch her green eyes sparkle with something.

"What?"

She shrugs. "Everything is perfect."

"You know," I start, whispering so she can just hear me. "You can officially move in this break if you'd like. We don't have to wait."

Her lips curl into a smile and it's contagious, bringing my own smile to my face. "Really? You know that'll mean I can start decorating then."

"I don't doubt you for a second, *Corazón*." I glide my free hand under her chin and lift it so she's closer to me. I give her a quick peck.

"I love you," she breathes out happily.

"You're my world," I whisper back. Her cheeks have a dusting of rose on them at my words and I shake my head. "Actually, not even that."

"Oh?" she laughs.

"*No, eres mi universo.*"

She's silent for a moment as she translates what I said. It's cute watching her do this. I love talking to her in Spanish and seeing her try to translate.

"Universe?" She asks.

I nod.

"I mean it."

Without answering, she leans in and kisses me. I lean into it, pushing my tongue into her mouth. She moves her hand to grasp my shirt, trying to pull me even closer than we already are.

"Woah! Love birds!" Lena screams, causing us to separate. She places a tray of shots on the table while Malcolm holds a cup full of lime and a salt shaker.

"We're celebrating!" Eliana giggles before we all take our shots and lift them. We look around our little group and then cheers, clinking our glasses together before throwing them back.

"Whew!" Malcolm belches after. My lips turn at the bitter and strong taste of the liquor and Eliana squeals, shaking her head.

"Fuck, that was awful!" she belts, leaning over the table to grab a lime and biting into it.

I follow suit and so does Lena and Malcolm.

"More?" Lena asks once we've recovered.

"Why not," Eliana says.

"We'll get them this time," I say, shifting in the booth and Eliana scoots out of it and I follow.

"Thank you!" Lena screams behind us as we make our way to the bar. Eliana keeps close to me and I breathe in her scent as she wraps her arm around my waist and presses her head to my shoulder.

We order the shots and head back to the table, continuing on with our celebration. It might be the start of winter break for us, but it feels like it's also the start of a new chapter and new leaf with Eliana.

I couldn't be fucking happier.

Epilogue

ELIANA

TWO AND A HALF YEARS LATER

"Is that all?" Julián asks loudly from the living room. I giggle as I finish up one last duffle bag of clothes and slip in some pieces of lace lingerie I bought the other day.

"*¿Corazón?*" his voice drifts throughout the apartment and I giggle again before stuffing the rest of the lingeries into the bag and zipping it closed. I hear his footsteps before his arms are wrapping around my waist. His lips are instantly on my neck before he's littering kisses all over.

My stomach flutters from his touch and I take a deep breath before turning around and wrapping my arms around his neck. "We could stay," I tease.

His hands roam my body as he ponders for a moment, looking up at the ceiling before hooking his fingers on the waistband of my leggings, getting hold of the fabric of my thong.

"If you keep talking like that, we'll miss our flight. And the beautiful hotel I booked. And the food… And the list of things I planned to do to you over there," he whispers.

"Fine, you win. But can you give me a hint of what you'd do? Or a sneak peek?"

He chuckles. "You'd love that, *mi amor*, huh?"

I nod. "Yes, please."

His eyes grow dark and his grip on me tightens before he pulls me closer to him, our cores brushing against each other and I can already feel his erection through his pants. A moan escapes my lips and he smirks.

"If we don't leave now," he says, trailing a hand around my waist to my front before dipping it lower and pushing past the fabric of the leggings and the thong. My skin instantly jolts at his touch and shivers run up my spine.

"We'd never make our flight," I finish his sentence. He leans his face in closer before he kisses me. His hand makes it between my legs and slips a finger through my folds.

"So fucking wet for me, baby," he whispers and I whimper once he inserts a finger and starts massaging my walls and I constrict around him. His thumb presses softly against my clit and I bite back a moan.

"You know what would be fun?" he whispers in my ear.

"What?" I breathlessly respond.

"If I got you riled up, edged you, and then never let you come. Make you have to wait the entire flight *and* the drive to the hotel before I can fuck you properly."

I whimper at his words as I open my mouth to protest. "You wouldn't." I move my hips vigorously to get some kind of friction against his finger and thumb so I can chase this high.

"Hmm," he hums before slipping his finger out of me and out of my pants. I yelp from the sudden movement and tears spring my eyes from not getting my release.

"Julián!"

He smiles. "You love it, just admit it."

"Never!"

"You love me," he pulls me close to him and lifts the finger that was just inside me and presses it against my lips. I part them and suck his finger, keeping eye contact. He licks his lips before moving his hand and replacing it with his lips. He tastes me as we kiss passionately and he moans through it.

"I love you," I whisper in between kisses.

"*Mi reina, mi universo,*" he mumbles before kissing me one more time. He pulls away and grabs the handle of the duffle bag on the bed and gives me a look.

"Another?"

"There are some great *presents* in there that you'll unwrap once we land."

He lifts a brow before walking out of the room and not saying anything else. I bite my lip as I saunter after him and grab my coat and purse with our passports.

We're going to Egypt for two months so he can show me his favorite country. I'm ecstatic to go to a place I've only been to when I was little, but can barely remember.

Julián even promised to take me to his favorite spots and meet some of his friends that live there.

He's mostly excited for me to see the Cairo night sky in real time. Not the simple fabrication of it at the museum the night we met. He even reserved one of his favorite restaurants that have an outdoor seating area where we can enjoy our first night in Cairo under the pretty sky.

He seemed so excited yet *nervous* when he told me about the plan, but I don't want to think too much of it.

"*¿Lista?*" he asks, opening the door for me to walk through first. He's got our bags stacked in a way where he can roll them on top of the main suitcase with wheels. I nod and clap my hands.

"I'm more than ready," I brush past him and wait for him to get out into the hallway before I close the door and lock it.

"*Vamos, Corazón,*" he smiles and we make our way out of the apartment to where our taxi is waiting to take us to the airport.

Once we're settled inside with our luggage in the trunk, Julián takes my hand and squeezes it three times. I look at him and he winks, causing me to have all the flutters in my tummy.

"Don't," I warn him.

He leans in and kisses my nose before pulling away. "I've been there so many times, but I will say I'm *very* excited about this trip."

"Well, yeah," I giggle. "I'll be there."

"Mhm," he hums, a smile breaking his face. "Exactly."

I give him a look and he just gives me another wink, causing me to smile.

He's up to something. But I hate trying to figure out surprises or any kind of plan. I'm going to keep pretending I don't know that he's got something up his sleeve.

I don't know what, but I have a feeling it'll be good. Anything with him is amazing, so I won't be surprised if whatever he's got planned will either bring me to my knees or make me cry with joy.

I hope it's both, because I've got the perfect outfit planned for that night.

"What are you thinking about, *reina*?"

"Wouldn't you like to know?"

He laughs before squeezing my hand three times.

I love you.

I squeeze his hand back three times.

THE END

Coming Soon

BY G. ELENA

IN DESPERATE RUIN
A Best Friend's Dad Forbidden Romance

Thank You

As always, I have to begin my list of thanking people with you, the reader. Thank you for giving this forbidden romance a chance and for giving me a chance as a dark romance author.

To my promotional team, thank you for supporting every post on social media. I can't do this without you.

To my beta readers Bianca, Cassidy, Cyndi, Jenni, and Lindsey thank you for helping me get this novel into better shape. It was a mess and you thankfully took your time to give me your feedback.

To my editor Jenni, you're always my life saver. I can't thank you enough for taking this novel into your hands and doing your magic. I also want to thank you for being such a supportive friend in my life even though we're miles away. I cherish our friendship and can't wait for the day we can finally meet and hug.

To Pamela, thank you so much for being willing to edit the Spanish in this book. I can't wait to continue working with you in the future! You are amazing and I'm so glad we met.

To Bianca, *mi reina*, your enthusiasm for any idea I have will always mean the world to me. I love you so much and can't thank you enough for your endless support. My sanity is intact because of you and allowing me to randomly bombard you with book ideas and questions at all hours of the night. *Te amo.*

To Lizzie, you are a bright light of sunshine. There aren't words to describe how much you mean to me. Thank you, thank you, thank you for all your support and your constant encouragement. You've helped me in so many ways throughout this publishing process and you've become such a great friend in the end result. I'm forever grateful for you and love you so much.

To Emily and Kelsey, as always, thank you for just being here. This book is a wild ride and I hope you enjoy it!

To Emily and Shelby, you guys were here when this novel was six chapters deep and a complete mess. I hope you like this finalized version. Love you!

To my parents, thank you for all your continuous support. Even though I specifically told you to never read books under this pen name, I have to thank you in it. *Los amo.*

To Sandy, thank you for being here for almost two decades. You've been such a rock in my life and I'm so thankful for you.

To Milo, the amount of times I wanted to call you up and talk to you about this book… I hope you're proud of me. I love you endlessly.

About the Author

G. Elena is the dark romance pen name for Grace Elena. Please check out her main author page for Romcoms, small town romances, and contemporary romances. She is a Mexican-American author who loves to write with strong Latinx leads.

You can keep up with her on Instagram (graceelenaauthor) or visit her website at graceelenaauthor.com for more insight to her books. If you'd like to get access to sneak peeks to her future novels before anyone else, join her Facebook Private Group "Grace Elena's Vineyard".

www.ingramcontent.com/pod-product-compliance
Lightning Source LLC
Chambersburg PA
CBHW011850300726
48970CB00009B/2733